"What is that?" She points to the numbers on the shirt.

"The year. Old Navy puts the year on all their flag T-shirts. It's sort of a racket, I guess—you have to buy a new one every year."

"That . . . is . . . the . . . year?" She looks sort of sick. Her face is suddenly almost the same color green as her eyes. She begins to sob again. "Oh, my . . . oh, no." She crumples back onto the floor, as she was when I first saw her. "It cannot be true. It cannot."

I kneel beside her. "What's the matter now? I thought you were fine."

She looks at me, then starts screaming. "Fine? Fine? I have been asleep nearly three hundred years!"

Also by
ALEX FLINN

A KISS IN TIME

ALEX FLINN

HARPER TEEN
An Imprint of HarperCollinsPublishers

HarperTeen is an imprint of HarperCollins Publishers.

A Kiss in Time
Copyright © 2009 by Alex Flinn
All rights reserved. Printed in the United States of America. No part of this book may
be used or reproduced in any manner whatsoever without written permission except in
the case of brief quotations embodied in critical articles and reviews. For information
address HarperCollins Children's Books, a division of HarperCollins Publishers,
10 East 53rd Street, New York, NY 10022.
www.harperteen.com

Library of Congress Cataloging-in-Publication Data
Flinn, Alex.
    A kiss in time / Alex Flinn. — 1st ed.
        p.   cm.
    Summary: Sixteen-year-old Princess Talia persuades seventeen-year-old Jack, the
modern-day American who kissed her awake after a three-hundred-year sleep, to take
her to his Miami home, where she hopes to win his love before the witch who cursed
her can spirit her away.
    ISBN 978-0-06-087421-6
    [1. Princesses—Fiction. 2. Blessing and cursing—Fiction. 3. Witches—
Fiction. 4. Family life—Florida—Fiction. 5. Fate and fatalism—Fiction. 6. Miami
(Fla.)—Fiction.]   I. Title.
PZ7.F6395Kis   2009   2008022582
[Fic]—dc22   CIP
                                                                                     AC

Typography by Michelle Gengaro
10   11   12   13   14   CG/RRDH   10   9   8   7   6   5   4   3   2   1
❖
First paperback edition, 2010

172 - 1301

For Joyce Sweeney. Thanks for everything!

Thanks to Marjetta Geerling for her insightful reading and for setting up our incomparable YA retreat group. Thanks also to my agent, George Nicholson; my editor, Toni Markiet; her assistant, Jayne Carapezzi; and especially my mother, Manya Lowman, for all her behind-the-scenes support that allows me to keep going as a writer.

Part I

Talia

Chapter 1

If I hear one more syllable about spindles, I shall surely die!

From my earliest memory, the subject has been worn to death in the castle, nay, in the entire kingdom. It is said that *spindle*, rather than *Mama* or *Papa*, was my first word in infancy, and I have little doubt that this is true, for 'tis the word which lights more frequently than any other upon my most unwilling ears.

"Talia, dearest, you must never touch a spindle," Mother would say as she tucked me into bed at night.

"I will not, Mother."

"Vous devez ne jamais toucher un axe," my tutor would say during French lessons.

"I will not," I told him in English.

"If ye spy a spindle, ye must leave it alone," the downstairs maid said as I left the castle, always with my governess, for I was never allowed a moment alone.

Every princeling, princess, or lesser noble who came to the castle to play was told of the restrictions upon spindles—lest they have one secreted about their person somewhere, or lest they mistakenly believe I was normal. Each servant was searched at the door, and thread was purchased from outside the kingdom. Even peasants were forbidden to have spindles. It was quite inconvenient for all concerned.

It should be said that I am not certain I would know a spindle if I saw one. But it seems unlikely that I ever shall.

"Why must I avoid spindles?" I asked my mother, in my earliest memory.

"You simply must," she replied, so as not to scare me, I suppose.

"But why?" I persisted.

She sighed. "Children should be seen, not heard."

I asked several times more before she excused herself, claiming a headache. As soon as she departed, I started in on my governess, Lady Brooke.

"Why am I never to touch a spindle?"

Lady Brooke looked aggrieved. It was frowned upon, she knew, to scold royal children. Father was a humane ruler who never resorted to beheading. Still, she had her job to consider, if not her neck.

"It is forbidden," she said.

Well, I stomped my foot and whined and cried, and when that failed to produce the desired result, I said, "If you do not answer, I will tell Father you slapped me."

"You wicked, wicked girl! God above will punish you for such deceit!"

"No one punishes princesses." My voice was calm. I was done with my screaming, now that I had discovered a better currency. "Not even God."

"God cares not for rank and privilege. If you tell such an awful lie, you will surely be damned."

"Then you must keep me from such a sin by telling me what I wish to know." Even at four or five, I was precocious *and* determined.

Finally, sighing, she told me.

I had been a long-wished-for babe (this I knew, for it had been told to me almost as often as the spindle speech), and when I was born, my parents invited much of the kingdom to my christening, including several women rumored to have magical powers.

"You mean fairies?" I interrupted, knowing she would not speak the word. Lady Brooke was highly religious, which seemed to mean that she believed in witches, who used their magic for evil, but not fairies, who used their powers for good. Still, even at four, I knew about fairies. Everyone did.

"There is no such a thing as fairies," Lady Brooke said. "But yes, people *said* they were fairies. Your father welcomed them, for he hoped they would bring you magical gifts. But there was one person your father did not invite: the witch Malvolia."

Lady Brooke went on to describe, at great length and in exhausting detail, the beauty of the day, the height of the sun in the sky, and the importance of the christening service. I closed my eyes. But when she attempted to carry me into my bedchamber, I woke and demanded, "What of the spindle?"

"Oh! I thought you were asleep."

I continued to demand to know of the spindle, which led to a lengthy recitation of the gifts I had received from the various guests. I struggled to remain attentive, but I perked up when she began to describe the fairies' gifts.

"Violet gave the gift of beauty, and Xanthe gave the gift of grace, although surely such qualities cannot be given."

I did not see why not. People often remarked upon my beauty and grace.

"Leila gave the gift of musical talent . . ."

I noted, privately, that I was already quite skilled on the harpsichord.

". . . while Celia gave the gift of intelligence. . . ."

It went without saying. . . .

Lady Brooke continued. "Flavia was about to step forward to give the gift of obedience—which would have been much welcomed, if I do say so myself." She winked at me, but the wink had a hint of annoyance which was not—I must say—appreciated.

"The spindle?" I reminded her, yawning.

"Just as Flavia was ready to step forward and offer her

much-desired gift of obedience, the door to the grand banquet hall was flung open. The witch Malvolia! The guards tried to stop her, but she brazened her way past them.

"'I demand to see the child!' she said.

"Your nurse tried to block her way. But quicker than the bat of an eyelash, the nurse was on the floor and Malvolia was standing over your bassinet.

"'Ah.' She seized you and held you up for all to see. 'The accursed babe.'

"Your mother and father tried to soothe Malvolia with tales of invitations lost, but she repeated the word 'accursed,' several times, and then she made good the curse itself.

"'Before her sixteenth birthday, the princess shall prick her finger on a spindle and die!' she roared. And then, as quickly as she had arrived, she was gone. But the beautiful day was ruined, and rain fell freely from the sky."

"And then what?" I asked, far from interested in the weather now that I understood I might die by touching a spindle. Why had no one told me?

"Flavia tried to save the situation with her gift. She said that since Malvolia's powers were immense, she could not reverse her spell, but she sought to modify it a bit.

"'The princess shall *not* die,' she said. But as everyone was sighing in relief, she added, 'Rather, the princess shall sleep. All Euphrasian citizens shall sleep also, protected from harm by this spell, and the kingdom shall be obscured from sight by a giant wood, unnoticed by the rest of the world and removed from maps and memory until . . .' People were becoming more nervous with each pronouncement. '. . . one day, the kingdom shall be rediscovered. The princess shall be awakened by her true love's first kiss, and the kingdom shall awake and become visible to the world again.'"

"But that is stupid!" I burst out. "If the entire kingdom is asleep and forgotten, who will be left to kiss me?"

Lady Brooke stopped speaking, and then she actually scratched her head, as persons in stories are said to do when they are trying to work some great puzzle. At the end of it, she said, "I do not know. Someone will. That is what Flavia said."

But even at my tender age, I knew this was improbable. Euphrasia was small, bounded on three sides by ocean and on the fourth by wilderness. The Belgians, our nearest neighbors, barely knew we existed, and if Euphrasia disappeared from sight and maps, the Belgians would forget us entirely. Other questions leaped to mind. How would we eat if we were all asleep? And wouldn't we eventually die, like old people did? Indeed, the cure seemed worse than the original punishment.

But to each successive question, Lady Brooke merely said, "That is why you must never touch a spindle."

And it is nigh upon my sixteenth birthday, and I have never touched one yet.

Chapter 2

Tomorrow is my sixteenth birthday. I do not suppose it necessary to explain the furor this has occasioned in the kingdom. 'Tis a heady occasion. Each year on my birthday, guests come from around the world to celebrate—and they bring gifts! Diamonds from Africa, crystal from Ireland, cheese from Switzerland. Of course, my sixteenth birthday is of special import. Rumor has it that a ship has sailed the world over, collecting items and persons for my pleasure. They say it has even visited the British colony on the other side of the world. I believe it is called Virginia.

But more than guests, more even than presents, is the actual hope that this whole spindle business will end today. *Before her sixteenth birthday.* That was what the witch Malvolia had said. So tomorrow Mother and Father will rejoice at having completed the Herculean task of keeping their stupid daughter away from a common household object for sixteen years, and then I can live the ordinary life of an ordinary princess.

I am ready for it.

It is not merely spindle avoidance that has been my difficulty thus far. Rather, because of this, I have been effectively shut out from the world. Other young maidens of my station have traveled to France, India, and even the wilds of Virginia. But I have not been permitted to make the shortest trip to the nearest kingdom, lest one of the populace there wished to attack me with a spindle. In the castle, the very tapestries seem to mock me with their pictures of places I have never seen. I am barely allowed outside, and when I am, it is only under the boring chaperonage of boring Lady Brooke or some other equally dull lady-in-waiting. I am fifteen years old, and I have never had a single friend. Who would want to be friends with an oddity who has never seen anything or done anything and is guarded night and day?

Likewise, a young princess my age would ordinarily have dozens of suitors questing for her hand. Her beauty would be the subject of song and story. Duels would be fought for her. She might even cause a war, if she were beautiful enough, and I am.

But though my beauty has been spoken of, raved of, even, there has not been one single request for my hand. Father says it is because I am young yet, but I know that to be a lie. The reason is the curse. Any sensible prince would prefer a bride with freckles or a hooked nose over one like me, one who might fall into a coma at any instant.

There is a knock upon the door. Lady Brooke! "Your Highness, the gowns are ready for viewing," she calls from outside.

The gowns! They have been prepared especially for tomorrow. It will be the grandest party ever. The guests will arrive at the palace door in carriages or at the harbor in ships. There will be a grand dinner tonight, and tomorrow a ball with an orchestra for dancing and a second orchestra for when the first tires. There will be fireworks and a midnight supper and magnums of a special bubbling wine made by Benedictine monks in France, then a week of lesser parties to follow. It will be a festival, a Festival of Talia. I will be at the center of it, of course, courted by every prince and raja, and before it is over, I will have fallen in love—and I will be sixteen, cured of the curse.

"Your Highness?" Lady Brooke continues to knock.

The gowns—I need one for tonight and several for the ball tomorrow and a dozen or so more for the coming week—must be perfect. And then, perhaps Father will speak with the tailor who designed the loveliest one and have him create fifty or so more for my wedding trip around the globe.

Truth be told, it is the trip, rather than the wedding, which appeals to me. I care not for marriage at someone else's whim. But it is my lot in life, and a cross I must bear to gain the wedding trip. I am more than ready to leave Euphrasia, having been trapped here for almost sixteen years. And, of course, my husband shall be handsome, and a prince.

I fling the door open. "Well? Where are they?"

Lady Brooke produces a map of the castle.

I take it from her. One has to admire her organization. I see now that Lady Brooke has marked out the rooms which will be used to house our numerous royal guests. Other rooms are marked with a star. "What is this?"

"On the occasion of your last birthday, you told your father that, upon the occasion of *this* birthday, you required 'the most perfect gown in all the world.' Your father took this request quite literally and sent out the call to tailors and seamstresses the world over. China's entire haul of silkworms has been put to this task. Children have been pulled from their cottages and huts to spin and sew and slave, all for the pleasure of Princess Talia of Euphrasia."

"Very good, Lady Brooke." I know she thinks I am silly and spoiled. Was I not gifted with intelligence? I also know this not to be the case. How can I be spoiled when I never get to do a single thing I want? I did not ask that children be pulled from their cribs to slave for me, but since they were, is it not only courteous to gaze upon their efforts and, hopefully, find a dress or two that will be acceptable? I can already picture the gown in which I shall make my grand entrance at the ball. It will be green. "The map?"

"Yes, the map. Each tailor was asked to bring his twenty best creations, all in your exact measurements. Your father believed that you might be overwhelmed, gazing upon so many gowns at once. Therefore, he decreed that they be placed in twenty-five separate rooms of the castle. In this way, you may wander about, choosing as you will."

Twenty gowns times twenty-five tailors! Five hundred gowns! I grow giddy.

"We had best get started," I tell Lady Brooke.

We begin to walk down the stone hallway. The first rooms are on the floor above us, and as we climb the stairs, Lady Brooke says, "May I ask what you will do with the gowns which do not meet with your approval?"

This is a trick question, I know, like all of Lady Brooke's questions, designed to prove that I am a horrid brat. Why care I what Lady Brooke thinks? But I do, for much as I loathe her, she is my only companion, the closest thing I have to a friend. So I rack my brain for an acceptable answer. Give them to her? Surely not. The gowns were made to my exact measurements, and Lady Brooke, who has not been blessed with the gift of beauty, is an ungainly half a head taller than I, and stout.

"Give them to the poor?" I say. When she frowns, I think again. "Or, better yet, hold an auction and give the money collected to the poor. For food."

There! That should satisfy the old bat!

And perhaps it does. At least, she is quiet as we enter the first room. Quiet disapproval is the best I can expect from Lady Brooke.

Dresses line the walls, covering even the windows. Twenty of them, in different fabrics, different shapes, but every single one of them blue!

"Was it not communicated to the tailors that my eyes are green?" I ask Lady Brooke in a whisper loud enough for the tailor to hear. I want him to. Of all the stupidity!

He hears. "You want-a green dresses?" He has an accent of some sort, and when he moves closer, I see beads of sweat forming upon his forehead. Ew. I certainly hope that he has refrained from sweating over his work, which would make the fabric smell.

"Not *all* green," I say. "But I would not have expected all blue."

"Blue, it is the fashion this year," the sweaty tailor says.

"I am a princess. I do not follow fashions—I make them."

"I am certain *one* blue dress would be acceptable." Lady Brooke tries to smooth things over with this peasant whilst glaring at me. "Talia, this man has come all the way from Italy. His designs are the finest in the world."

"What?" I say, meaning, what does this have to do with me?

"I said . . . oh, never mind. Will you not look at the dresses now? Please?"

I look. The dresses are all ugly. Or maybe not ugly but boring, with boring ruffles. Boring, like everything else in my life. Still, I manage to smile so as not to call out another lecture from Lady Brooke. "Lovely, thank you."

"You like?" He steps in my way.

Would not I have said if I liked? But I tell him, "I will

think upon it. This is the first room I have visited."

This seems to satisfy him. At least, he gets his sweatiness out of my way, and I am allowed to pass to the next room.

This room and indeed the two after it are little better. I find one dress, a pink one, which might be acceptable for a lesser event like Friday's picnic, some event at which I would not mind looking like the dessert, but nothing at all to wear on the Most Important Night of My Life.

"Talia?" Lady Brooke says after the third room. "Perhaps if you gave more than a cursory glance—"

"Perhaps if they were not all so hideous!" I am devastated and hurt, and Lady Brooke does not understand. How could she? When she was young, she could go to shops and choose her own clothing, even make it if she liked. I will never be normal, but barring that, I would like to be *abnormal* in a lovely green dress without too many frills.

"Here is a green one," Lady Brooke says in the next room.

I glower at it. The ruffles would reach my nose. "This would suit . . . my grandmother."

"Could the ruffles be removed?" Lady Brooke asks the tailor.

"Could you create a gown that is not entirely hideous?" I add.

"Talia . . ."

"It is naught but the truth."

"*Pardonez moi,*" the tailor says. "The frock, I can fix it."

13

"*Non, merci,*" I say, and flounce from the room.

In the next, I spy a lavender velvet with a heart-shaped neckline. I reach to touch the soft fabric.

"Beautiful, is it not?" Lady Brooke asks.

I pull my hand back. I am thoroughly sick of Lady Brooke and dresses and my life. I am certain she despises me as well and, suddenly, the company of even Malvolia herself seems preferable to that of the detestable Lady Brooke.

"Do you have anything better?"

"Talia, you are being terrible."

"I am being truthful, and I would thank you to remember that you are in my father's service."

"I know it. Would that it were not the case, for I am ashamed to be in your presence when you are behaving like a horrible brat."

She says it with a smile. The tailor, too, smiles stupidly. I stare at him. "Are there any gowns which are less likely to make me want to vomit than this one?"

The man continues to smile and nod.

"He speaks no English," I say. "So what care you what I say to him?"

"I care because I am forced to listen to you. You have grown more and more insolent in recent weeks. I am ashamed of you." She nods and smiles.

I feel something like tears springing to my eyes. Lady Brooke hates me, even though she is required to like me. Probably everyone else hates me, too, and merely pretends because of Father. But I hold the tears back. Princesses do not cry.

"Then why not leave me alone?" I ask, smiling as I was trained. "Why does no one ever leave me be for one single, solitary instant?"

"My orders—"

"Were your orders to yell at me and call me a brat?" I begin to pace back and forth like a caged animal. I *am* a caged animal. "Tomorrow I shall be sixteen. Peasant girls my age are married with two and three babes, and yet I am not permitted to walk down a hallway within my own castle without supervision."

"The curse—"

"You do not even believe in the curse! And yet it has come true, not the spindle part, but the death. . . . I am living my death, little by little, each day. And when I am sixteen and the curse ends, I shall be given over to a husband of someone else's choosing, who will tell me what to do and say and eat and wear for the rest of my life. I can only pray that it will be short, pray for the blessed independence of the grave. I will always be under someone's orders." I begin to cry, anyway, to sob. What difference does it make? "Can I not simply walk down a hallway on my own?"

Through it all, the tailor smiles and nods.

Lady Brooke's expression softens. "I suppose it would be all right. After all, the tailors have been thoroughly searched and the spindle regulations explained to them."

"Of course they have." I sigh.

Lady Brooke turns to the man and speaks to him in French.

"Thank you!" I sob. I point to the lavender gown and say, in French, "It is beautiful! I shall take that one, and that one as well." I point to a charming scarlet satin with a neckline off the shoulders in the style of Queen Mary of England, a gown I had purposely ignored before, which now looks quite fetching.

"Very well." Lady Brooke hands me the map. "Just point to what you want, and they will put it aside."

I nod and take the paper from her. I am free—at least for an hour!

Chapter 3

Free of the encumbrance that is Lady Brooke, I fairly skip down the stone hallways. I would swing from the chandeliers, could I reach them, but I content myself with jumping up toward them. My life is no less horrible than before, but at least there is no dour Lady Brooke to remark upon its horribleness.

In short time, I have chosen five dresses, none blue, but none special enough for my grand entrance at my birthday ball. Although one is green, it does not match the exact shade of my eyes.

"It will look lovely on you," says the tailor, who is from England.

Of course he thinks so. I know what he is about. Having his dress worn by a princess on an occasion of such import will increase his renown. For the rest of his life, he might call himself "Tailor to Talia, Princess of Euphrasia."

But his apprentice says, "Indeed. It may not be the same shade as your remarkable eyes, but it will bring them out."

The tailor quickly shushes him, lest the boy disgrace them both by speaking so to a princess. But I turn toward him and smile. He is my age, no more, perhaps the tailor's son. And—I find it difficult not to notice—he is handsome. For a commoner. His eyes are the color of cornflowers.

"Do you think so?"

He looks down, blushing. "I meant no disrespect, Your Highness. But yes. It will look lovely on you, as any dress would."

I wonder what it would be like to be a common girl, who could flirt with such a handsome tailor's apprentice with impunity. Or, better yet, to *be* the apprentice himself, to be a boy, so young, yet traveling far from home. And to learn a trade such as making a dress. In all my life, I have never created anything, never *done* anything at all other than silly paintings of flowers for my art master, Signor Maratti. Father hung them in his bedchamber, where they would be seen by no one. Is it enough to be a princess, when being a princess means nothing?

I nod and turn reluctantly to the old tailor. "I shall wear it tonight for dinner. Many noblewomen will be in attendance, and if they compliment my gown, I will tell them your name."

I start for the door. The tailor bows, but the boy does not move. He is staring at me, entranced by my beauty. I get the shiveriest sensation across my arms. Of course he thinks I am beautiful, but I like that he sees me. I wonder if this is what it will be like when I meet my prince. Maybe it will not be so bad.

Five more rooms, then ten, and still the dress I desire has not been found. It seems a small task, certainly one the best tailors in the world should be able to accomplish. And yet they have not. I sigh. Perhaps I will wear the English tailor's dress to the ball after all.

I reach the end of the hallway. I have never been in this part of the castle before. Amazing. These rooms have barely been used, but surely a child—a normal child—would explore every room at some time. But I had not been a normal child.

I spy a staircase in the shadows. This is not one of the stairways I am accustomed to using to reach the fourth floor, and when I check Lady Brooke's map, I see that it was not included. How odd. I am seized with a sudden urge to run up its steps, even slide down the banister. But that is silly, and if I do that, I will be delayed. And then Lady Brooke will come looking for me. I turn back down the hall.

Suddenly, I hear a voice.

It was a lover and his lass,
With a hey, and a ho,
And a hey nonny no . . .

A lover.

In the spring time, the only pretty ring time . . .

A woman's voice, singing. Entranced, almost, I start up the stair.

When birds do sing,
Hey ding a ding, ding!
Sweet lovers love the spring!

At the top of the stairs, there is an open door. I stop. There is no tailor. I knew there would not be. But instead, there is an old woman sitting upon a bench. I see not what she is doing, for she is surrounded by dresses, so many dresses, much more than twenty. But that is not the remarkable thing.

Each and every dress is exactly the same shade of green as my eyes.

"Lovely!" The cry comes from me unbidden. I run into the room.

"Good afternoon, Your Highness." The old woman attempts to rise from her chair with great effort. She begins to curtsy.

"Oh, please don't!" I say. She is, after all, very old.

"Ah, but I must. You are a princess, and respect must be accorded certain positions. Those who do not take heed will pay the price."

She is almost to the floor, and I wonder how long it will take her to right herself. Still, I say, "Very well." I wish for a second—but only a second—that Lady Brooke were here so that she might see how I follow her directions about not arguing with my elders.

I step back and study the dresses. It seems there is every style and every fabric: satins, velvets, brocades of all designs, and a lighter fabric I have never seen before, which will float behind me like a cloud of butterflies.

Finally, the woman rises. "Do you like anything?"

I had nearly forgotten she was there, so enchanted was I with the gowns.

I sigh. "Yes, I like everything! It is all perfect."

She laughs. "I am honored that you believe so. For you see, I am from Euphrasia. I have seen you all your life, Your Highness, and have flattered myself that I knew better than any foreigner the designs that would suit my own princess."

"Indeed." I try to recall if I have seen her before, perhaps in the crowds at a parade. But why would I have noticed an old woman who looks much like any other? Only her eyes are unusual. They are not glazed over with a film of white, like so many very old people's are. Instead, they are lively, black and glittering like a crow's.

"Have you a special favorite?" she asks.

"This one." I start toward the lightweight dress. "I shall rival the fairies in this!"

"'Tis my favorite, too. Do you mind, Your Highness, if

I sit back down? I know it is not the correct way, but I am quite old, and my knees are not what they once were when I was a young woman like yourself, dancing at festivals."

"Of course." I am flooded with gratitude toward this stranger who knows what I want, who understands me as Mother and Father and wretched Lady Brooke do not. I approach the dress. The old woman has settled back onto her stool and has begun some sort of needlework. There is a contraption in her hand, something that looks like a top with which children play. It is nearly covered in wool that has been dyed a deep rose.

"What is that?" I ask her.

"Oh, 'tis my sewing. I make my own thread. Do you wish to try?"

Sewing? I step closer. The contraption is a wooden spike weighted at one end with a whorl of darker wood. A hook holds the thread in place, and when the thread is finished, it winds around the stick below the whorl, to be used for sewing. There is a quantity of unfinished wool at the top. "Oh, I should not."

"Of course not. I misspoke. 'Twould be unfitting for a young lady such as yourself to make dresses. You were born merely to wear them. Humble souls like myself were meant to create."

I nod, approaching the dresses again.

"Only . . ."

"What is it?" I am touching the fabric, but I glance back at her.

"They say 'tis lucky. 'Twas handed down to me by my mother and her mother before her, and all who make thread with it are entitled to one wish."

"A wish?" I know what Lady Brooke would say on the subject. Her thoughts on wishes are much like her thoughts on magic. Superstition is the opposite of God. Still, I say, "Have you ever wished upon it?"

"Aye." She nods. "I have indeed, when I was young. I wished for a long life."

I stare at her. Her face is like crumpled silk, and her hair the color of paper.

"How long ago was that?"

"When I was your age, fifteen. So nigh upon two hundred years."

I gasp, but the old woman holds my gaze.

"What would you wish for, Your Highness? I know you must have wishes, trapped as you are in this castle, longing to marry if only to get out, not daring to hope for freedom." Her voice is very nearly hypnotic. "Be not afraid. What do you wish for?"

My freedom. Or love. Or . . . travel. I wish to travel the world, to be not a princess trapped in a protected existence, but a human girl. *Silly thought. I cannot do that.*

"I think . . ." I say, "I will try it."

She nods and moves aside to make room for me on the bench. Her movement is less labored than before. She pats the space beside her. "Sit, Princess." She hands me the object, stick first. "This in your right hand. Then take the thread in your left, and spin it clockwise. When the thread has begun to spin, you make your wish."

I take the stick. I am distracted, thinking of my wish, my freedom, of seeing the world. As I reach for the thread, I feel a stab of pain in my finger. The hook at the end has punctured my left ring finger. When I glance down, I see a drop of crimson upon my skirt. Blood.

It is only then that I realize what the object is.

A spindle. *The princess shall prick her finger on a spindle.*

I hear the old woman's laughter as I begin to sink down.

Malvolia!

My last thought as I hit the ground is, *I should have listened to Lady Brooke.*

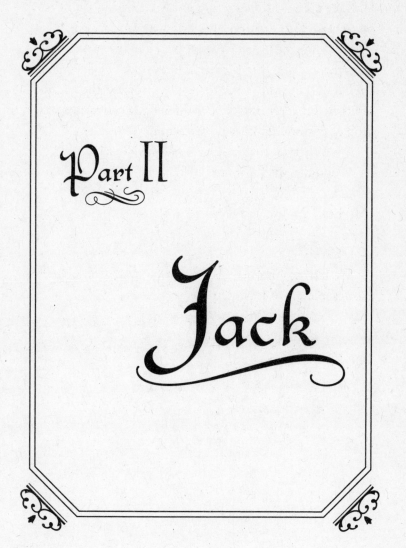

Part II

Jack

Chapter 1

What they don't tell you about Europe is how completely lame it is.

I should have guessed, though. It was my parents' idea. They're not exactly renowned for their coolness. They sent me on this tour of Europe, supposedly for my education but really to get me out of their hair for a month, while simultaneously being able to brag to their friends that "Jack is on tour in Europe, getting something interesting to write about on college essays."

Painful admission here: I didn't totally mind because my girlfriend, Amber, dumped me like last year's cat litter when some college guy asked her out. At least being here keeps me from seeing her with the new guy, and also forces me to appear like I have some pride and not call her. And who knows? Maybe I'll meet someone.

I was picturing clubs with Eurotrash nobility, riding on Vespas, lounging in French cafés and Greek tavernas, and, of course, the occasional topless beach (although it is a well-known fact that European women aren't big on shaving their, um, pitular area—I planned to look elsewhere). I thought at least there'd be some cool gardens, something outdoors. I never imagined the suckitude I was about to experience—one big bus tour to every museum that offers a group rate. In Miami, where I'm from, we have maybe five museums, if you count the zoo. Here in Europe, every podunk town has ten or twenty. The bus pulls up in front of a museum and lets us out. Our tour guide, Mindy, has this little blue-and-white flag with a picture of a bird on it, which makes walking behind her the ultimate in humiliation. She walks backward to whichever great work of art the museum's famous for. The assembled peasants gawk for a full two minutes. Then it's off to the gift shop to spend our Euros on stuff we wouldn't pay two cents for if it was in the Walgreens back home.

It's not doing a thing to get my mind off Amber.

At least my friend Travis is here. Guess his parents wanted to get rid of him, too. I don't even know what country we're in now. One of those lame ones you don't learn much about in geography, like Belgium, or maybe one of the "L" ones. I don't pay much attention to Mindy, but yesterday I heard her say the magic word: *coast.* We're near the beach. That's when I started formulating my plan.

I shake Travis awake.

"What the . . . what time is it?"

"Five thirty, man."

"In the morning?"

"No, at night. It's almost time for dinner."

That gets him up. But when he sees how dark it is, he slumps back on the bed.

"It's still dark."

Can't put anything over on Travis, at least not where food or sleep are concerned.

"Okay, I lied. But I need to get out of this Tour of the Damned and have some fun. That's not going to happen unless we can beat the seven o'clock meet-up time."

"Know what would be fun?"

"What, Trav?" I'm hoping maybe he has some ideas, since I know his parents roped him into this tour, same as mine.

"Sleeping."

"It's not like they're going to let you sleep in, anyway. Soon they'll be banging on the door, telling us to get ready. This way, you can sleep when we hit the beach."

"Beach?"

Back home in Miami, Travis is a serious sun god. Now he's the color of marshmallows.

"Sure, the beach. Think of it, Travis. Topless French chicks."

"We're not in France."

"Okay, topless German chicks. Does it make a difference?"

"Will there be food?"

"Sure. There's a café across the street. We'll get breakfast and some sandwiches, but first we have to get out of here."

Finally, I manage to get him out of bed. I'd actually sort of wanted to go look at this National Botanic Garden of Belgium (Belgium! That's where we are!) we passed yesterday on the way to Museum Number Three. I could see this huge giant sequoia from the road. Of course, we didn't have time to look at it. But I knew that Travis was way more likely to go along with me to the beach. At least it's not another dusty art museum, and maybe we can hit the garden on the way back.

I drag Travis to the concierge desk to ask for directions.

"You couldn't have done that while I was getting ready?" Travis asks.

"You'd have gone back to sleep."

"You know, sometimes it's like you *work* at being a slacker."

"I prefer to spend my summer not working at anything."

We have to stand there for a while, while the concierge guy makes time with the desk clerk. If he doesn't get over here soon, Mindy might catch us.

"Hey, little help here . . ." I look at his nameplate. "Jacks?"

He ignores us.

"Hey! Don't want to take time from your busy schedule."

When he finally figures out that we're not leaving, he comes over.

"Which way to the beach, Jacks?" I ask.

"It is *Jacques*." He gives me that special glare hotel concierges always give you when they figure out you're American or that you don't speak the language, like he ate a bad niçoise salad. Like I'm supposed to speak every language in Europe. I took Spanish in school. Of course, we haven't been to Spain yet. At least, I don't think we have.

"The beach?" I repeat. *"La playa?"*

"Le plage," Travis tries.

"Ah, *oui*. *La plage*." We've pushed a magic button, and suddenly the concierge is our best friend and now speaks perfect English. "The autobus leaves at nine thirty."

"We can't wait until nine thirty, Jacks."

Jacques shrugs. "That is when it goes."

If we have to wait until nine thirty, we're going to get caught, and I'm going to get stuck in another museum. My girlfriend dumped me, my summer vacation is ruined, and this guy can't even help me have one decent day? Isn't it, like, his *job* to be helpful? "Is there another bus, maybe? Is this, like, the completely lamest country in Europe?"

Travis nudges me. "Jack, you're gonna get him mad."

"Who cares? He doesn't understand me, anyway. Everyone in this country is—"

"Ah, you are correct, *monsieur*," Jacques interrupts,

31

"and I am wrong. I have just remembered there is another autobus, a different route. A different beach."

I give Trav a look like, *see?*

"Would you write it down for us?" Travis asks. "Please?"

"But of course."

The concierge hands us a bus schedule with the routes and times circled. "You want to get off here and then walk to the east." He sketches a map. It looks pretty complicated, but at least the bus leaves in twenty minutes.

"Thanks," Travis says. "Listen, is there a place to get sandwiches?"

My cell phone rings. I check the caller ID: Mindy, looking for us. I grab Travis's arm. "We've got to go."

"But I'm hungry."

"Later." I drag him away.

"Thanks," he yells to Jacques. "See you later."

Jacques waves, and he's actually smiling. He says something that sounds like "I doubt it" but is probably just some weird French phrase. I pull Travis out the door just as I spot Mindy stepping out of the elevator.

Luckily, she's already walking backward and doesn't see us.

Chapter 2

"Good thing we got food first," Travis says on the bus.

"Yeah, you mentioned that."

Actually, Travis has mentioned that seven times, once every ten minutes that we've been on this bus ride.

"But it *is* a good thing. Otherwise, we'd be starving. In fact, I'm thinking about breaking out one of the sandwiches now."

Travis brought enough sandwiches and beer (the legal drinking age here is sixteen!) for a family of four for a week. He also ate a four-egg omelet, a stack of pancakes, and ten strips of bacon (the waitress called it the "American breakfast"). Plus, since he got it to go, he actually just finished eating about twenty minutes ago.

"Forget food for a minute. Doesn't this bus ride seem a little long to you? I mean, this is a small country. I brought my passport, but I wasn't planning on using it."

"It's long," Travis agrees, eyeing the bag with the sandwiches.

I pick it up and hold it shut so he has to listen to me.

"And isn't it going—I don't know—sort of in the opposite direction of the way you'd think the beach would be?"

"The guy said it was a different beach, but maybe he lied."

"I think that guy messed us up on purpose."

"You did say his country was lame."

"It is lame. So you think we're going the wrong way, too?"

"Maybe." Trav's looking at the bag with the sandwiches. "It's hard to think straight when you're hungry."

I'm about to give him a sandwich just so *I* can think when the bus driver announces that we've reached Jacques's stop.

"Finally. Time to get off."

"Does that mean I can't have a sandwich?"

"Think how good it will taste when we're sitting on the beach."

Twenty minutes later, not only have we not found the beach, we haven't even found the first street Jacques wrote on his map.

"It says go three blocks, then turn on St. Germain," Travis says. "But it's been more than three blocks. It's been, like, six. Maybe we should turn back."

I'm about to agree when I see a street called St. Germain. "This must be it."

But the next street isn't where it's supposed to be, either, even when we've walked three times as far as the map says. "Maybe you're right," I say.

When we turn back, nothing looks the way it did the first time. The first time, there were houses and stores and bicycles. Now there's nothing but trees and, well . . . nature everywhere I look. "What happened?" I say.

"To what?" Travis is munching on a sandwich.

"To everything—the town, the people?"

Travis wipes his mouth on his sleeve. "I didn't notice."

I see a little dirt road I hadn't seen before. I turn down it, gesturing to Travis to follow me. "Come on."

But this isn't where we were before, either. It's like everything just disappeared into a fog. Travis isn't noticing, since he's in a fog of his own, created by the sandwich. But then we run into something he can't ignore.

It's a solid wall of brambles.

"Now what?" I say.

"Go back."

"Back where? We're lost. This isn't where we were before. Besides, look." I gesture around me. "All this natural stuff. Back in Miami, if you had all this nature around, you'd definitely be near the beach."

In fact, the hedge looks a lot like bramble bushes in Miami. It has fuchsia flowers a little like the bougainvillea that grows there. The weird thing is that it must be three or four stories high.

"So where's the beach?" Travis asks.

I shrug. "Not back there."

"But this road's a dead end."

"I know. But listen." I cup my hand to my ear. "What do you hear?"

"Chewing," Travis says.

"Well, stop chewing."

Travis finishes the last bite. "Okay."

"Now, what do you hear?"

Travis listens real carefully. "I don't hear anything."

"Exactly. Which means there must be nothing on the other side of that hedge—no city, no cars, just nothing. The beach."

"So you're saying you want to go *through* the hedge?"

"What have we got to lose?"

"How about blood? Those bushes look prickly."

It's true. But I say, "Don't be a wuss."

"Can I have another sandwich at least?"

I grab the bag from him. "After the hedge."

Fifteen minutes later, there's nothing on any side of us except brambles.

"I bet I look like the victim in a slasher movie," Travis says. "What's the French word for 'chain saw'?"

"It's not that bad. The flowers sort of smell nice." I inhale.

36

"Right. You stay and smell the flowers. I'm going back."

I grab his wrist. "Please, Trav. I want to go to the beach. I can't handle another day of the tour."

He pulls away. "What's the big deal? My parents are going to ask me what I did today."

"That's the thing. My parents won't. They won't ask me what I did the past week. They don't care what I'm doing. And I hate going to all those stupid museums. Looking at all that boring art makes my mind wander, and when my mind wanders, all I can think of is Amber kissing that frat boy."

Travis stops pulling. "Wow. That really hit you hard, huh?"

"Yeah." I thought I was just making stuff up to get Trav to do what I want, but I have this sort of sick feeling in my stomach. I'm telling the truth. My parents haven't called in two weeks, except once to ask me if I signed up for AP Government next year for school, and this trip is doing nothing to make me forget about Amber. I see her face in every painting in every museum—especially that Degas guy, who painted girls with no faces at all. I can't get away from her. "Yeah. I just want to go to the beach for one day. I need to be outside."

"Okay, buddy. Only you go in front."

So I go up front, taking the full scratchy brunt of the brambles for another twenty minutes—twenty minutes during which I don't think about my parents *or* Amber but only about the fact that if I lose too much blood, there'll be no one here to help. When we finally reach the other side, I stop.

"Wow," I say.

"What is it?" Travis is still behind me.

"Definitely not the beach."

hapter 3

When I was a kid, back when my family was still pretending to like one another, we took a trip to Colonial
Williamsburg. It's this place where everything's like Colonial times—horses and buggies on unpaved streets. There's
stuff like blacksmith shops, too. My sister, Meryl, and I had
fun with the employees because if you ask them stuff like
which way to Starbucks, they act like they don't know what
you're talking about. But it got weird after a while. You
wondered if they seriously didn't know it was the twenty-
first century. I was ready to go home at the end of the day.

The place on the other side of the hedge is sort of like
that. I mean, not just *old*. Pretty much everything in Europe
is old and falling apart and important, but this place takes
historic preservation to a whole new level.

"Do you think it's, like, a theme park?" I say to Travis.

"No one here."

"Maybe it's just not open yet. Or closed. Is today Sunday?"

The streets are unpaved, and even if they were, they're barely wide enough to get one of those little European cars down. But the transportation here is horses, judging from how many are tied to hitching posts, sleeping. There's not a McDonald's or a Gap anywhere, only one building with ALEHOUSE painted on it in peeling, old-fashioned lettering. And the plants look bad. Some are overgrown, but a lot of stuff is bare, like the grass died years ago.

"Definitely not the beach." Travis starts pushing through the brambles.

The brambles have settled into the same shape they were before we went through them. I do not want to go through those bushes again.

Travis must think the same thing because he steps back. "Maybe we should eat lunch first."

Something about this place is really weirding me out. "Let's wait for a while. Who knows how long it will take to get back to civilization . . . and sandwiches."

Travis thinks about it and gets this worried look on his face. "Okay. Then we should get out of here." He starts pushing through the brambles again.

"Wait! Maybe we should start looking for a different way out or at least see if anyone around here has a chain saw."

"You see any people here?"

"There's horses. And they're tied up. That means there are people somewhere." The weird thing is, I sort of want to look around a little bit. This place is cooler than anything else we've seen on this trip. At least it's outside, and Mindy's not here telling us what to think. "We should look for them."

Travis glances around. "If there's people here, they're really not into mowing and weeding. But if you say so. . . ."

"I do."

He shrugs but follows me. We walk down the street, which is really more of a pathway with weeds and stuff growing on both sides. I point to the alehouse. "Let's try in there."

He nods. "It doesn't look like the type of place where they'd card."

The alehouse has steps in front of it. When I put my foot on one, it squeaks and moves under me. I step on a better, less rotted part, but even so, it quivers and shakes.

"This is really weird, Jack. You think maybe the whole town died or something, and there's nothing but a bunch of dead bodies?"

I remember when we went to Colonial Williamsburg, they told us about all the diseases people got in those days, like yellow fever, black plague, and scarlet fever. Meryl and I joked that all the diseases back then sounded really colorful. But now it's kind of freaky thinking about some sickness taking out the whole town. Maybe Travis is right, not necessarily that everyone died, but maybe a lot did and the rest decided to get out of Dodge.

But I say, "That's stupid. There's no abandoned town in Europe. If there were, someone would turn it into a museum. They'd widen the streets and bring people here by the busload and torture kids on tours."

"I guess you're right."

"Of course I am."

And to prove how right I am, I walk to the door.

But I still can't bring myself to go in, so I look through the window. It's easy because there's no glass in it, and I remember that a lot of places didn't have glass windows in the old days, only shutters to pull down at night or if it got cold. I can't see much. There's no light inside and nothing moving. We stand there so long that I'm almost expecting someone—possibly a ghost—to come up behind us and ask what we're doing here. So when Travis says, "Come on!" I jump about three feet.

He laughs. "Not afraid of dead bodies, huh?"

"Nope." I push open the door.

The room is dark. There are lanterns, but none are lit. It takes my eyes a minute to get used to it. Even so, I see there are people there, sitting on barstools, but they're really quiet. No music, no laughter, no talking, and when my pupils finally dilate, I realize the people aren't moving at all, like they're dead.

But they can't be dead. If they died long ago in some plague or massacre, their horses wouldn't still be tied outside, and they'd be reduced to skeletons.

Unless they got mummified. I saw this movie once where this guy killed someone. He mummified her body and sat her in an upstairs window. You couldn't tell the difference unless you saw her face.

I take a deep breath and let it out real slow, prepping myself to walk around and look at their faces. That's when it happens.

One of them snores.

"What was that?" Travis says. He's hugging the door.

"It sounded like a snore."

"A snore? Like they're sleeping? All of them?"

"I think so." I walk over to the side of one guy. He snores, and I see his stomach moving in and out. He's alive. He's definitely alive. I'm saved! I don't have to touch a mummified corpse!

I tap his shoulder. "Hey, bud."

He doesn't answer. I shake him harder and yell louder. "Hey! Dude! Hey, you!"

Now that it's that obvious they're not zombies or anything, Travis steps forward and starts shaking a different guy. "We're sorry to bother you, but we're looking for directions."

Nothing.

There are five guys on stools and the bartender asleep on the floor. Trav and I spend five minutes shaking, yelling, pulling, and practically dancing with them. They're definitely alive, but they're totally asleep.

"I think we need to try another place," I tell Trav.

There's only one person at the next shop, an old lady asleep with a bunch of falling-apart hats on stands. We shake her, but she doesn't wake.

We try three more places, and they're all the same.

"Freaky," Travis says when we step out of the greengrocer's. There was nothing in the bins, not a single grape or carrot. The grocer was napping on the floor. "Can we leave now? A grocer without groceries is just . . . wrong."

I sigh. "I guess so."

But when I turn the corner, I stop.

"Whoa!"

Chapter 4

It's a castle. Not a modern-looking one like Buckingham Palace, with electricity and toilets (when we visited it, the plumber was there—his truck said THE DIPLOMAT OF DRAIN AND SEWER CLEANING—and Trav and I had fun joking about what the queen had done to stop up the drains), but a real castle, the kind that comes in a set with a bunch of plastic knights and horses. It could even have a dungeon.

"Check it out." I start toward it.

"Hey, wrong way. I want to go back."

"Suit yourself." I walk faster. "But I have the sandwiches."

"Hey!" Travis starts running after me, but he's got on flip-flops. I have sneakers, and I was on the track team at school, so I can outrun him.

The castle is farther than I thought because it's bigger

than I thought. It's big enough to put a whole city in. I finally reach it about ten minutes later. There's a moat around it full of brown, sludgy water.

"Oops. Can't go in," Trav yells from way back.

I walk around the perimeter until I see where the draw-bridge is. It's open, and there's a castle door at the end of it. I start across.

"Are you sure you should do that? Someone might behead you."

"Come on, Travis. What are we going to do, go crawling back to Mindy? This is the first interesting thing we've seen in the past three weeks. I just want to look around."

At the door, I see two guards. Surprise—they're sleeping. I grasp the handle and pull on it. It opens with a loud squeal. I step inside.

We're in this huge room with three-story ceilings.

"Wow, it's like the ballroom in *Shrek 2*," Travis says.

I nod and hand him a sandwich. It lightens the load, and we've still got six or seven more. To be safe, I hold on to the beer.

"Hey, look." I point at a suit of armor standing in a corner. "Let's try it on."

"There could be someone in it."

I jump back. I hadn't thought about that. I don't think the sleeping people around here look like they date back to medieval times, but better safe than sorry. I slowly, gingerly lift the bill of the knight's face mask.

It's empty.

I breathe out. "Maybe this place won't be as freaky as the rest."

This is so cool. All the castles and towers we've been to, you're either not allowed to look around inside at all, or if you are, you just get to stand behind velvet ropes and see stuff in climate-controlled boxes. This place is real, even if it is a little dusty. I start down a hallway that goes out to the side. I look in the first room. "Hey."

"What is it? The kitchen?"

"Better."

It's an actual throne room like in the movies, and there are people in it, peasants maybe, waiting to see the king or something. The king isn't there, though.

"They're asleep like everyone else in this town," Travis says.

"But look."

Two guards sleep off to one side. Each has a pillow in his lap. On each pillow is a crown encrusted with diamonds, emeralds, and rubies. It's just like the stuff we saw in the Tower of London, only it's out where we can touch it.

"I'm trying one on," I say.

"Are you sure you should? What if they wake up?"

"We've practically stomped on these people, and they haven't woken up."

Still, when I take the crown off its velvet pillow, I almost expect an alarm to go off or something. None does, and I place the crown on my head. "How do I look?"

Travis laughs. "Kind of stupid."

"You're just jealous. Try the other."

"It's a girl's crown." Still, he puts it on. We fool around, sitting on the thrones and patting the peasants on the heads. After a while, Travis says, "We should take them."

I shake my head. I don't like the idea of stealing anything. "Let's look around first and see what else there is."

We put the crowns back and go into more rooms. On the third floor, there's a bunch of rooms with nothing in them but dresses.

"Wouldn't you think this stuff would get eaten by rats and bugs?" Travis says.

"You see any rats and bugs? Maybe they're sleeping, too."

When we reach maybe the tenth room of dresses, Travis says, "This is boring. Let's try on the armor."

I'm about to say okay when I notice this weird little staircase going off to the side. I saw a turret when we were outside. I wonder if this goes up to it.

"Let's go there first," I say.

Before Travis can protest, I start upstairs. I didn't think the staircase was very tall, but it curves around and goes higher. Then it curves again and again.

When we finally reach the top, the door is closed. I open it and find a room with nothing but a girl, sleeping on the floor.

She's the most beautiful girl I've ever seen.

Chapter 5

I stare at her. I've never seen a human being who looks like her, and I'm from Miami, where good-looking people go to spawn. But this girl isn't just beautiful. She's perfect in a way that's unreal, like one of Meryl's Barbie dolls.

What I'm saying is, this girl is . . .

"Wow, she's hot," Travis says when he finally reaches the door.

Yeah. That. She's lying on the floor with these golden curls all around her, like someone arranged them that way. Her body, I can tell even in her long dress, is totally perfect. She's taller than almost everyone else here, and thin in all the right places with these great . . .

"Would you look at her?" Travis interrupts my thoughts again.

I am. I stare at the top of her dress, which she's really filling out, let me tell you. I feel this incredible urge to touch her, but I know it's wrong because she's asleep.

But the weird thing is, it's not her body I notice the most. It's her face.

Her skin is the color of milk with just the tiniest bit of strawberry Nesquik mixed in. Her eyes are closed, but I can tell they're huge, with long eyelashes that curve upward.

And her mouth. It's full and red, and her lips definitely don't look like lips that haven't been moistened in hundreds of years.

For some reason, looking at her makes me think of Amber. Not that she looks like Amber, because she doesn't. Amber's beautiful in a normal, human way. But, compared to this girl, Amber's total chopped liver.

And somehow, just looking at her, I know she isn't like Amber. She wouldn't dump someone for a guy with a cooler car.

"What are you, in love with her?" Travis says. "You're staring like an idiot."

The weird thing is, I think I am.

Stupid.

"She's asleep. You could . . ." Travis looks at the door. ". . . do anything."

"That's sick."

"You know you were thinking about it."

"No, I wasn't. That would be wrong."

"Right and wrong's getting kind of fuzzy for me. Was it

50

wrong to ditch the tour? Was it wrong to lie to Mindy? Was it wrong to sneak in here?"

"I guess." I keep looking at the girl. I can't stop looking at her.

"Come on. I dare you to touch her."

"Okay." I want to anyway. I lean toward her, wishing she'd wake up.

I reach down and touch one of her curls.

Soft. So soft. I comb my fingers through it to make it last. She stirs in her sleep, and I imagine she's enjoying my touch, but of course, that's impossible.

"Not her hair, dorko. She can't even feel her hair."

"She can't feel anything. She's asleep like the rest of them."

"So why not touch an important part?"

It's not because Travis says to. It's because I want to. I move my hand back up the length of her hair to her face.

It feels like—God, this is hokey—flower petals. Roses, maybe. I move my finger across her cheek, to her mouth, her lips. They're parted slightly, and suddenly, I can't keep from admitting it: I want to kiss her. Crazy, because ten minutes ago I was still completely thinking about Amber, but I really want to kiss this comatose chick. I lean closer.

"Not her cheek, idiot!" Travis leans down. "God, get out of the way."

"No!" I block him. It's impossible to say that I totally, like, respect this girl even though I don't know her. I can just tell she's someone special.

God, I wonder if she's a princess!

I stand. "Look, I want to kiss her, but not in front of you. Why don't you go downstairs and steal those crowns? The princess and I need some time alone."

"For real?"

"Sure." I can get him to put them back later. "But give me ten minutes."

"Okay, but I'll be back soon." He starts toward the door and then turns back. "Hey, you don't think it's really stealing when they're, like, never going to wake up?"

I sort of do, but I'm not the one doing the stealing, and I want Travis gone. "Of course not."

"Okay. See ya." And he's gone.

I'm alone in the room except for the girl. I touch her hair again, and her cheek, now that I can do it without Travis ragging on me. She sighs softly in her sleep. She's so beautiful, I wish she'd wake up so I could talk to her. But it's probably better this way. If she were awake, she wouldn't be into me.

That's when I think of *Snow White.*

Snow White was Meryl's favorite fairy tale. Of course, being a boy, I thought it was lame. Still, she watched the DVD maybe a thousand times, so I couldn't help but know the story, which is about a princess who eats a poisoned apple.

Everyone thinks she's dead. But then the prince kisses her. She wakes up, and she and the prince live happily ever after.

Maybe I could wake her up.

Except, of course, I'm no prince.

And there's all those other sleeping people. That didn't happen in *Snow White*.

Still, it wouldn't hurt to kiss her. I'd feel less like a sicko if I think I'm trying to wake her.

I raise her up toward me. Her body is warm, and it's like nothing to lift her. Her dress is made of this soft velvet, and when I pull her close, I can feel her heartbeat.

I wish I could see her eyes, but her face . . . her lips . . .

It's kind of weird to kiss a girl if you don't know her name. But maybe I can make one up.

Talia.

The name just comes to me. I don't know where I got it from. I've never known a Talia. Still, I'm sure it's the perfect name.

"Talia," I whisper.

She sighs in her sleep.

"Oh, Talia." I pull her toward me, one hand in her hair, supporting her head. I bring my face close to hers, and it's like I can see her whole life, being in this castle, isolated, wishing for something more. I don't know how I know it, maybe the same way I know her name. Talia.

My lips are on hers. It's a long kiss. I hold her closer, feeling her hair, her body, her mouth, and then her hands in my hair.

What the—?

I don't want to stop kissing her, especially since she's

53

kissing me back, even if it's in her sleep.

Still, finally, I have to pull away from her to breathe. So I do.

"You're so beautiful, Talia."

I look straight into her grass green eyes. I've never seen eyes that color before.

"Thank you, my prince," she sighs.

Then the green eyes widen.

"Who are you?"

And that's when she screams.

Chapter 6

She's awake! It really is like *Snow White*! Holy crap! But I'm no prince. I'm just this regular guy from America—a totally prince-free country—and she's still awake.

She opens her mouth to scream again.

"Don't scream." I put my fingers over her lips, not like a kidnapper or anything. "I'm not going to hurt you. Please don't scream."

Not that it would matter if she did. I mean, there's no one awake to hear her.

She pushes my hand away.

"Explain yourself! Who are you? Why were you . . . kissing me?"

"I'm Jack. I wasn't kissing you, exactly. You were passed out. I was giving you mouth-to-mouth resuscitation." I lie because I don't want her to think I was attacking her or something.

"Mouth to . . . what? What are you saying? What is that?"

Geez, she's stupid. Beautiful, but dumb. Isn't that always the way?

Unless they don't have mouth-to-mouth where—or *when*—she's from.

"Jack? Are you one of the dressmakers? What is that you are wearing?"

I look down. I have on kind of junky clothes, an Old Navy Fourth of July flag T-shirt from last summer, and jeans. The shirt's all torn up from going through the bushes. At least I pulled the jeans on over my swim trunks at the last minute. "It's a flag T-shirt."

She looks confused at the word *T-shirt* and squints at it. "Flag? From what country?"

"The United States. America. *Yo soy Americano.*"

"Where is that?"

"Other side of the ocean? Head west?" Maybe she hit her head.

Her eyes light up with recognition. "Oh! You mean Virginia?"

Which is weird. Colonial Williamsburg is in Virginia. Maybe all these people who pretend they're historical figures know each other, like some sort of club. "Yeah, sort of. Not Virginia, exactly. Florida. But they're both in America."

"And this is your flag? It is a custom, then, to wear it on your chest?"

It seems kind of weird when you put it that way. "Not always."

"I see. So you have come from . . . ?"

"Florida."

"Then you must be here to show me dresses, for you are certainly not visiting royalty."

I'm not sure I like the way she says "certainly," but I let it go. The girl has definitely had a bad day. "What dresses?"

She gets a sort of faraway look on her face, then stands.

"Now I remember. Before I . . . fainted, I suppose, I was looking at dresses, such beautiful dresses, each the exact shade of my eyes."

She looks at me, and I notice again what gorgeous eyes she has. I imagine what it would be like to have those eyes focused on me.

"They are gone," she says.

"I didn't see any dresses. I swear."

"But you were not here, either. It was just me and one other person. A boy." She smiles. "No. That was earlier. But then there was a lady, an old woman. It was she who brought the green dresses. She was spinning thread. She told me I could make a wish."

She stops speaking and turns away from me, toward the window. "But why can I not remember? It just happened."

"Maybe I can help you," I say, kneeling beside her. "Close your eyes."

She gives me a look, like maybe I'm trying to trick her, but she closes them. With her eyes closed, it's like the lights have gone out, and now it's nighttime.

"Okay," I say. "Now, try to picture it. You're looking at the pretty dresses, and there's an old woman there. What does she look like?"

"I could tell she was once beautiful. She had black eyes that glittered like onyx."

"She said you could have a wish, and then what?"

She places her hand over her eyes. "Oh, I have a headache."

"What's the next thing you remember?"

She breathes in deeply, then sighs. Finally, she says, "A dream. It must be, for I was kissing a prince, my prince. He was telling me how beautiful I was."

"Your boyfriend?"

"No! I have no friends, certainly none who are boys. I have been nowhere, met no one." She shakes her head. "It was but a dream. Then I opened my eyes, and you were kissing me." She looks down a moment, examining something on her skirt. It looks like a spot of blood.

And suddenly, her eyes open fully, wider and greener than before.

"Oh, my!"

"What?" I back away. "What is it?"

"A kiss! You say I was sleeping, and you happened upon me?"

"Yeah."

"Yes. And did you think I was quite beautiful?" I grimace, and she says, "Oh, never mind. Of course you did. Everyone agrees that I am utterly stunning."

"Modest, too."

She ignores me. "So you saw me, and I was so beautiful that you immediately fell in love with me."

This girl's pretty full of herself, but it's not far from the truth. "Well, not—"

"You fell in love with me, and you leaned over and kissed me. Love's first kiss. And when you kissed me, I woke immediately. Is that true?"

"Yeah."

And suddenly, she begins to cry. "Oh, no. Oh, no. I am a fool. Old pudding-faced Lady Brooke was right. I am a stupid girl and ought never have been trusted for even a minute on my own."

"What are you talking about?" I want to put my arm around her or something, but I get the feeling that wouldn't be a good idea.

"The curse, stupid!"

"Now I'm stupid? What happened to you being stupid, and what curse?"

"The curse. *The* curse. Everyone knows about Malvolia's curse. Oh, my father will kill me. They will probably lock me up in a convent!" She begins to sob again, and then seeing that I am still not with the program, she says, "Before her sixteenth birthday, the princess shall prick her finger on a spindle and die."

"But you're not dead."

"No. The fairy Flavia changed it so I would merely sleep. The whole kingdom would sleep, to wake only when *I* was wakened by true love's first kiss."

"Uh-huh." *She's nuts.*

"The old lady was Malvolia, do you not see? She came with the dresses, gained my trust. She had probably been watching me all my life. She brought with her a spindle. She knew I would make a wish, and when I did . . ."

"You're saying she stabbed you with that spindle thing?"

"Exactly. It is the curse. I have made the curse come true."

And she starts blubbering harder.

"Hey, calm down," I say. "It's going to be okay."

Now she stands and begins pacing. "They warned me so many times. It is practically the only subject upon which I conversed with my parents. It was their worst fear, and it has come true."

I try to think of what my parents' worst fear is—me not getting into college, maybe. Or having to go to one of those community colleges that's *near* a good school, so they could just tell everyone "Jack went to Boston" or whatever. They'd die.

But I say, "Exactly. It's over. You went to sleep, and you're awake now because of me and my magical kiss. Your parents will probably be so happy you're okay that they won't even be mad."

"Do you really think that?"

"Sure. It's like this one time I totaled my car. My mom was driving by, and she saw the wreck. She was so happy I wasn't dead that she didn't even . . ." I stop. The princess is staring at me like I'm speaking in tongues. "Anyway, I'm sure they'll just be okay with it. You're their little princess, right?"

She's stopped crying, and now she nods. "Perhaps you are right."

"I know I am."

"What is the date? I need to know how long I have slept."

I check my watch's date feature. "It's June twenty-third."

"Oh, that is not so bad then. A month. I missed my birthday party, which is a shame, and they will need to explain to the guests, but still . . ."

Her eyes fall on my watch. "What is that?"

"A watch."

She picks up my wrist, examines it, then holds it to her ear. "A clock? On your wrist? How strange." She pulls back from me and examines my clothes, the flag T-shirt.

"What is that?" She points to the numbers on the shirt.

"The year. Old Navy puts the year on all their flag T-shirts. It's sort of a racket, I guess—you have to buy a new one every year."

"That . . . is . . . the . . . year?" She looks sort of sick. Her face is suddenly almost the same color green as her eyes.

"Well, I got it last year. We always get them for when we

go watch fireworks. But I probably won't get one this year, come to think of it, because—"

"That is the year? The year!"

"Well, last year."

She begins to shake. "Oh, my . . . oh, no." She crumples back onto the floor, as she was when I first saw her. "It cannot be true. It cannot."

I kneel beside her. "What's the matter now? I thought you were fine."

She looks at me, then starts screaming. "Fine? Fine? I have been asleep nearly three hundred years!"

Outside on the stairs, I hear a commotion, people running, then yelling.

"Stop! Thief!"

Travis appears at the door. "Jack, we gotta go. They're all awake, and they're after me for stealing the crown!"

Chapter 7

Things get a little crazy then. There's Travis at the door and then two guards with actual swords. When they come in, Travis starts yelling, "I don't have them! Search me if you don't believe me—just don't behead me!" One of the swords swings around, and he jumps. "Get those things away from me!"

Then a bunch more people show up. Most of them are holding fancy old dresses.

Next is a woman, who I'm guessing is the one the princess called "pudding-faced Lady Brooke," because her face does look as beige and bland as vanilla pudding. Talia runs to her, screaming with anguish. "Lady Brooke! I have done it! I have done it!"

"Done what, dear?" Lady Brooke says.

"Ruined everything. I am so sorry."

Travis has managed to edge away from the guards in the confusion when the dressmakers showed up. Now, he tugs my arm. "Come on, man."

I start to go, glancing back at the princess, who's still wailing away.

"Wait!" the princess screams, loud enough to make everyone in the room stop what they're doing and look at her. Everything is silent, and I realize that no one but Talia and I know that they've been asleep for hundreds of years.

Finally, pudding-faced Lady Brooke says, "What now, dear?"

The princess points at me. "He cannot leave."

"Why not?"

"Because he has kissed me!"

Every eye in the room turns on me. The guards notice Travis again, but this time they grab both of us.

"Have you defiled the princess?" one guard demands, getting close with the sword.

"No . . . I mean, I don't think so."

"No!" Talia says. "I am not defiled in the least. But he must stay."

"Who are you?" Lady Brooke asks.

"I'm Jack O'Neill . . . from Florida . . . I guess I broke some spell. No need to thank me. If you'll just call off your guard before he removes something, I'll get going."

The princess lunges toward me. "You cannot go. You have broken the spell. Do you know what that means?" When I don't answer, she says, "It means you are my true love."

"Cuckoo! Cuckoo!" Travis whispers.

I ignore him. "True love? But I don't even know your name."

"My name?" She looks surprised. "Oh, well, that is easy enough. Everyone knows that."

"Except me." *Once you tell me, can I leave?*

"Very well. It is probably best to have a proper introduction." She looks at Pudding Face and says, "Lady Brooke."

Lady Brooke nods, although she doesn't look happy about it, and gestures toward me. "Jack O'Neill, of Florida, you are presented to Her Royal Highness, Princess Talia."

Talia.

"It is customary to bow at this time," Talia says.

"Your name is Talia? I didn't know . . ."

"And yet, that is what you called me when you . . ."

"I know." I shake my head. "I mean, I didn't know your name, but somehow I guessed or something. It was weird, like someone told it to me."

She nods. "True love. It was meant to be."

"Look," I say, "I might want to go out sometime, but as far as true love—"

"But you woke me! And I can only be awakened by true love's kiss. And besides, I am a beautiful princess. How could you *not* love me?"

Easy.

Travis looks at Talia, then at the hands of the guards who are holding him, and then back at Talia. "So, um, Your Royalness, do you think you could maybe let us go?"

"Yeah, it's—ah—getting late." It's actually only twelve thirty, but who knows if these people can even tell time. "Our tour group's waiting for us."

"Highness, this one is a thief!" the guard behind Travis says. "And if this person was with him, he must be an accomplice."

"I'm no thief," I say, "and neither is Travis."

"The crown was in his hands!" says the guard.

"He didn't take anything, and I'm the one who broke the curse and saved you all. Doesn't that count for anything?"

"What curse?" Lady Brooke says. "What is he talking about?"

Talia ignores her. "Yes. Guards, you must unhand this gentleman at once. He is an honored guest and a friend of my future husband. You must both stay for supper."

Future husband? Does she mean me? "Excuse me, but I'm not—"

"Talia . . ." Lady Brooke says. "You cannot mean to invite this . . . this . . . commoner to supper. It is the eve of your birthday ball."

Talia starts to cry again. "No, Lady Brooke. Do you not understand? I have touched a spindle! A spindle! We have all been asleep for a great while, and this . . ." She gestures toward me. "This commoner has awakened me."

"You have touched a spindle, you say?" Lady Brooke's puddingy jaw is hanging.

Talia nods.

"A spindle, you say?"

66

"Yes!"

Lady Brooke cradles her forehead in her hands. "I have left you alone for ten minutes, and you touched a spindle and slept for . . . for . . ."

"Three hundred years."

"Ah!" Lady Brooke looks like she's been stabbed. "Oh, not again, not again . . ." She recovers. "And you have been awakened by a . . . a . . ."

"Really great guy?" I volunteer.

Talia nods. "He will stay for supper." She looks at me. "You *will* stay for supper?"

I nod. I can handle it if that's what it takes for them to let me go—even though they'll probably serve squirrel or something. "That's fine. Just let me call the hotel and tell them where we are." I take out my cell phone.

"What is that?" Princess Talia says.

"A phone." She keeps staring at it. In fact, everyone stops what they're doing, gathers around, and stares. "You can, um, talk to people on it."

Except I can't get a signal. Duh. There's no tower here. Suddenly, it dawns on me what Talia said: *I have been asleep nearly three hundred years!* If that's true, this place is like a time warp. Princess Talia really did screw things up.

And all I'm thinking is, *How did they go so long without eating or peeing?*

Everyone's still staring at the phone, which lights up and makes beeping noises. Think how jacked they'd get if it actually worked.

"We have to go there," I say. "They'll be waiting for us."

"But surely your friends must have known of your journey," Talia says.

"We sort of sneaked off."

"Then we must send a messenger," Talia says. "Simply tell me the name of the inn in which you are staying, and it shall be done."

Problem one: I have no idea where the hotel is. Problem two: There's a huge hedge around the whole country. Problem three: I am not—and I mean not—marrying this princess.

"Does this help?" Travis pulls a postcard out of his pocket. It has a photo of our hotel on the front. This causes another spasm of activity as everyone has to gather around to look at the photo. Finally, Travis says, "The address is on the back, I think."

Talia hands it to Pudding Face, who looks dangerously close to fainting. She examines it a moment, then says, "That is two days' journey."

It seemed pretty far but not two days.

"Nah," Travis says. "It was about two hours on the bus."

Pudding Face looks puzzled. "Bus?"

"Yah. It's sort of like a car only . . . you got the wheel here? Has that been invented yet?"

Talia straightens her shoulders, and even Lady Brooke seems to have recovered enough to glare at Travis.

"I guess it has," Travis says. "Well, a bus is sort of a wheel thing with a motor, and fast." He looks at them. "Okay, I can see you don't get the bus thing. Maybe I could, like, take your guards out and show it to them if, um, they'd let go of me and get their swords out of my butt."

Talia nods. "Do as he says."

The guards look disappointed, but they let go of Travis, and he gestures to them to follow him. "Hey, do you guys have a chain saw?" Travis is saying as they leave.

When he is gone, Talia turns to me. "Well, then, we must find you some proper clothing. If we are to marry, you must meet my father." Then, in case I don't get it, she adds, "The king. So we can arrange the wedding."

Lady Brooke finally topples to the ground. I'm pretty close to joining her.

I should have stayed with the tour!

Part III

Jack and Talia

Chapter 1: Talia

My life is ruined.

I dispatch Lady Brooke to find Jack a room and some clothing. Then I go back to the task I began, I thought, this morning, but apparently almost three hundred years ago—choosing dresses for the ball. There is no reason not to have a ball. Yes, I am three hundred sixteen years old (give or take a year) rather than sixteen years old, but since I have neither starved to death, nor died of thirst while asleep, it seems as though my body has been somehow suspended in time all these years. Besides, Jack would not have kissed me had I been a crone. Therefore, tomorrow will still be my sixteenth birthday, and I am still entitled to my party, so I still need dresses.

The bad news is that the most beautiful dresses were

supplied by someone whom I now know was an evil witch bent upon destroying me because she was annoyed at not being invited to a previous party (I will say, Father and Mother were rather shortsighted in not simply inviting her—what would it have cost, an extra pheasant and perhaps some turnips?), so I will need to continue my search.

I venture into the first, then the second room. I know I should go looking for Mother and Father, but I simply cannot face them yet. I do not want to tell them what I have done. They will never forgive me.

It is in the third room that I see Father. He looks distraught.

"Talia, I am so glad to have found you."

Although, truthfully, he does not look glad in the least.

"I have terrible news," he continues. "The ball must be canceled."

"But why?" Although I have some idea why. He has discovered my folly with the spindle, and he means to punish me. I prepare to bawl, possibly to wail. I am an excellent wailer.

But Father says something even more surprising.

"I do not know, my pet. It seems there are no guests."

"No guests? Whatever do you mean?"

"It is the queerest thing. The lookouts saw the first ships off in the distance at nine o'clock. By ten thirty, some were on the verge of entering the harbor. But then they simply disappeared."

"Disappeared?" I repeat what he has said to give me time to think.

Father nods. "I fear, daughter, that there is something afoot here, that we might be on the verge of war, or worse, that I may have been victimized by black magic, the dark art of the witch Malvolia."

Malvolia. Oh, no. In an instant, I understand what happened to the ships. They did not turn around, nor were they bewitched, not really. They may have tried to enter our harbor. But when they did, it was not there. The kingdom was obscured from sight by a giant wood, as Flavia said in her idiotic spell. They thought they had gone to the wrong place. The guests, the visiting royalty, even the special prince who might have been my husband, they have been dust for centuries, and I am merely a three-hundred-sixteen-or-so-year-old princess with absolutely no prospects whatsoever.

It will take a great deal of tact to explain this to Father.

"I am sorry, my dear daughter."

He is sorry. Would it be possible simply to feign ignorance of the whole situation? Pretend I have no idea what happened to the ships, no comprehension of what caused—I am certain—numerous additional changes to the kingdom?

But I remember Jack's clothing and the strange flashing object he carried with him, Travis's talk of buses. Certainly the world changed during our three-hundred-year hibernation, as surely as it changed during the three hundred years before that, and as soon as Father remarks the changes, he will understand their cause. If he does not, Lady Brooke will be certain to tell him.

"Father?" I touch his shoulder.

"Yes, my princess?"

"I believe . . ." I take his arm, sweet as I can, and guide him toward a chair. "I believe you should sit down."

He does, and when he does, I begin to tell my story.

"I touched the spindle, and then at the next moment, a commoner named Jack was waking me up," I conclude.

Father is silent.

"Father? Are you . . . is everything quite all right?"

"You say you touched a spindle, Talia? A spindle?"

"It was no fault of mine."

"No fault of yours? It was every fault of yours." He looks, suddenly, like God's revenge against murder. "Have we taught you nothing? How many times have we told you—cautioned you—about spindles? It was the first word you learned, the last thing you heard before bed at night, the one lesson of any import: Do not touch spindles. And you forgot it—*ignored* it?"

"I said I was sorry."

"Sorry? Do you not understand that we are ruined?"

"Ruined?" Father is making quite a fuss. "Certainly it is inconvenient, but—"

"Inconvenient! Talia, do you not understand? Could you be so stupid?"

I feel tears springing to my eyes yet again. He has never spoken to me in this manner. "Father, your voice. Everyone will hear you."

"What does it matter? If, as you say, we have all slept these three hundred years, we are ruined, destroyed—you, I, the entire kingdom. We have no kingdom. We have no trade. We have no allies to defend us. Mark my words, it will not be long before everyone realizes that my daughter is the stupidest girl on earth."

"But . . . but . . ." I can hold back my tears no longer, and when I look at my father, I see something horrible. He is struggling to hold back his own. My father, the king, the most powerful man in all Euphrasia, is weeping, and it is my fault, all my fault.

"It was a mistake!"

"You cared for no one but yourself, Talia, and we are paying the price. It would have been better had you engaged in any other youthful indiscretion—running away, even eloping—rather than this one. This has affected everyone, and it is unforgivable."

My father's words strike like daggers. He would rather see me gone than have me do what I did. He hates me.

"I am sorry, Father."

He looks at the floor. "Perhaps, Talia, you ought to go to your room."

Yes. Perhaps I should go and never come out—which is probably what is planned for me, anyway. I nod and start for the door. Then I remember something I must tell him, although at this point, I would much rather not. Still, if Father despises me, I have nothing to lose. I have already ruined everything.

"Father?"

"What is it now, Talia?"

"The boy, the one who woke me from my sleep . . . I have invited him to stay at the castle and to have supper with us."

Father stares at me. "Supper?"

"Yes. It seemed the proper thing to do."

He makes an attempt to straighten his shoulders but fails. "Yes." The word comes out as a sigh. "Yes, I suppose it is."

And then, before I can say anything else, Father turns on his heel and leaves. I wait a minute to make sure he is gone before leaving the room myself.

I am passing through the guest chambers on the way to my own room when I hear a voice.

"Excuse me? Talia? Um, Your Highness."

I stop. Jack! They must have placed him in this room.

I approach the door. "Yes?"

Indeed, it is him. This commoner, this *boy* I am supposed to marry, this nobody who has ruined everything.

And yet . . . he is wearing more appropriate clothing, in which he looks handsome, yet quite uncomfortable at the same time, as befits a member of the nobility. "Um, sorry to bother you, Princess."

"No bother." Although, in truth, I would much rather be alone with my grief. My face burns. Soon, everyone will know of my stupidity and humiliation, that I have ruined the kingdom, and soon *I* will be the most ruined of all.

"Your dad seemed upset."

I nod, unable to speak. So he had heard.

"But what he said," Mr. Jack O'Neill continues, "about the hundred years' sleep?"

"Three hundred."

"Right. Sorry."

"Three hundred! We have slept three hundred years, and we are ruined, and it is all my fault." I try not to sob again. Were I a few years (or a few hundred years) younger, I could throw myself on the floor with impunity, but as it is, I simply stand there, gasping for breath.

Jack stands there, too, looking down. I wonder if he heard Father call me the stupidest girl on earth. Probably the whole castle did. Finally, he says, "Can I get you something, like a Kleenex?" I have no idea what a Kleenex is, but he reaches into his pocket and procures a bit of paper, sort of a paper handkerchief.

I take it and sniffle into it. I try not to snuff too loudly. However, I have been crying very hard. So finally, I have to give in and snort like one of the horses so that, in addition to being the stupidest girl in all Euphrasia—nay, the world—I might also be the most disgusting.

To his credit, Jack pretends not to notice, and his kindness sends forth the torrent of tears I have been trying to avoid.

When I finish, he says, "My dad can be kind of a jerk, too. But I didn't think princesses had to deal with that."

"I am not even certain I *am* a princess any longer. Can I still be a princess if Euphrasia is no longer a country? It is all my fault! I am so stupid!"

"You're not stupid. You messed up. I mess up all the time."

Messed up? I move away from him, wondering if my face is blotchy, if I am hideous now, in addition to being stupid and disgusting. But I catch a bit of my reflection in the mirror attached to the wall. No, Violet's gift has held true. I am still beautiful. Perfect, in every way save one.

He continues. "From what I'm getting, you had a curse placed upon you—that before your sixteenth birthday, you would prick your finger on a spindle. Right?"

I nod. "Right."

"My dad, he's a businessman, and he's always looking at the wording of things. So that's how it was phrased? 'Before her sixteenth birthday, the princess *shall* prick her finger on a spindle . . .' not 'the princess *might* prick her finger' or 'if she is not careful, she will'?"

I nod. "But I was supposed to take care. Mother and Father always said—"

He holds up his hand. "Meaning no disrespect to them, either. I guess they were trying to protect you, but I don't think you could have kept from getting pricked with the spindle if it was part of the curse. It had to happen."

"But . . ." I stop. I rather like the way this young man is thinking. In fact, he is quite handsome for a peasant. "Do you really think so?"

"I do." There is conviction in his eyes. "This witch put that curse on you, and that was that—you were going to touch it. Maybe she even enchanted you to *make* you touch the spindle. It was your destiny."

"Destiny." I like the sound of it, particularly because it means that this whole fiasco is not my fault.

"Yeah, destiny, like how it was Anakin Skywalker's destiny to be Darth Vader."

I have not the slightest idea what he is talking about. "But that does not change the fact that Father believes me a fool and thinks it is all my fault that our country is ruined." I remember what Father said earlier, about how he would rather I had run away and eloped. I gaze at Mr. Jack O'Neill. He is tall, and his brown eyes are quite intoxicating, and in that moment, I see my escape. "Do you think perhaps . . . ?"

I cannot ask it.

But he says, "What, Your Highness?"

His eyes are kind as well.

"Talia. Call me Talia, for I am about to ask you to . . . take me with you."

"What?" He backs away three steps, as if he has been pushed. When he recovers himself, his voice is a whisper, and he glances at the door. "I can't."

"Why not? If it is because I am a princess and you are

81

a commoner, this matters not. I am an outcast now. Father despises me. They all . . ." I gesture toward the window, indicating the ground below, the land, the people. "They all shall hate me soon enough. Their crops are dead. Their food has rotted. They should be long dead and rotted themselves, but because of me, they are alive still, only the whole world has changed around them."

"But I'm only seventeen. I can't be responsible for a princess. I can barely get my homework done."

"Whyever not? Seventeen is a grown man. Surely, you must be learning a trade—like blacksmithing or making shoes."

"Sort of. I go to school. That's what everyone does now."

Now. Everything is different now. But I must change it. I was destined to prick my finger upon a spindle, and I did. But there was another part of the curse. I was to be wakened by true love's first kiss. That kiss was Jack's. Therefore, he must be my true love, even though he seems rather lazy and unpleasant, and I wonder how he could have gotten through the wood to the kingdom. He does not seem to appreciate the great opportunity he has been given, marriage to one gifted by the fairies with beauty and grace and musical talent and intelligence. I must make him realize it. I must make him my true love, if I am going to fulfill my destiny.

"Well," I say, "in any case, you must join us for supper."

"Okay," he says. "Supper's okay. Marriage—not so much."

I pretend to agree, but I know that I must make him fall in love with me, whether he wants to or not.

Chapter 2: Jack

I'm wearing something halfway between pants and tights, a *red* jacket, a ruffly shirt, and boots, all too small. At least they don't wear kilts in this country.

I crack the door (which is ten feet tall) open and look into the hallway.

A guard rushes toward me. "May I help you, sir?"

"Um, is there any food around here?"

The guy looks down. "I shall check, sir."

He doesn't move.

I close the door, my stomach growling like an ATV pulling through mud. It's been four hours since I kissed the princess. I know that from checking my cell phone, which is now useful only as a clock. I turn it off again to save the battery. It's not like there's any place to recharge it.

Of course, Travis took the sandwiches with him when

he ditched me to go to the hotel. Bet he doesn't come back. I kept the beer, but it's probably not a good idea to drink it on an empty stomach. I wonder if this is just a really fancy dungeon.

I go to the window for about the tenth time. There's no chance of escaping out the door. The hallway is crowded with people waiting to do my bidding. But no one wants to help me escape (and, really, where could I go in these pants?). The window's not much better. It's at least four stories up and made of this thick glass like in churches. No, my best bet is to have dinner, then sneak out when they all go back to sleep.

Of course, after three hundred years, they're probably pretty well rested.

I should have stayed with the tour group. Sure, the museums were boring, but at least the people were from this century.

Someone knocks at the door.

"Come in!"

They knock again. The door's so thick they can't even hear through it. I walk across the room and open it. "What?"

"Begging your pardon, sir." It's some servant guy in an outfit that is—I need to mention—way less froufrou than what they gave me to wear. "His Majesty apologizes for the delay in getting supper. There have been . . . difficulties."

My stomach growls loudly.

I'm scared to find out what these people eat. My mom's

a real freak about germs and salmonella, and this doesn't seem like the type of place that has sanitary cooking facilities or even a decent oven. Didn't people used to die at, like, age thirty-five in the 1700s, or even younger? And didn't they have plagues with rats and stuff?

If I have to die, I hope I don't die in tights.

What we're having for dinner is meat. Lots of meat and mushrooms and strawberries.

Talia's parents are there. Her father—the king—is a skinny guy with red hair, and he actually looks sort of like the Burger King, only the Burger King looks a lot friendlier and happy about burgers and stuff.

"I apologize for the fare," he's telling the group. Besides Talia and me, there's Pudding Face, the queen (an older version of Talia), and a bunch of other people introduced as lords and ladies. There are also two women Talia says are fairies, but I must have heard her wrong. "But, you see, all our crops died when my daughter put us to sleep for three hundred years, and the food we had has long since spoiled."

Talia looks away, but I can see her hands are trembling.

She looks great, though, especially in that dress she's wearing, a green one you can see down. She's stopped crying. She sits beside me and keeps staring at me with those eyes of hers.

"I am sorry, Father," she says. When the king doesn't answer, I see her glance toward the door.

I decide to change the subject. "So where'd you get the mushrooms . . . um, Your Highness?"

"Your Majesty," Talia whispers.

One of the fairy women turns to the other, and when she does, I see that there are wings sprouting from her back. She whispers, "*Him? He's* her destiny?"

"Shush," whispers the other.

"That is quite all right, Talia," the king says. "I am certain this young man is unused to dining with royalty in . . . Florida, is it?"

I nod.

"A Spanish colony, if I recall, and rather a wasteland. Has it changed much in three hundred years?"

"Um, a little."

"The hunters found the mushrooms in the forest," the king continues.

"Are they okay to eat?" I ask. It's probably a rude question, and actually a hallucinogenic mushroom could hit the spot right about now.

The king shrugs. "Does it truly matter at this point?" Talia flinches when he says that. The king takes a large forkful of the mushrooms, chews, and swallows them. We all watch. He doesn't fall over or barf or anything.

"They are acceptable," he says finally.

I don't ask what the meat is, but Talia says, "Is not the peacock excellent?"

"A bit tough after it has been drowsing three hundred years." The king glares at Talia. "But it will have to do."

Hoo-boy. And I thought my parents were rough. This guy's acting kind of like a spoiled brat. But then, that's how his daughter is, too.

Again, I try to change the subject.

"This is peacock?"

"Certainly," the queen says.

"Wow." I've tried it now, and it's sort of gamy and tough, like duck in a really bad Chinese restaurant. I move it around on my plate.

"Do you not have peacocks where you are from?" Talia seems even more eager to change the subject than I am.

"We have peacocks. We don't eat them, though."

"What do you eat, then?" Talia asks.

I think about it. "Lots of stuff. People in America are from all over the place, so we eat pizza from Italy . . ."

Talia sighs loudly. "I have never been to Italy."

". . . hamburgers . . ."

"I have not been to Germany, either."

". . . French fries . . ."

"I have not been to France."

". . . tacos from Mexico . . ."

"I do not even know where that is. Would it not be grand, Jack, to go off and see the world?" She gazes at me, smiling.

"Talia . . ." The king seems to be having some trouble with the chewy peacock and the chewier mushrooms. Still, he opens his mouth to speak to her. "That will be enough."

"Enough of what? All my life, you have made me stay in this castle, doing nothing, all for the fear of spindles."

"Obviously, we did not do enough for fear of spindles. Perhaps we should have locked you in a cage."

"Louis . . ." The queen's voice is whispery.

"It is the truth."

"No, it is not!" Talia bursts out. "There was nothing you or I could have done to prevent it. The curse said, '*shall* prick her finger.' It was preordained—my destiny. You would have been better off had you pricked my finger yourself, making certain a prince was on hand to kiss me. This is all your fault! *Your* fault!"

Wow, it's weird hearing her quoting me, like I'm a lawyer or something.

Nah. I'd never be a lawyer.

"If that is the case," the king says, "you would have been awakened by your true love. Where is he, then?"

Talia points to me. "Here! Jack. He loves me. He has to love me."

There is silence. The lords and ladies stop in midchew. The king is obviously not used to being yelled at. From the fairies, I hear a small voice say, "He could *not* be her true love. But how could my spell have gone so wrong?" With a small sigh, she turns into a small, birdlike creature and flies off. The other follows.

"Hey," I say to King Louis, "you want to listen to my iPod?"

The king looks shocked. "What—or who—is an iPod?"

89

"It's something from the twenty-first century. You can listen to music on it. Do you like music?"

"I adore music," Talia says.

The king sighs. "I used to—three hundred years ago." He glares at Talia once again.

"Here." I take it out. I'm glad this getup they put me in has pockets and that I thought to put the iPod in one of them. I wish I had something classical, maybe Gregorian chant. The closest I have is classic rock, some Beatles songs my sister likes. I find "Yesterday." "You put in these earbuds."

"In my *ears*?"

"Sure. That way, you can listen to music without anyone else hearing it."

The king looks like he still doesn't get it, but he sticks the earbuds in. "Now what?"

"You push that. Here. I'll do it for you." I lean over and push it for him. Obviously, these people are button-challenged.

"Can he hear us?" Talia whispers. When I say no, she turns to the queen. "Mother, please make him stop being so cruel. This is not my fault."

The queen shakes her head. "Oh, Talia."

"Then you are against me, too? I hate this! I wish I could simply run away." She turns to me. "How did you get here? To Euphrasia?"

"I already told you, I came through the hedge."

"No. Before that. How did you get to Europe from . . . Florida?"

King Louis takes out the earbuds. He sighs. "How I long for yesterday."

Which is a line from the Beatles song.

"You mean to say, young man," he continues, "that in your century, they have found a way to preserve this man's singing and put it into a minuscule box, all so that one can listen to music without the bother of having it performed, without having to dress and gather and dance, that in your time—which, by unfortunate accident, is now *my* time as well—each man can live entirely in his own world?"

I nod. "Cool, isn't it?"

The king hands me back the iPod. The lord across from me looks like he might want to have a listen, but he doesn't dare ask. "I should have been dead three hundred years ago," the king continues. "I should have . . ." He glares at Talia again. ". . . and I *would* have, had you merely kept away from spindles as you were told."

"By all the saints!" Talia cries.

"Talia," her mother cautions. "Do not swear."

"I *will* swear, Mother. I am done being obedient. Obedience has done me no good. Father may be peevish to me, but I will not stand to see him being so to our guest. We are very much in Jack's debt. Had he not kissed me—"

"He what?!" the king roars.

Uh-oh. Did he not know that?

"K-kissed me. That is how I happened to awaken. Surely you must—"

"You!" The king points a trembling finger toward me.

"You, a commoner, dared to take advantage of my daughter's sleeping state to . . ."

"I didn't know she was a princess, Your Highness . . . Majesty . . . sir!" I push my chair aside. "I'm sorry. I should get going." I take a few steps backward and stumble into a servant holding a tray of mushrooms. I'd better get out of here before they come up with the idea of—oh, I don't know—*stoning* me to death.

"No! You will go nowhere. You have defiled my daughter."

"I didn't! It was a kiss. A little one."

"Yes, you are right, Father," Talia says. "He defiled me."

"What?" I yell. "I didn't . . . I barely touched you!" I want to scream at her, but I try to keep in control. Hurling insults would probably get me in more trouble than I'm in already. "Tell the truth, you . . . brat!" Oops. That slipped out.

She glares at me, then continues. "It is true. I am quite sullied. There is nothing for me to do but marry this young man and go to Florida with him immediately."

"Marry you? Ma—"

"Impossible!" the king declares.

"Why not?" Talia says. "All the princes I might have married are long dead. You do not wish me in your presence."

The king nods at the guards behind me, and I feel hands on my arms. "This young man is an offender of the most contemptible kind, a rogue who would take advantage of a young lady's—a princess's—sleeping state to . . . desecrate her. Death is too good for such an offender."

There it is. Death.

"But I didn't . . . I wouldn't touch her if you paid me!"

"He must be brought to the royal dungeon to await a suitable punishment."

I plead with Talia, even though I can barely look at her, I'm so mad. "Can you say something to him? Please."

She shrugs. "I do not know what to say."

"How about, 'he didn't sully me'? That would be a good start."

"He will not listen to me. He thinks me a fool." She begins to pout.

"You *are* a fool!" the king roars. "To think that we hoped and prayed and protected you, only to have you stupidly ruin the kingdom! I wish we had remained childless!" To the guards, he says, "Take him away!"

And the next thing I know, three guys who look like they could work for the WWE are dragging me down a very long, dark flight of stairs.

To the dungeon.

Chapter 3: Jack

My mom will be happy. I'm seeing something not many people get to see in Europe. An actual dungeon.

It's not like I'd have pictured a dungeon. Maybe that's because it's so dark I can't see my own froufrou tights, much less any beds of nails or cat-o'-nine-tails, or that thing where they stretch people. It just seems like a cold, damp, dark room, like my grandmother's basement in New York.

And it's quiet. I never really thought about quiet before, but at home, there's always the stop-start of the air-conditioner, the buzz of the computer fan. But there's nothing except silence here, and I have nothing to do but think about it. The walls are thick around me, and the ceiling is thick above me, like being dead. There is no one here but me.

And the rats.

The more I get tuned in to the silence, the more I realize there *are* noises after all. Little ones. Little ones like feet. Scurrying feet.

I bet the rats are really hungry after sleeping for three hundred years.

Don't think about this!

The guards didn't take away my iPod, so I turn it on. It starts in at the same song the king was listening to.

I said something wrong, now I long for yesterday.

Hoo-boy, did I. And I *did* something wrong. I kissed some stupid, spoiled brat princess who couldn't even trouble herself to tell her father I didn't "defile" her. And now I'm stuck here, rotting, maybe forever.

And why did I do it? Because she was hot-looking. You'd think I'd have learned from Amber.

I switch to another song. Rap. Loud. One of those songs about what some guy's going to do to some other guy's girlfriend. Good stuff.

Maybe they'll let me out tomorrow.

Maybe they'll decapitate me.

No. There are rules about how you have to treat prisoners. I read about that in school. Geneva Convention.

Except I'm not sure the Geneva Convention's been invented yet here.

Also, that's just for prisoners of war.

I am a prisoner of *love*.

I close my eyes and try to sleep. But I can't, so I just close my eyes and try not to hear the rats in the darkness. It sounds like a big one's creeping up.

I feel red-hot liquid on my arm.

"Ouch!"

Are they torturing me? Boiling me in oil?

"Be quiet!" a voice whispers. It's Talia.

"But that hurt."

"It is but a candle. The wax dripped. Do not be such a baby."

"I'm in a dungeon!"

Suddenly, she's all, "Oh, you poor, poor dear . . . yes, I do apologize for that. Father is in a peevish mood."

"You don't say. How'd you get down here?"

"Everyone is asleep, except the guard. He let me pass."

"But are you allowed down here?"

"I am a princess. I am allowed wherever I wish to go."

"You'd better go," I say. "I know how it is. You come in here, and then in a few minutes your lady-in-waiting or whatever notices you missing. You lie about what happened . . . and all of a sudden I don't have a head."

"Do you wish to escape?"

"That would be a yes."

"Then you must speak to me. If not, I shall be forced to—"

"Don't . . ."

"I will. I shall be forced to scream, and everyone will come running. I will tell them this knave has abused me grievously. The kiss will be nothing in comparison. I will be pitied, and perhaps it may affect my marriage prospects, but they were slight in any case. You, however, shall be stoned at sunrise . . . but only if you do not let me stay and talk to you."

A chill runs through me when she says "stoned at sunrise." Do they actually do that? In any case, she's clearly not going to stop them.

"You know, you're not as sweet as I thought you were," I say.

"I am sweet."

"Could have fooled me."

"I am. Sweet and compliant. Or I was, my first sixteen years, the most docile, malleable creature one might ever imagine. I would have made someone a fine wife. But then everything changed. Or rather, nothing did. I am grown up, and I am still being treated like a child, or an animal. Do you know what it is to be treated as chattel?"

I don't even know what a chattel is. "Sorry. I was too caught up in the whole being-locked-in-a-dungeon thing."

"To be treated like you have no choice in what you do in life?"

"My dad wants me to take over his business when I grow up. He's a developer, like he builds communities where all the houses look alike. I hate it, but he won't take no for an answer. I guess it's irrelevant, though, if I'm going to die here."

"You wish to leave, then?" When I don't answer, she says, "Well?"

"That was a question? Of course I wish to leave."

"Then I shall help you leave, but upon one condition."

I think I know what the condition is.

"You must take me with you." She grabs my hand and squeezes it.

And we have a winner.

I know I should keep my mouth shut, but I say, "Yeah, about that. I know I'm supposed to be your true love and marry you and all, but I'm only seventeen. It might be perfectly normal to get married at seventeen in your time—your *old* time. But no one gets married that young now."

She laughs. "Marry? I do not wish to marry you!" She laughs so hard I'm worried stuff will start flying out of her nose.

She doesn't need to laugh *that* much. "You don't?"

"Hardly. Let us not forget that *you* were the one who kissed *me*."

"Oh, I get it. It's because I'm not a prince."

She sighs. "It does not signify. I do not wish to marry you, and you do not wish to marry me, but I do wish you to take me with you when you go."

"Look, Princess . . . Your Majesty . . ."

"Talia will do."

"Talia will not do. Don't get me wrong. You're beautiful, and there're a lot of guys who'd love to take you wherever they're going."

"No."

"No?"

"No. Those others are all dead. Every suitable consort is dead and has been for nearly three hundred years."

"But your father will never let you go away with me, especially if we're not married."

"No, of course he will not."

"Okay, so we understand each other." I try to shake off her hand, which is difficult with her grasping mine. "Anyway, it was nice meeting you. Good luck with the princess thing. Now, if you can just get your father to let me out of here—"

"No!" She's still holding my hand. "I am not asking to marry you, nor am I going to ask my father's permission to let you go or to leave with you. I wish to sneak out, under cover of darkness, and leave Euphrasia. I wish to go with you, not as man and wife, but merely as friends, travel companions, the sort of happy-go-lucky chums about whom rollicking old ballads of the road are written." She grips my hand even harder. "You owe it to me."

"I *owe* you? How do you figure?"

"You woke me up. You ruined everything. Had you not come along with your intrusive lips, someone else would have woken me, someone who loved me and could have saved me and Euphrasia. A prince. Or perhaps we would have slept forever."

"And that would be a *good* thing?"

"It seems preferable to waking and having everyone know that I am the ruin of my kingdom, to having my father despise me. Jack, you desire to escape. I wish to run away. I thought we might help each other. And if you don't . . ." Her voice trails off.

"And if I don't?"

"Well, then, I shall run away on my own, venturing out into the cold, cruel world full of buses and telephones and other matters of which I know nothing. I have no map and no money, save a large quantity of priceless jewels."

Did she say jewels?

"Without you," she continues, "I might be robbed or . . . worse."

"And me . . . ?"

I feel her shoulders go up. "I suppose you shall rot here . . . although once Father finds out I am missing, he may have you riding the three-legged mare."

"What?"

"The gallows. He shall order you hanged."

She had to say the H word.

And that is how I end up running off with Princess Talia.

Chapter 4: Talia

Helping Jack escape is simple work. At first, I think to trick the guard by saying I saw a mouse and asking him to come nab it, so Jack can escape, or perhaps bribe him with one of the many necklaces in my jewel case. But when I see who the guard is, I know what to do.

One advantage of being forever in my parents' custody is that I have been privy to many secrets of the castle, secrets discussed in my presence, simply because I was always there. From this, I know such tidbits as which upstairs maid is joining giblets with which footman, which coachman was arrested for beating his wife with too thick a stick, and which groom stands accused of bilking an ale draper.

I also know that the guard at the dungeon door is a drunkard.

I suspect that the bag upon which Jack kept so close a hold earlier may contain ale.

"What is in your bag?" I ask when he finally agrees to accept my help.

"N-nothing."

"This is no time to be secretive. You are imprisoned, and I suspect that you have the item, more precious than jewels, that may buy your freedom. Give me the ale."

He tells me where to find the bag, and I find what is needed—six bottles full. When the guard grasps what the contents are, he fairly weeps with joy, and I know it will be short work. I need only wait until he has consumed the beverage, and then, when drunkenness causes his jowls to droop onto his ample chest, I steal the key to secure Jack's freedom.

"Took you long enough!" Jack says when we issue forth from the castle door.

"Shhh!" I whisper. "And hurry."

"Easy for you to say," he whispers back. "You're not carrying anything."

It is true. I took the trouble to secure Jack's other possessions and those, along with my clothing and jewel case, present a heavy burden. But *I* am certainly not going to carry anything. He is the man, and I am the princess. "Go as slowly as you wish, but I am told that ale-induced sleep is not of long duration. If the guard wakes—"

"Okay, okay." Jack trudges faster. When he has gone a short way, he says, "What's in here, anyway?"

"Only the items necessary for our journey."

"Which are?"

"Gowns . . . and my jewels. I have no currency, so I brought the contents of my jewelry box." He mutters something I cannot understand, something about credit cards.

"Excuse me? Would you prefer to return to the castle . . . to the dungeon?"

"No. That's okay."

Now that I have made my escape and aided Jack in making his, I must make him fall in love with me—even though he detests me. I lied when I said I did not wish to marry him. A necessary lie. Marriage to Jack is my destiny, just as it was my destiny to prick my finger upon a spindle. I had hoped that my destiny would make me happy. However, Jack is not being very cooperative. Hence, the lie.

I would think it should be short work to make Jack love me. After all, I am quite beautiful. But the fact is, I have never made anyone fall in love with me before.

Still, I must marry Jack. For if I do so, it will show that it was all predestined—my spindle-pricking, the kiss, and our inevitable happily-ever-after. Once Jack falls under my spell and we marry, Father will have to acknowledge that what happened was not my fault. Perhaps then he will love me again.

But, on the other hand, if Jack does not fall in love with me, then—well—Father must be right. None of this was destiny. It was my fault.

Oh, I prefer not to think about that!

"Do you wish me to help you to carry some of that?" I ask, to convince him that I am nice, even though I think it entirely unreasonable to expect a princess to carry anything.

But he says, "That would be great."

"All right. I just thought that since you were so big and strong, you would be able to handle it all." I place my hand upon his shoulder.

"Well, you thought wrong. Here. Carry the jewelry box. It's heavy."

He shoves it into my hands and continues walking.

Chapter 5: Jack

I trip for about the fifteenth time on the overgrown trees and bushes (and, once, a pig). "God, this is the darkest place I've ever been."

"It is nighttime," Talia points out unhelpfully.

"Yeah, but where I come from, we have lights at night."

"We do, too. They are called stars. They are quite romantic."

Like I'd want to get romantic with her. When I stopped to change out of that monkey suit they gave me, she spent the whole time whining about how it was improper for me to disrobe in her presence, even though I went in the bushes to change. And I'm back to carrying the jewelry box, because when she was carrying it, she slowed to a crawl. "No. Not stars, better than stars. Lights in the houses and outside on the streets."

"Fire? We have had that for quite a while here as well. We Euphrasians are not as primitive as you might believe."

At least they've discovered fire.

"Electricity," I tell her. "See, there was this guy, Benjamin Franklin. He was a little bit after your time, maybe fifty years, and he was American. He discovered electricity one day when he was out flying a kite in the rain."

She chuckles.

"What's so funny?"

"It sounds a mite foolish to fly a kite in the rain."

"He did it on purpose. He was trying to discover electricity."

"If he had not yet discovered it, how did he know he would discover it by flying a kite in the rain? He must have gotten very wet, and he sounds very silly."

This girl is totally annoying, and I don't even really remember the whole story about Ben Franklin. We learned it in fourth grade. Still, I say, "He wasn't silly. He discovered electricity, and a hundred years later, a guy named Edison—another American—invented the lightbulb. So now we have electricity, and if you were sneaking out of the castle in the dead of night, you'd at least have a—"

"Watch out!" Talia screams just as I bonk into something large and wooden. A tree? Yep. Roots. Bark. Really big trunk. It's a tree. I just crashed into a tree.

I rub my forehead. "How'd you know that was there? Was it there in your time?"

"In my time, we can see ahead of us. I suppose we are used to darkness." She laughs.

"It's not funny."

"Oh, I am sorry. In my time, a man running into a tree was considered the height of amusement, indeed." She giggles. "But I suppose everything is better in your time."

I rub my forehead again, to show that it still hurts and that I don't appreciate her laughing. "Well, yeah. Let's see . . . we have electricity, indoor plumbing, fast food, cars, airplanes, computers, movies, television, iPods. Yeah, I think it's pretty much better."

"You think so?" Her voice rises an octave. "Well . . . we have things in Euphrasia that are better than what you have now."

"Like what? Chamber pots? Indentured servants? Bubonic plague? Name me one thing you had in your time that's better than what we have."

"Love!" she cries. "Respect for one another. In my time, people did not go around kissing other people they did not love and had no interest in marrying. In my time, a man who did such a thing would be considered a cad and thrown in the dungeon for his crime. In my time, ladies were respected!"

"If your time is so wonderful, you should go back there!"

"I cannot. You have ruined everything with your selfish, selfish lips!"

"I'm selfish? I'm not the one who touched the spindle."

"You said that was not my fault!"

"That was before I knew you. I changed my mind after I saw what a self-centered brat you are! You probably did it on purpose, just to ruin things for everyone else!"

"Oh!" She stomps her foot.

"That's right. Stomp your foot! Brat!"

"I shall never speak to you again!"

"Good! I'll enjoy the quiet."

"I shall . . . I shall go home!"

"Good! Go! That's exactly what I want!"

She stops walking for a second, and I think she'll turn around, that I'll actually be rid of her. I keep walking. Maybe I should throw her jewelry box on the ground. If I don't, she'll probably accuse me of stealing it.

But a moment later, I hear her footsteps, running to catch up.

"Forget something?" I say.

"I cannot go home. You know I cannot."

"Why not? They'll get over it. You're their little princess."

"They will not 'get over it'! All is ruined! I must go with you—distasteful though the prospect may be." She starts walking.

I'm distasteful. I like that. I'm not the one who begged her to go with me. "I could just ditch you, you know? I don't have to take you with me."

She gasps. "A gentleman would."

"A gentleman of your time, maybe. They sound like

saps. In my time, we don't think girls are fragile flowers. We think they should be responsible if they mess up—just like guys."

"All right, then. You will take me with you because, if you do not, I shall scream. I shall run to the nearest house and cry to the people there—my subjects—and they will come out with pitchforks and torches. They will hold you until my father comes."

She has a good point, I guess—even though she makes it like a brat. I look around, and I can see houses full of people—extremely well-rested people who will probably rush to defend their princess, since they don't know what she's really like.

And, the fact is, I shouldn't have kissed her. I know it's wrong to take advantage of girls who are passed out. If I hadn't done it, I wouldn't be in this mess. So, okay, I'll take her across the border. That's it, though. After that, she's on her own.

So I say, "Okay. Come on. But take back the jewelry box. I don't want anyone to think I stole it if they catch us together. And go faster."

She starts to protest but then says, "Oh, all right."

We keep walking. I wonder how far we are from the border or whatever that giant hedge is.

I'm about to ask Talia when she says, "Why *did* you kiss me?"

"Look, I'm sorry. I didn't know I'd wake you."

"That is not what I meant. I meant why did you kiss

me? I was supposed to be awakened by my true love's kiss, and then we were supposed to marry."

"I got that."

"So if you did not love me, why did you kiss me? Someone else might have, if you hadn't."

I hear her implication, *someone better.* I shrug.

"What does that mean?"

I forgot she can see in the dark. "I don't know. I just wanted to. In my time, we sometimes just kiss for fun."

She doesn't answer for a minute. Then we both say, "I like our way better."

She reaches toward me to touch my forehead. Her hand is cool and soft. "Does it hurt very badly, where you hit the tree?"

I pull away. I don't want her touching me, even though it feels good. "Ouch."

I want to ask Talia why she kissed me back, if it was so horrible, but I'm not speaking to her. Besides, maybe someone will hear. Someone with a big dog. Or a dragon or something. So we trudge along, and the only sound I can hear is my feet hitting the dirt and the dirt hitting my feet, over and over with no light in sight.

After about a thousand more footsteps, we reach the hedge.

Chapter 6: Talia

I am trapped in a bramble bush and have been for the past hour! I am bruised. I am scratched. I am bleeding. I can see nothing on any side. I hear nothing but my thoughts.

And Jack is no closer to falling in love with me than before. If anything, it is worse. When I tried to touch his forehead—his forehead!—he pulled away. He must think me a very silly young girl.

I *am* a very silly young girl.

Father loathes me. Mother is disappointed. My suitors-to-be are dead.

And now I am stuck in a thicket with a boy from a country of which I have never heard, who is wearing a costume suspiciously resembling brightly colored undergarments.

And I have reason to believe that everyone else where we are going will be dressed thus.

A thorn nearly jabs me in the eye.

"Ouch!"

"I told you it was prickly. You have to go in the direction the branches grow." Jack has been pushing ahead of me, doing a poor job of parting the branches so I can make my way through. The oaf obviously has no idea how a princess should be treated.

"This isn't even as big as it was when we first came through it. It seems to have shrunk."

"Yes. That was part of Flavia's spell. She said that after the spell was broken, the kingdom would become visible to the world again. I daresay the hedge is shrinking."

Jack does not answer this. I do not think he believes in fairies. Or spells. Or, certainly, that he is my destiny. Still, he has taken me with him. I should be patient, lest he leave me in the middle of all this. And he is to be my true love, no matter what he thinks.

"I apologize for complaining," I say. "It—this hedge— is not what I am used to."

"I think you should go back."

I note that he does not say that *we* should go back, only me. He wishes to be rid of me, like everyone else.

"You know," he continues, "it's not going to be easy out there. It would be better if you went home."

I sigh. "It will be difficult anywhere, but I prefer to go somewhere where no one knows me. I want to go somewhere princesses do not exist."

"Yeah, sure you do," he says.

"It is true." At least, I think it is, although it will be hard to be a commoner. They have to do a great deal of work, and sometimes they smell bad. "I want to go someplace where everyone is not angry with me, then."

He laughs. "I get that. People are always mad at me, too. They have this weird idea that I'm a slacker." And then, suddenly, he stops pushing. "Hey!"

"What?"

Jack moves aside and draws my hand toward him. "We made it."

I emerge from the brush. I can see his face because, even though it is still nighttime, there are lights in the distance, lights almost like daylight but twinkling like stars.

It is as he said. It is wondrous!

We have walked at least a mile since pushing through the hedge. Rather than bringing my jewels, I might have been better off stealing a sturdy pair of boots. But I dare not complain. Finally, we reach the edge of the wilderness, and Jack says, "We should find someplace to hide you until morning."

"Hide? Why?"

"This may come as a shock to you, but in the twenty-first century, girls don't dress like that. It'll freak people out."

I examine Jack's attire and shudder to imagine what ladies must wear in his time. Brightly colored corsets, perhaps?

"I cannot wait here," I say. "What if they see me?"

"If you hear someone coming, you could hide."

With no other argument, I voice my greatest—my real—fear. "How do I know that you will not abandon me here?"

He shrugs. "You don't. I was thinking about it, actually."

"You were?" There is nothing I can do if he leaves. Nothing. Now that we have escaped, I cannot make him stay.

"Yeah, but I'm not going to. If I'd wanted, I could have left you in the bushes. Or back there, when you were walking so slowly because of your shoes. But I didn't."

"Why not?"

He shrugs. "Don't know. I feel sort of sorry for you, I guess. Besides, this is the most adventure I've had since I got to Europe."

"Truly?" Despite myself, I thrill at this flattery. I have spent little time in the company of boys. But what if it is merely a trick to get rid of me? He is being nice now, but I still remember that he called me a brat.

"I won't leave. I feel sort of . . . responsible." He thinks of something and reaches into his pocket. "Here. Take this."

A present! I take the object from him.

"It's a telephone," Jack says. "You can talk to people on it."

I recognize it from before. "But it did not work."

"It will now. Watch." He takes it from me once again and presses several numbers. He waits.

"Travis," he says. "Her Royal Highness wishes to speak to you." A pause. "What? Tell them I'm puking my brains out. I had some bad *crème brûlée* last night. . . . I just told you, I'm with Talia . . . we ran away after she got me out of the dungeon . . . dungeon. . . . It's not like you did very much to help me when I was trapped in a dungeon. . . . Soon. Okay. Just . . . here. Talk to her. I'm showing her how to use the phone." He hands me the object . . . the telephone.

"Hey, Talia."

I shriek and drop it. It bounces once, then falls to the ground. Jack grabs it.

"What's the matter?" Jack says.

"Your telephone! Your friend Travis is inside it."

Jack shakes his head. "Geez."

"Is it . . . witchcraft? I expected him to sound far away, but he is inside it!"

Jack speaks into the telephone. "You still there, Trav? She's freaking out." He looks at me. "He's not in the phone."

"He is."

"Nah." Into the phone, he says, "Tell her where you are, Trav." He hands it to me.

"I'm back at the hotel, trying to sleep for once. I gave your guys the slip last night. They couldn't get through the hedge with that horse-drawn carriage. And then, when I tried to tell the police to come back and get Jack, they didn't believe me about Euphrasia."

"They knew nothing about Euphrasia," I say. I look at Jack, and he shrugs, then takes the phone from me.

"Cover for me, Trav, huh? I'm leaving her with the phone. Don't let anyone call me. Okay?" A pause. "A few hours. . . . Hey, can you call it once, so I can show her how it works?"

He hands it back to me.

An instant later, the phone begins to jump about in my hand, and another man's voice—not Travis's—begins to shout from it. He sounds so angry.

"Do it to me! Do it to me!"

I cannot help it. The phone leaps from my hand, and I begin to scream. "Who is that? What is he saying?"

Jack catches it. He speaks into it. "Trav, you there? Yeah, she's a little freaked around technology. Call back in a sec and I'll put it on vibrate . . . yeah, I know."

I have the distinct impression these young men are making jokes at my expense.

"You need to lighten up," Jack says.

"Lighten? Nothing is heavy."

"It's an expression. It means chill . . . don't take everything so seriously." Jack does something to the phone, then hands it back to me. "Okay. It's gonna move around. When it does, *don't throw it.* Just open it up, say hello, and *don't throw it.* Okay?"

I nod.

"What are you *not* going to do?"

"Throw it." I smile. He thinks me a simpleton. Perhaps I am.

The blessed thing commences vibrating and, once again, I am seized with the urge to toss it aloft. I restrain myself. "What now?"

"Open it."

I do.

"Now hold it to your ear and say 'yo.'"

I hold it to my ear. "Yo?"

"'Sup, Talia? Will you tell Jack he owes me big-time?"

This I repeat to Jack, although I have no idea what it means. He shrugs and checks his watch. "We should go. Say good-bye to Travis."

"Good-bye."

"Now, close it up."

Jack finds me a place in some trees. He buries my jewels under some leaves, in case of robbers. It must be very dangerous in Jack's time, if a young princess cannot go out safely in her gown and jewels. He leaves the telephone. "Don't answer if anyone else calls."

"How shall I know?"

Jack begins to explain some new, difficult concept that, apparently, even a buffoon like Travis has mastered in Jack's time. My eyes glaze over, as they do when Lady Brooke reads to me from the Reverend Phelps's *Sermons for Young Ladies*. Jack must see it, for he says, "Forget it. No one's going to call, anyway."

And then he leaves.

With no book or other form of entertainment, I while the time away by listening to the calls of birds. When I was little, Father taught me to pick out the tune of a sparrow, the morning song of a lark. I miss Father and Mother. Still, as I watch the sun journey higher up on the horizon, I appreciate that, for only the second time in my entire life, I am alone, blessedly alone, with no one to tell me what to do or what to wear, no one to have to be polite to. Nothing.

But I do not wish to be alone, not entirely. Now that I am finally alone, it feels . . . lonely.

Soon, the lark's song ceases. Hyperion continues his journey across the sky, and I become aware of other sounds, not merely birds, but a cacophony of something like metal clanking together. It is like nothing I have ever heard in Euphrasia. Suddenly, I realize I am afraid to know what it is.

Never have I been afraid before. I miss home. I even miss Lady Brooke.

I could return.

The castle is waking, noticing that I am not there. Soon, they will send out search parties. There will be panic, accusations made, rewards offered for the safe return of their much-beloved princess. It is like something in a book.

And if I creep back through the bushes and am found, scraped and battered after many hours' absence, Father may be too relieved to be angry. All will be forgiven.

And I shall spend the remainder of my days under the constant supervision reserved for little children and the feeble-minded.

No. I can never go back, only forward. I must go to Florida, to my destiny.

I stare at the horizon once again, and my vision blurs. I have been up all night, rescuing Jack, fighting the brambles. Perhaps it would not be a terrible idea to close my eyes a spell. . . .

I am awakened by vibrations. At first, I jump, believing someone has found me. Then I remember. The telephone. *Do not throw it.* I pick it up, open it. I see a word. *Amber. Amber?* What is Amber? A jewel? I press the button.

"Hello?"

"Who is this?" a female voice demands.

It is surely not Jack. What am I to do?

"Hello?" the voice repeats.

I recover myself. "Yes?"

"Who is this?"

"Talia," I say, leaving out the princess part.

"Where's Jack?"

"I do not know, exactly. He went to purchase clothing for me, you see, and—"

"He went to buy you *clothes*?"

"Yes."

"What time is it there?"

Has this angry young lady called Jack's telephone strictly to ascertain the time? "Have you no clock?"

"Listen." The voice is extremely loud, and I am forced to hold the telephone away from my ear. "I don't know

119

who you are, or why you have Jack's phone, but he is *my* boyfriend, and—"

Boyfriend? What is a boyfriend? Perhaps it is something like a beau. "Is he engaged to you, then?" I hope not.

"What? No. Of course not."

"Oh, what a relief. He is *my* true love, and you do not sound very nice."

"What? Listen, you . . ."

And then, strangely enough, she calls me a female dog.

She continues talking. She is vile and coarse. And then I realize that Jack told me not to speak with anyone else, and here I am, speaking.

"I beg your pardon, what did you say your name was?"

"I didn't. It's Amber."

"Amber, I cannot go on being insulted by you. Jack may be trying to call."

"Why would he do that?"

"We have run away together. I must go."

I close the phone as Jack taught me.

A moment later, it begins to vibrate again. This time, however, I see the name Amber and know not to answer it. I am quite proud of myself for having learned this.

It is close to noon now. I cannot go back to sleep, and the sun is blazing. Why *do* we wear so many clothes?

Jack has not called.

Perhaps he has abandoned me to be eaten by wolves or whatever is making that noise.

Perhaps I should leave.

Perhaps I should go into the city and find a bus—whatever that may be—and sell my jewels myself and live on my own.

Perhaps I—

"Hey."

It is him.

"Oh, thank goodness! I thought you had left me to die!"

"I wouldn't do that." He hands me a small sack of some sort, made of a smooth blue material. It has writing on it which I do not understand. GAP.

"What is this?"

"Your clothes."

"They fit in there?"

It is more horrible than I imagined.

Jack laughs. "Girls don't wear ball gowns anymore, Princess—not even to balls."

I open the sack. The horror continues. Men's trousers, a green piece of fabric, and two objects which might be some sort of tools. How am I to make Jack fall in love with me when I shall be dressed in such ugly clothing?

"I will be disguised as a man, then?" I ask, holding up the trousers. Jack glances at my bosom and shakes his head.

"They're women's clothes. Try them on. You'll look hot."

"With so little fabric, I shall more likely be cold." But I hate to hurt his feelings, so I say, "Very well. Where is my dressing room?"

He gestures toward the trees. "I'll turn around."

"See that you do."

It is very difficult to dress without a lady's maid. There are so many buttons to unbutton, stays to unlace, and of course I cannot ask Jack for assistance. When I am finally done, I am quite winded. I put on the little shirt (at least it is green), then the trousers. Finally, I add the tools, which are apparently meant as shoes.

I stand a moment, allowing the breeze to touch my naked arms. I would be quite comfortable, were I not worried that Jack has dressed me up as a hedge whore.

"Are you quite certain this is all?" I ask.

"Can I see?"

I sigh. "I suppose."

He turns. "Wow, you look great. Most girls would wear a—ah—bra with that, but they didn't have them at the Gap."

"What is a bra?"

"It's for your . . . ah . . . ." He blushes red and gestures toward his chest. "Um . . . ."

"Never mind. I understand." I remember my manners. I need to be nice to this boy, so he might fall in love with me. "I . . . I thank you for the clothes."

He nods. "We should get going." He starts to walk, not looking at me again.

The shoes are even worse than my old slippers. They slap against my foot with each step and pinch my toes. I am still carrying my jewelry box and now my old clothes, too, as Jack did not wish anyone to find them abandoned. But soon we reach a clearing.

"Princess Talia, welcome to the world."

"The world" proves to be a rather loud and very foul-smelling conveyance called a bus. We are in what was known as the Spanish Netherlands in my time, but Jack tells me it is now called Belgium. There are many people on the bus—peasants, no doubt, on their way to market. They are all dressed as I am or worse. No waistcoats! No dresses! Not a single corset! I see four women whose bosoms are revealed to a degree more suited to the ballroom than to daylight.

Although my own attire is modest by comparison, everyone stares at me.

"Why are they looking at me?" I whisper to Jack.

"Duh. Because you're so beautiful," he whispers back.

At least he noticed that I am beautiful.

There are no seats available on the bus, and no gentleman (and I use the term loosely) offers to surrender his. One man does, however, pat his lap and say, "Sit with me, angel."

I look at Jack to ascertain if this is now an established custom. I am relieved when he shakes his head and says, "No, thanks. We'll just stand."

Once started, the bus is faster than the fastest carriage, wilder than the wildest horse. I resist the urge to shriek, but it is difficult. I try to see the streets and houses and people, but it all goes by much faster than I can take it in. There is writing everywhere. Most of the peasantry in Euphrasia cannot even write their names. Can all the people in Jack's time read?

I ask Jack.

"Sure," he says.

"But how can they all be taught? And why would they all need to read, if they are just going to be field workers and such?"

"Well, that's why you have to learn to read—so you won't get stuck being a field worker."

"But what if they wish to be field workers?"

"Why would anyone want backbreaking labor and low pay?"

"But the peasants in Euphrasia always seemed so merry."

"Did you spend much time with the peasants, then?"

"No, but I saw them at festivals and such." I stop. Of course they were happy at festivals. For then, they were not working in the fields. Why *would* they wish to be field workers? I was led to believe that the workers in Euphrasia were happy, but in all probability, the field workers in Euphrasia were born to be field workers and sentenced to their lot in life, just as I was born to be a princess and sentenced to mine.

Put into this perspective, being a princess does not seem bad at all.

"Amazing," I say to Jack. I look around the bus with new respect. It is quite impressive to think that each and every one of the peasants here can read.

The bus makes many stops and people get on and off. Finally, it is our turn to get out in a gray sort of place, gray streets, gray buildings, gray people.

"Where is the grass?" I ask Jack.

"Someplace else," he says, laughing. He nudges the sack that says GAP, into which he has placed my jewel case. "What's the smallest thing you have in there?"

"None of my jewels are small."

"A ring, maybe?"

I start to take out the box, but Jack stops me. "Not here." He rushes me behind a pillar and blocks me from sight as I extract the smallest bauble, a tanzanite ring given to me for my twelfth birthday.

"That's the smallest? The stone's as big as my eyeball."

A slight exaggeration. I am no more thrilled to part with it than Jack is to have to sell it. Still, I hand it to him, and he leads me into a store with all manner of things— guns, jewelry (nothing near as lovely as my ring), and other objects I cannot identify, although I do see something which resembles Jack's music maker.

Jack approaches the shopkeeper, a hairy and rather frightening sort of person, and holds up my ring. "We need to sell this. Her mother's, um, sick and needs medicine."

The bear-turned-man stares at us rather strangely, then asks, *"Parlez-vous Français?"* Jack does not respond. Ah! He thinks he is so smart, but the fool speaks no French!

"Oui. Je parle Français," I say. I turn to Jack. "Tell me what I am to say."

"Okay, but don't agree to his first offer."

I nod, then turn to the man and say in French, "We need to sell this."

"Fifty Euros," he says before I can even get out the part about my mother needing medication. This I add.

"I don't care if you need it to buy drugs," the man snarls. "Fifty."

I repeat this to Jack. "Are you kidding?" he says. "This is worth thousands."

The man must understand because he tells me, "I can't sell fancy stuff like that. This isn't an antique store."

I am about to tell him that my ring is no antique. Then, I realize it is. Indeed, *I* am an antique.

"Ask him if he can do any better," Jack says.

I do, and he says, "Two hundred. That's it."

I give him my sweetest look, the one that almost always persuaded Father to do my bidding, and I say, "Please, sir. If you could make it four hundred Euros for my poor, dear mother." And when I think of Mother, Mother whom I may never see again, whom I have disappointed, my eyes begin to tear up. "You know you are getting a bargain."

"Three fifty," the man growls. "Now, if *you* were for sale, for that I would pay a thousand."

Are all women for sale now? In my current attire, I can certainly see how one might think I was such a woman. But I say, "I will take three hundred seventy-five Euros, *monsieur.*"

The man opens a cash box under the counter, hands me

a wad of money, which he does not bother to count, then whisks away my precious ring before I have time to bid it good-bye. I note that he is chuckling, pleased with his bargain. I bite my lip and resist the urge to sob.

"Hey, you weren't a total disaster in there," Jack says, counting out the money as we leave.

I understand this is a compliment, and I manage a smile, accepting it.

Our next stop is a door with peeling green paint. Jack knocks upon it, and a man who might be the twin brother of the last man answers.

"What do you want?" he asks in French.

I look at Jack.

"Jolie sent us," he says in English.

The man nods and allows us to pass.

"You have money?" he says in English.

"How much for a passport?" he asks. "For her?"

The man gives a price, which is almost all we have, then says, "Let's see it."

"I am quite sorry, sir, but we only have one hundred fifty," I tell him.

He nods. "If you were to only have two hundred fifty, I might be able to do it. Can you find that?"

I rather enjoyed bargaining with the last gentleman. It made me feel like Father negotiating treaties, so I say, "I can find two hundred."

"Very well," the man says.

I look at Jack. He nods and hands him the money, taking care not to show all we have.

The man takes it with dirty hands. "What is your name?"

"My name? My name is Her Royal Highness, Princess Talia Aurora Augusta Ludwiga Wilhelmina Agnes Marie Rose of Euphrasia."

"It's Talia . . ." Jack interrupts. "Talia . . . um . . ."

I grasp his meaning. "Brooke. Talia Brooke."

"Is that your final decision?" the man growls.

"Of course," I say. "It is my name. The other name was in jest." I laugh. "Ha, ha!"

"Stand here." He pushes me toward a paper board hanging from the wall. When I stand before it, he takes out a small, square object, rather resembling Jack's telephone.

"What is . . . ?"

A bright light flashes. "Good! Wait here." He disappears into another room.

I stand quite still, attempting to touch nothing in the dark, cramped, dirty room.

"Ludwiga?" Jack asks.

"Father was sad at not having a male heir, so he attempted to name me after several great Euphrasian kings—Augustus, Ludwig, and Wilhem, alphabetically so no one would be offended. The other names—Agnes, Marie, and Rose—were Euphrasian queens."

"How about Aurora?"

"She was my grandmother on my mother's side, and she

was named for the goddess of the dawn." I glance around, spying a millipede making its way across the wall, dangerously close to nesting in my hair. I move closer to Jack. "Why are we here?"

"Getting a passport." At my blank look, he adds, "Travel documents. So you can get around, travel. I got this guy's name from a girl I met through a guy I met at the Gap."

Travel! The idea is wonderful and terrible at the same time, to be aboard a boat to a strange new place with this strange, messy-haired young man I met only yesterday. I shiver slightly.

"So I will go with you?" I ask Jack.

"With me? Look, I'm helping you out, getting you set up. But after that, you're on your own."

"On my own? But how can I . . . what will I do?"

"Sell some more jewels. I don't know."

I cannot do that. How will I know where to go, how to sell them? How will I obtain food or even know what to wear? Even in Euphrasia, I handled no money. I do not even know how Jack paid for the bus. And if I am on my own, I can never make Jack fall in love with me.

"Will you help me a bit, just with getting money and a ticket for the ship and such?" After he helps me with that, I will talk him into the next thing. And then the next. Surely, when he sees how much I need him, he will let me stay with him. Mother always said that men like to feel needed. I gaze up into his eyes, letting my lower lip quiver just a bit. It is not difficult.

He sighs. "I guess I can help you a little."

Now that I have achieved my goal, I clap my hands to show that I am keeping my chin up. "Thank you! It is my fondest wish to travel!"

Chapter 7: Jack

As soon as we get the passport and are out the door, my cell phone rings.

It's my mother.

"Jack, where are you? They said you ran away from the tour."

"Who is this?" I say.

"You know very well who this is."

Talia's still with me. I feel bad about just ditching her, but what else can I do? Right now, she's staring at the photograph on the passport. Every few steps, she touches her own face, like she's trying to see if it's really still there.

"Well," I say, "it sounds like my mother, but my mother never calls."

"Very funny. Don't change the subject. Where are you?

Amber says she called earlier and some girl answered the phone."

"Amber? She didn't call me. We broke up. She broke up with *me*." I see Talia's hand fly to her mouth. "Hold on a second, Mom." To Talia, I say, "Something you need to tell me?"

She purses her lips in thought before saying, "I am dreadfully sorry . . . in the excitement, I forgot. A person named Amber called. She sounded angry."

Amber? In my hand, my mother's voice keeps buzzing. "Jack? Jack? Where are you? Jack, did you hang up on me?"

I let her wait. "Amber called? What did you say?"

"I told her we ran away together," Talia says.

"You told her *what*?"

In my hand, Mom's voice says, "This girl told Amber you'd run off together."

Talia looks like she's about to burst into tears. "Was it wrong to say that? I am unfamiliar with telephones!"

Nah, you've just totally ruined any possibility of getting back with Amber. But she looks so cute, like a little girl who's afraid of getting in trouble. "No, of course not."

"Jaaaaaaaack!" the telephone shrieks.

Then my father's voice, loud but business-as-usual. "Jack, speak to me this instant."

"Sorry, Dad."

"Sorry? Your mother's crying."

"Why's she doing that?"

132

"Because she thinks you've run off with some girl you just met!"

Funny thought. "Oh, yeah. I guess I did."

"What?"

I'm enjoying this. It's the first time they've paid attention to me since the time I flunked science and crashed my car in the same week. It might be fun to mess with them more.

"Yeah, I met her yesterday. You'll like her, Dad. She's real pretty. Oh, and she's a princess. We eloped." *That'll get their attention.*

No answer from Dad. Maybe the call dropped. Maybe he passed out.

But no. Mom's there now. "What do you mean you eloped? I want you on a plane back home this minute. This minute!"

"Okay. Wire me some money, and I'll buy a ticket." This is fun. But as soon as I give them what they want, they'll start ignoring me again.

"Don't you get smart with me, young man."

"I wasn't—"

"I'll wire you the money, and you'll buy a ticket on the next flight."

Isn't that what I just said? What would happen if I just kept messing with them?

"All right. But I'm bringing Talia with me." I hadn't planned on saying that, but it just pops out. It'll really drive them nuts.

133

When I get off the phone, Talia says, "Thank you."

"For what?"

"For saying I can go with you."

I shrug. "At least I get to go home. Who wants to travel around and see all this junk?"

"You do not like to travel."

I shake my head, then smile, thinking about it. "Boy, are my parents going to freak when they see you."

"Much as my parents, er, freaked when you appeared. Will it be a long journey? How many weeks will it take? I have so many questions. Will we need to acquire more clothes in order to conduct our journey in style? What if the ship sinks? Or there is an outbreak of cholera? I might never see my family again."

I start laughing.

"What is so funny?"

"Weeks? Try a day."

"What sort of ship can journey to the other side of the earth in a day?"

"The kind that can fly."

Mom works like a fiend when she's freaking out. Within twenty-four hours, Talia and I are at the airport.

"Remember what I told you," I say to Talia as we wait in line for security.

"My name is Talia Brooke. I am from Belgium. And if anyone questions my jewels, I am to say they are part of the new Royal Euphrasian line of . . . what is it called again?"

"Costume jewelry."

"Costume jewelry, which I am going to South Beach, Florida, to model. But how would anyone believe that such lovely jewels are false?"

"Because no one wears real jewelry that big anymore, not even the Queen of England." We had to sell another one of Talia's rings to buy her plane ticket, but that doesn't help much with the weight. "Can you remember that?"

"Yes. Costume jewelry."

A few minutes later, we reach the front of the line. I think I'll hold my breath until we're on the plane.

I show my passport. The woman barely looks at it. Just another boring American student. When she gets to Talia's, she examines it more carefully and begins talking to Talia in rapid French. Does she know Talia's passport's a fake?

Talia responds in French, and a lot of it. What is she saying? Why didn't I take French?

What am I, kidding myself? If I'd taken French, I'd have only learned the swear words, like I did in Spanish.

The conversation goes on for approximately eight hours, but finally the employee lets Talia go.

"What was that about?" I ask her when we're safely past.

"She noticed my passport was new. It only has the one stamp, from when we crossed into France. So she asked if it is my first time traveling outside Europe."

"To which you said . . . ?"

"I said, yes, as a matter of fact, it is. I have been sleeping for three hundred years, so I have never been on an airplane before. Oh, and, by the way, I am heir to the throne of Euphrasia." She sees the look on my face. "Lighten up! I was joking."

"Don't joke about that. It's not funny."

"It is so."

I whisper, "I was sure we were going to be busted . . . um, get sent to the dungeon."

"But you would not be going, in any case. It would be only I who was in trouble."

"You think I'd let you take the fall for it, that I'd just leave you and go home?"

"We barely know each other. And you hate me."

"Still, I wouldn't do that. I couldn't."

I hadn't realized it before, but it's true. Could I be falling for Talia? No. It's just that I feel responsible for her, since I kissed her and ruined her life and all.

I point to two seats by our gate, but Talia's looking at me. "What?" I say.

"You are a wonderful person," she says. "In Euphrasia, everyone was kind to me because I was a princess. But I always wished . . ." She stops and sits down.

"What?"

"Lady Brooke used to take me on long rides through the Euphrasian countryside, since I was not allowed to go anywhere on my own. Once, on a very cold day, I happened to spy a peasant couple. Each wore a thin, threadbare coat, and the woman shivered. The man took off his own coat and put it over her shoulders, even though this left him quite exposed. When the woman tried to stop him, he refused to take it back. He allowed the coat to fall to the ground, then placed it again upon her shoulders, until finally, she accepted it. I could see that he was trying to walk more rapidly to get to shelter, but he did not complain."

"Wow. What did you do?"

"What I did was of no importance."

"But you did something?"

"I suppose." She glances down. "I made the driver stop the carriage and then asked Lady Brooke to give the couple our cloaks."

"That was nice."

"It was a small sacrifice for me. I had numerous cloaks at home. The man made a much greater sacrifice. I always wanted someone to sacrifice for me, as that man sacrificed for that woman, not because I was royalty, but simply because he lo . . . liked me. And you have."

I shrug. "It's not a sacrifice."

And it's true. It's not. I wanted to go home early, wanted to try and get back together with Amber or, at least, be able to spend my summer sleeping and going to the beach instead of touring the Museum of Napoleon's Nose Hair. Talia gave me a great excuse. If I'd known running away would work, I'd have tried it sooner.

The fact that my parents are completely riled is just an added bonus. Of course, they didn't believe the truth about Talia.

"Jack, that's not funny," Mom said when I told her to prepare for visiting royalty.

"I'm not trying to be funny."

That's when Dad picked up the phone again.

"This has gone on long enough, Jack. Your mother's all upset."

"It's true, Dad. She's a princess. Why would I make that up?"

"I have no idea, but I don't think—"

"Okay, Dad, you win. She's some girl I picked up on the street. You never should have chosen a teen tour that went through Amsterdam's red-light district."

That pretty much ended the conversation.

Since then, I've decided it's probably better if I don't tell anyone that Talia's a princess. I mean, who'd believe it?

Now they're calling us to board the plane. I check to make sure that Talia has her boarding pass. She does, and she's making a minute examination of the bar code. I nudge her. "It's time to get on."

Her eyes widen. "Onto the flying ship?"

"Onto the airplane. It's called an airplane."

She stands, then looks at all the people jockeying for space in line. "Will the ship . . . er, airplane, leave without all of them?"

"What do you mean?"

"I mean, is it necessary to push and shove, as these people are doing, or can we wait patiently?"

I never thought about it. People just usually do push

and shove to get on the plane, but then you just end up waiting on the runway, anyway. "We can wait," I say. I would have thought she'd expect to go first, being a princess and all.

"Good. I do not like to shove."

She takes her place at the end of the line, behind an elderly woman. "This is my first time on an airplane," she tells her.

"Are you frightened, dear?"

"I am excited."

And the woman looks excited for her.

We finally reach our seats. I give Talia the window, even though it means I'm stuck in the center.

"What is this?" Talia asks, holding up a plastic-wrapped package.

"Slippers. They're to keep your feet warm."

"How nice!" She starts to put them on. She's got the cutest little feet. They look like they've never walked anywhere. Probably, she has servants who spread cream on them every day. She had a complete spaz about the blister she got walking. A moment later, she holds up another package. "What is this?"

"A mask. It's to cover your eyes so you can sleep."

Talia takes out the mask and examines it. "I have slept quite long enough already." She tucks it into the seat-back pocket.

Hoo-boy. I remember last night at the hotel in Paris—a hotel with two queen-size beds with down comforters—

Talia refused to sleep at all, instead running to the window over and over to look at the city lights. "Well, some people like to sleep," I tell her, "so you'll have to be quiet."

She pouts for a full ten seconds before holding up something else.

"And these?"

"Earbuds, so you can listen to music or watch a movie."

She purses her lips in this weird way she does. "What is a movie?"

"It's like television." She saw TV last night at the hotel. "You watch it to kill time on the plane."

Please, please, let her at least watch a movie.

"Kill time?"

"You know, make it go faster."

"Why would you want to do that?"

"Because it's boring, sitting and doing nothing."

"But you are doing nothing in the sky! How can that be boring?"

I shrug. "To most people, it is."

"Try being asleep for three hundred years. Then you will know what boring is."

I don't say anything. I'm one of those people who wants to sleep.

"Everything is boring to you, isn't it?" she says.

"That's not true."

Is it?

"Oh, no?" She tips up her feet to look at the airline

slippers again. "Let me see . . . your parents sent you on a tour of Europe for . . . how long?"

"A month. I've been gone three weeks. But I don't know what that's got to do—"

"Three weeks at great expense. And during that time, you've visited how many countries?"

I count on my fingers—England, the Netherlands, France, Belgium . . . "I'm not sure. Five or six, maybe. It's all a blur."

"It's all a blur," she mimics, then laughs. "But in any case, you have viewed great masterworks, marvels of architecture, historical sights, and you have generally found it to be, on the whole, quite dull. Is that the case?"

When she puts it that way, it does sort of make me sound like a jerk. But she's not getting the reason why I didn't want to go.

"Look, you don't understand. My parents, they just sent me to fulfill some fantasy they have about having a son who's into that stuff. I never get any choice about what I do in the summer. After I get home, they're going to want me to take an SAT course and get a job. It's all about them."

"*I* do not understand about not getting a choice as to how to live one's life?"

I shrug. "Besides, the tour bus sort of sucked."

"Ah. So, in order to get away from the sucking tour bus—"

"Sucky."

"Beg pardon?"

"Sucky. You would say the bus was sucky. That's what Americans would say."

"Thank you. So, in order to get away from the sucky tour bus, you sneaked off, found a lost kingdom, entered a castle, kissed a princess—an incredibly beautiful princess who had been asleep for centuries due to a curse placed upon her at birth by an evil witch—caused a fracas, were thrown into a dungeon, escaped, and traveled cross-country with that same incredibly beautiful—"

"Not to mention modest." I know I shouldn't interrupt her or I'll never get my earbuds in, but it's tempting.

"Incredibly beautiful and intelligent princess. And still, you are quite bored, Jack, so bored that you cannot wait to put in your earbuds and be done with this conversation and this voyage."

I fumble with the earbuds guiltily.

"So my question to you, Jack, is what is it that you do *not* find boring?"

She stops speaking and looks at me. I look at her. If anyone else, my friends from school, even Amber back when we were dating, had asked me such a question, I'd have blown them off, said something like, "partying" or "raising hell," just to end the conversation. But with Talia, I know that won't work. She won't think it's funny. She'll think I'm stupid.

So instead of saying the first thing that comes to mind, I think about it, really think about the last time I wasn't bored with something, the last time I was excited. She's right. It's been a while. My life has been this long series of hoops to jump through—school, activities Dad thinks would look good on my college apps, whatever, so I have to think back a long time.

"I apologize." Talia interrupts my thoughts. "Do people not talk to each other in your time, then?"

"It's not that. I was trying to think."

"Obviously an activity of great difficulty for you." She giggles.

Difficulty. That makes me remember something.

When I was a kid, I used to be in Boy Scouts. I quit the year Dad started talking about how good being an Eagle Scout would look on my college applications. But back when I *was* still in Scouts, one of the projects we did was this park.

"I like to plant stuff," I say.

She looks surprised. "Plant? You mean, like a farmer?"

"More like a gardener. This one time in Boy Scouts, we did a project, a park in a bad neighborhood. It was all over-grown with weeds, and we pulled them out and planted flowers and trees. Most of the guys sort of fooled around, didn't do much, but me . . ." I stopped, picturing it. "I really liked making it look better. I liked the work, putting my hands in the dirt or whatever." I shrug.

"I do not think I have ever handled dirt. How does dirt feel?"

"Clean," I say. "I mean, not clean like it's been through the laundry, but . . . honest. And when we finally

143

finished and saw how it looked, I felt really—I don't know—proud."

It was true. I'd gone back to look at that park after I got my driver's license, even though I'd quit Scouts by then. I'd even pulled some weeds.

"I think I'd really like to be a gardener or maybe a landscaper." I've never thought about it before, but I realize it's true. When I think of what Dad wants me to do—wear a suit all day and sit at a desk—it just sort of makes me want to cry. "It would be cool to spend every day out in the sun, making things look beautiful."

She smiles. "Then I think you should do so."

I laugh. "Yeah, right. I can just see me telling my dad I want to plant stuff for a living. He thinks gardening's for losers. He hires people to mow the lawn."

Once, after the Boy Scout thing, I said I thought it would be cool to get a summer job at Disney World, working in their gardens. They have these beautiful gardens with topiaries. Dad said working outdoors was for illegal aliens.

"You should tell him that that is what you wish to do."

"Yeah? How would that work with your parents?"

She shrugs, then smiles. "They cannot keep an eye on us all the time, can they?" Then she yawns. "My! Perhaps it is the power of suggestion, with the slippers and the sleep mask, but I am, indeed, rather tired."

She places her sleep mask over her eyes and, in a

moment, she is sawing wood, her head drifting sideways onto my shoulder. I know I should take the opportunity for a nap of my own, but instead I take out a sheet of paper and pencil and start drawing a plan for a garden. That was the problem with the tour: lots of buildings and paintings but no gardens. I draw one, a big one with roses and ivy.

A garden perfect enough for Talia's castle in Euphrasia.

The plane starts to taxi. Talia jolts awake.

"Jack? Jack?" She peers out the window, then at me, then back out the window. "We're flying. Oh, my!"

"It's okay. It just took off. They do it all the time."

"So you have told me. But I need to know something else."

I put down my pencil. "What?"

"Where is Euphrasia?"

I look past her out the window. The plane climbs higher. It is a clear day, so I can see pretty far, but I don't even know what direction Euphrasia would be in. "I don't know."

"But surely . . . we can see so far away."

"I don't know."

But then I do see it, a little wilderness near the shore, almost out of sight. I know it's Euphrasia because, through the trees, only visible if you know it's there, is a spire. The castle.

"I think that's it."

"That?" She stares where I'm pointing. "So small?"

"Yeah. Everything looks small from an airplane. You

can't even see people from here. It's not a big deal."

"But that is impossible! It cannot be so small! It was my whole world."

And then she leans her forehead against the window and doesn't say anything for a very long time, just stares at that tiny spire until we're high in the clouds.

Chapter 8: Talia

I wake due to Jack's repeated nudging.

"We're here," he says.

"In America? Your country?"

"In Miami."

I cannot speak. Does he mean to say that we have completed our entire journey? It seems barely longer than the time spent walking to the Euphrasian border. I wonder . . . if everything can be accomplished in so little time, does that mean people live longer?

"How long was I asleep, then? Three months? Six?"

Jack laughs. "The flight was long, but not that long—a few hours." He hands me a crinkly object, which I now know is a plastic bag. "Here. I got you some pretzels."

I have no idea what a pretzel is, but I take the bag. "Thank you. It is lovely." I gaze at it. It is blue and says

AMERICAN AIRLINES. "I shall treasure it forever."

He shrugs. "I thought maybe you'd eat it."

So I do. It takes a few attempts to open the bag, but once I do, the pretzels are crunchy and salty. I wonder if all American food is like this. If so, it is a bit dry. Still, I eat them politely. "Lovely."

Jack points to the window. "There it is."

I look. There are strange sorts of trees, tall with no leaves save for little hats on top, and there is water all around. I remember that we have been flying in the air all this time, ten hours, and it should be nighttime, yet it is daylight, glorious, sunny daylight, and I am free to go out into it if I please.

And suddenly, the pretzels taste not like salt but like freedom.

"I need my hairbrush," I tell Jack.

"What for?" He opens his travel trunk.

"We shall be meeting your family, shall we not?" When Father returns from a voyage, Mother and I and all the members of court meet his ship with flowers. If this is to be like that, I should comb my hair. In any case, a princess must keep up appearances.

I take out the simplest hairbrush I own, silver with hardly any jewels. Jack was appalled when he saw it. Modern hairbrushes, he says, are made of plastic. I know what plastic is now, and I must say that it has none of the appeal of silver. I threw out the plastic shoes Jack purchased for me, which pinched my feet so that I could barely walk.

Now, I have cloth shoes which tie in front. Still, I yearn for my own shoes, made of the finest kid and fitted exactly to my feet.

I miss my lady's maid, who brushed my hair one hundred strokes each morning and night. I miss being a princess.

But then I remember Father's anger. That I do not miss at all.

"Nah, no one will be there," Jack says, recalling me to the time and place.

"Beg your pardon?"

"My family. They're all busy. You'll meet them later on, I guess."

"But surely someone—"

"Nope. We'll take a cab."

I took a cab to the airport in France, and the most I can say for it is that it is not a bus. I shake my head but keep a civil tongue inside it. It seems incredible that a young man could journey across the ocean and come home to no fanfare whatsoever. I examine Jack's face. His lips are pursed, his brow furrowed, and I suspect that his thoughts on the subject are similar to my own. It strikes me that Jack and I suffer from the opposite problem: While my parents kept me too close at hand, Jack's do not keep him at hand at all.

Suddenly there is a giant bump that causes my seat, my body, my very bones to jump, and there is a sound like a thunderclap.

"What was that?" I cry.

Jack laughs. "Relax, silly. We just landed. We're on the ground." He takes out his telephone and turns it on.

"We are?" I glance out the window. It is true. We are. The trees and ocean are no longer visible, replaced by dull, gray land. But a moment ago, I was in the clouds! Me. Talia. After three hundred sixteen years isolated in a castle, apart from everyone, in three days I have met a boy, run away, and crossed the ocean in a magical flying machine. Who would have believed it possible?

Certainly not my father.

Chapter 9:  Jack

It takes a while to get off the plane with Talia's fifty-pound carry-on. But finally we make it.

I love when you enter the jetport in Miami, and you're met with that first blast of hot air through the cracks that reminds you you're home. I watch Talia's face as we walk off the plane.

"Ooh! So warm!"

I grin.

I told Talia no one would be there to pick us up at the airport, mostly because I didn't want her to spend an hour in the airport bathroom, fixing her hair with that ten-pound brush of hers and pinching her cheeks to make them pink or something. But I didn't really think no one was coming.

I check my cell phone to make sure I turned it on, and I

check to see if I have messages, even though I know I don't. I texted both parents when I got off the plane. Nothing yet.

We head downstairs to the baggage claim. Talia seems a bit dazed, and I nudge her. "You okay?"

She rests her hand on my arm. "I am glad you are here. I do not think I have seen as many people in my entire life as I have seen today."

"No problem." Her hand's still there. It's weird because I kind of like the way it feels, her sort of depending on me.

She points to the luggage carousel. "Ooh! What fun!"

"Yeah. Don't touch it. We have to look for our suitcases."

My parents still aren't here, so I dial home. My sister answers.

"Hey, Mer, where's Mom?"

"Out drowning her sorrows about getting stuck with such a bad son."

"Yeah?"

"I think she's playing tennis."

"I'm at the airport." I turn so Talia can't hear me. "Is anyone coming?"

"Hmm . . . I'm guessing that would be a no. That's weird. She came and picked *me* up from camp last week. They must love me more—but then, I didn't run away from camp."

"Very funny."

152

I call Dad. His secretary answers. Her name is Marilyn, which I know because making me work in his office is my dad's other favorite way to ruin my summer. Actually, that was the one selling point for the Europe trip.

"Oh, was that today?" she says when I tell her I'm at the airport.

"Uh, yeah."

"He's in Houston right now. Do you want me to call Super Shuttle for you?"

No way. If my parents forget to pick me up from the airport after I've been gone almost the whole time I was supposed to be, they're springing for a cab.

I see my suitcase, and I grab it. But I'm more worried about what I don't see, which is Talia. Where'd she go? She was holding my arm, but now she's not.

Which gets me thinking about all the things that could have happened to her. Like, what if she decided to take a ride on the luggage carousel and ended up in some kind of baggage dead-letter office?

Or maybe she decided to show the nice security guard her jewels.

Or someone offered her some candy if she'd help him find his lost puppy.

She'd go. That's what she'd do.

Stay calm. There are a lot of people here. She's probably just stuck in a crowd.

Where is she?

"Jack?" A whisper interrupts me. Talia!

"Jack?"

I look again, and I see her. She's pressed against a wall, the green hoodie I got her covering all her yellow hair and most of her body.

"Come on," I say. "I have the suitcases."

She looks over her shoulder, not really at me but out at the airport. "Is she still there?" she whispers.

"Is who still there?"

"Shh! There was a lady, an old lady in a black dress. It was Malvolia."

Malvolia? I try to remember where I've heard that name before. The fairy. Witch. Whatever. The one who cast the spell on Talia and made her sleep all those years.

I laugh. "She couldn't be here. She was alive hundreds of years ago, in Euphrasia."

"*I* was alive hundreds of years ago in Euphrasia, and I am here."

Good point. "Still . . ." I look around and see the lady Talia's talking about, an old lady in a black dress. A black *habit*, actually.

"That's not Malvolia," I say. "That's a nun."

"Not her. She was . . ." She turns the rest of the way around, using the hoodie to shield her face. "She has vanished."

"Good. Then we can go."

"I suppose." Talia keeps looking, walking as though she expects something or someone to swoop down on her from the ceiling.

"Ah, if she's still alive, she's probably forgotten you by now." I take her arm to lead her toward the exit. "How long can someone stay mad about not being invited to a party?"

"Perhaps. But she was a woman. Women never forget such slights. And I have learned the consequences of not heeding warnings. It shall not happen again."

Chapter 10: Talia

The taxicab ride is hot and barely faster than a horse, due to what Jack calls "traffic." Throughout it, I am picturing Malvolia's face.

What I failed to tell Jack, lest he believe me insane, was that she spoke to me.

"Ah, Princess." Her black eyes flickered. "You have been a naughty girl, indeed."

She did not look as she looked that day in the tower room, a sweet old lady. Now she was younger, taller, straighter. But her eyes were the same, black and glittering, as was her voice.

"You have awakened under false pretenses," she said.

"False pretenses?"

"Yes." She stepped aside to allow a man with luggage to pass. "This boy is not your true love. You should not be awake. But I will fix it, as I always do. Those who thwart me suffer the consequences."

She reached for me, clawed fingers brushing my sleeve. I started to run away through the crowds, putting as many people between us as possible. I hid. That was when Jack found me.

But perhaps Jack is right. I am insane. In my mind, the events with the dresses, the spindle, everything, happened days ago, not hundreds of years ago. Could Malvolia be alive? Even if she is, surely she would forget the small slight of not being invited to my christening party in so many years' time.

Of course. It was my imagination. It must have been. My insane imagination.

Still, I wonder what she meant by consequences.

Or what my imagination meant, since she was not real. She was not real.

I look over at Jack, asleep in the seat. I sigh. He is to be my husband, although he does not realize it. Can I love him? He is selfish and immature, and yet he did take me with him when he could easily have abandoned me. Why did he? For love, or for pity? Can pity be turned into love? I know not. I also do not know if the gratitude I feel to this silly boy for taking me with him can be turned to love on my side. But then, I probably would not have loved my chosen husband had I stayed in Euphrasia.

No, the important thing is not what I feel for him but what he feels for me. I must make Jack love me, to make my lie true. If he *is* my true love, even Malvolia cannot complain. And, just as important, I must make his parents love me, for no marriage can take place without their approval.

I can be very sweet when I wish to, not to mention beautiful.

I take out my hairbrush. It is so hot I feel my face may melt, but I can work on my hair.

Jack's home is not nearly as large as the castle. But it is much larger than the homes of the peasants in Euphrasia. Surely the family that lives here would be delighted to have their son marry royalty.

Jack knocks and knocks upon the door. "Guess no one's home, either," he says.

I relax a bit.

A rush of cold air greets us, as does the sight of a sullen girl of about three and ten. This must be his sister, Meryl. She is tall, as tall as I am, and a number of blemishes mar her cheeks. I have never had a blemish myself, of course, but one of my lady's maids had several, and they looked quite painful. Meryl also has metallic objects connected to her teeth. In one hand, she clutches a pad of paper. She scowls. "Oh. You're here."

"Hey, why didn't you get the door?" Jack says.

She shrugs. "Didn't hear it."

Jack laughs. "Aren't you happy to see your big brother?"

"Depends. Did you bring me anything?"

"Not a thing," Jack says. "This is Talia."

I put out my hand to her. "Charmed to meet you."

She sticks her tongue out at Jack and does not offer to shake my hand, much less curtsy. "Are you for real? You brought home a girl from Europe? Oh, you are going to be in soooo much trouble." She grins a bit, anticipating it.

"Jack," I say, "we did bring her a gift. Remember?" I want this girl to be on my side, if she is to be my future sister-in-law. I withdraw a cameo necklace from my jewel case. It is the smallest thing there, but I did not sell it to the man in Belgium because it was too precious to me. It is a portrait of my great-grandmother Aurora. In it, she is turned slightly to the side, her hair cascading over her shoulder, and she bears more than a passing resemblance to myself. "I would like you to have this. It is from my country."

She looks at it, then at Jack. "Oh, wow, I can wear it to school." She rolls her eyes.

Not the reaction I had expected.

"A thank-you would be nice," Jack says.

"Yeah, I guess it would." She does not thank me.

"Those objects on your teeth? Pray, what are they?" I ask her.

She scowls. "*Excuse* me?"

"You have some metal in your mouth. Is that a fashion accessory?"

She rolls her eyes yet again and starts upstairs without answering.

159

Jack shrugs. "My sister doesn't . . . like . . . people."
Then he takes my elbow. "Come on, Talia. I'm starving."

I follow him into a room which must be the kitchen, although I cannot be certain, for I have never been inside a kitchen before. We had one at the castle, of course, but it was the exclusive domain of the cook, Mistress Pyrtle, and her serving girls, and she did not take kindly to intruders.

The kitchen in Jack's home is pleasant enough. The walls are lined with shiny wooden cabinetry, and at the center is a large, metal object which Jack opens.

"Looks like Mom hasn't been shopping much lately," he says. "We've got leftover Chinese, leftover Mexican, leftover Chicken Kitchen. . . ." He turns to me. "What looks good?"

"I am sorry. Is that food?" I know what chicken is, but the rest is unfamiliar.

"Sort of." He closes the door and yells toward the other room. "Hey, Meryl, how old's this Chinese?"

No response.

Jack takes out a paper container with a picture in red. He sniffs it. "Smells okay. No hair on it." A chime rings.

Jack goes to get a dish from one of the cabinets. At the same time, two girls approximately the same age as Meryl enter the room. More sisters? Jack did not mention additional sisters. No. They must be friends of Meryl's. These girls are less awkward than Meryl, perhaps a bit more attractive. And yet there is something I do not like about them. For one thing, they both wear blouses which show their bellies and bosoms. Why do young women of this time not wear clothing that fits?

"Hi, Jack," one of the girls, a petite blonde, says, flouncing toward him. She ignores me entirely.

"Hey." Jack hands me a plate. On it, he begins to heap strange food from the box, which I now see has a picture of a pagoda on it. I learned about pagodas in my study of the Orient. I always wished to see one in person. "Are you here to see Meryl?"

The brunette wrinkles her nose. "We're here to see you. Heard you went to Europe."

"Yep." Jack gives me the remaining food and gestures for me to sit at a table on the other side of the room.

That's when Meryl enters. She glances at the two girls, as if comparing them to herself and finding herself lacking. "Hey, so what are you guys doing today?"

The blond girl does not look at her but says to Jack, "Gaby and I were going to go to the beach. Want to come?"

Jack does not answer but continues to shovel the "Chinese food" into his mouth. I take a cautious bite of my own. Salty, but rather interesting. I recognize some of the vegetables, but others, such as an ear of corn no bigger than my index finger, confound me. Jack's telephone makes its noise. He answers it.

The brunette girl drapes herself around him, much in the manner of Mother's Persian cat. "Please, Jack, please go with us."

The other girl follows suit. "Please, Jack. It will be fun."

Jack continues to speak into the telephone.

"Hey, guys," Meryl says, "I could probably talk to my brother and get him to—"

"Whatever." The blond girl's eyes never leave Jack.

Finally, Jack says, "Hold on a sec." He puts down the telephone and shakes the two girls off. "Hey, Jailbait, you mind? I'm trying to have a conversation."

The two girls look offended, then make an elaborate show of peeling themselves off Jack's shoulders. The brunette girl seems purposely to be shoving her rather ample bosom in front of Jack's eyes. Do these girls' mothers know they behave in this manner? Finally, both leave, and Meryl follows. I can still see them through the door a bit.

"Hey, Jennifer," I hear her say. "I can get Jack to take us to the beach another day. Maybe we could ride our bikes to the mall or something."

I watch through the kitchen doorway. One girl laughs, then both, exposed bellies bouncing inward as they do. "Why would we want to do that?" the blond girl says.

"Yeah, really," the brunette echoes. "It's not like we could meet any hot guys with you along."

"But I could . . ." Meryl stammers. "I have money. I could buy us lunch in the Grove or something."

"Hey, what's this?" The blonde reaches for the object in Meryl's hand. "Your diary?"

"It's nothing," Meryl says, holding it away.

The brunette takes up the mockery. "Let me see." She pulls it from Meryl's hand, then opens it. I see that it is a book of sketches. "Look, Jen. Meryl's an artist."

Jennifer grabs the sketchbook. She opens it to a portrait of a mermaid on a rock. "Ooh, is this your girlfriend?"

"Give it back!" Meryl appears near tears.

"I'm just looking. It's such beautiful art." Despite the words, her tone is nasty.

"Jen, give it back!"

"Why should I?"

"Because I say so," I interrupt. I hadn't even realized I'd left the room, but now I am standing before the girls, holding out my hand. "Please return it."

I fix them with my best princessy look. Although I am no longer in Euphrasia, I am still a princess, and these girls are still common. I will make them obey me.

"Who are you?" Jennifer says, but she hands me the pad. "I was just looking at it."

"And now you have stopped. Thank you." I give the pad to Meryl and go back into the kitchen.

"What's up her butt?" the blonde says. "Let me know if your brother's free later."

"But . . . okay . . ." Meryl watches as the two girls leave.

Before the door closes, I hear one say to the other, "Can you believe a dog like that has such a hot brother?"

Horrible things! Meryl undoubtedly heard her, for she looks down and her mouth twists in an awkward manner.

I do not know what to say. Although I spent months learning about diplomacy, we never once discussed what to do if someone is deliberately cruel to another person in one's presence.

Jack continues on the telephone. Why did he not come to his sister's rescue?

Meryl is still standing by the door. She looks at me, and I realize she must be embarrassed at my witnessing this exchange. I take a rather too-large bite of my Chinese food. Some of the sauce dribbles down my throat, causing me to cough, then disgorge the food onto the ground. "Oh, my goodness!" I cough again.

Meryl brightens, laughing. "Eat much?"

I attempt to retrieve the piece—one of the miniature corn ears—with my napkin. "No, not much at all."

"It shows."

I hold out my plate. "Would you like some? It seems not to agree with me."

She begins to shake her head, then nods. "Okay." She gets her own plate and scrapes some of the food from my plate to hers. She sits down. We eat in relative silence, other than Jack's conversation. I wish I could think of something to say.

Finally, I say, "Are those girls friends of yours?"

She looks down. "We *were* friends . . . before they turned into complete . . ." She says a word I do not understand.

"Bee . . . I am sorry, but I do not know this term."

164

"Oh, I forgot you're Dutch." She sighs. "It's kind of like *skank*? *Ho*?" Seeing my confusion, she says, "Don't they have hos in your country?"

I begin to understand, particularly in light of the way the young commoners dressed . . . not to mention the way they pressed themselves against Jack. I nod.

"Jennifer—that's the blond one—she lives next door. She's hot for Jack, and she's always trying to jump on him."

"I understand." I nod and take another bite of the Chinese food. I begin to warm to its exoticness.

Meryl takes a bite, too. I glance out the window. The two girls are still outside, looking into the window, possibly at Jack. When the brunette girl sees me staring at her, she nudges her friend, then makes a face. I do not like these girls. I remember when I was seven or eight, there was a girl, the daughter of one of Mother's ladies-in-waiting, who teased me quite relentlessly about not being allowed out, saying she was going to prick me with a spindle. I despised her.

"Well, then," I say to Meryl, "why allow them in, if they are so unkind?"

The question appears to take her by surprise. Still, she manages to swallow her food before saying, "I don't know, 'cause we used to be friends, I guess. It seems like if you know someone since birth, they should at least be nice to you."

I nod. "Why are they not, then?"

Meryl rolls her eyes as if I am the stupidest person she has ever seen and takes another bite of her food. She does not answer. Jack continues to prattle along on the telephone, never once suspecting that I am making a complete idiot of myself in front of his sister.

Finally, Meryl says, "I'd rather not talk about it, Barbie."

"My name is Talia."

"Whatever. You wouldn't understand. You probably have a gazillion friends. You're totally gorgeous."

I sigh. "No, actually, I have often been quite lonely."

I do not get the chance to elaborate upon this statement, though, as Jack finally closes his telephone. "Good news—we're invited to a party at Stewy Stewart's house tonight."

"A party!" I glance down at my attire, blue trousers and something Jack called a tank top. "Shall I wear my blue gown?" I ask Jack. "Or my red one?" I am fairly jumping up and down, for I love parties. This one shall perhaps make up for the birthday celebration I missed at home. In fact, perhaps it will be like my birthday celebration in one important particular—that it will be the day upon which my true love will find me. When Jack gazes upon me on the dance floor, he will surely—

"Whoa, whoa . . ." he says. "It's not that kind of party."

I glance at Meryl. She is laughing at me.

"What kind is it, then?"

"The fun kind."

I have never heard of a party without gowns. This is turning out to be a very disappointing century.

Within a few minutes, Jack has invaded Meryl's room (over her protests) and procured for me a shirt with the words ABERCROMBIE & FITCH emblazoned across the chest. There was a Fitch family in Euphrasia, but they were plagued by insanity. I decide not to mention this. He also tries to get me to wear something called a bathing suit, which consists of a rather small scrap of yellow cloth.

"I cannot wear that," I say. "It is immodest. It is . . . obscene."

I have a fleeting notion that Jack is playing a trick on me, that this garment is merely an undergarment and his insistence that I wear it merely a ruse to see me unclothed. Although he will be within his rights to demand such privileges *after* our nuptials, I cannot consent before.

"It's a one-piece," Jack says.

"One piece of what?" I demand. "I cannot wear it."

"I don't want her to borrow it, anyway," Meryl says. "You go, girl! Tell him you won't wear it."

"Not helpful," Jack says. To me, he says, "That's what people wear to go swimming nowadays . . . in this century."

"Well, then, it is very simple, then," I say, "because I cannot swim."

Jack sighs, and I know he is angry. For this, I am sorry,

as he has been kind and I wish to please him. I wish to marry him, in fact.

"Can you get out of my room now?" Meryl asks. I note that she is once again clutching her sketch pad. "Some people are trying to work."

"I am sorry," I tell Jack. "Perhaps American young ladies wear such garments and swim and . . ." I think of the young girls—I would not call them ladies—who have just left. ". . . and hang on to young men in a shameless manner. But I am not an American young lady. There are certain compromises I am unwilling to make. I do appreciate your kindness."

If Jack is indeed my destiny, he should understand, and love me for myself.

Of course, at the moment, he does not love me at all.

Chapter 11: Jack

I'm sitting on the sofa with Talia, eating Doritos and watching *Judge Judy*. Meryl's in her room, sulking.

"This is fascinating." Talia licks Doritos cheese off her fingers.

"What's fascinating?" I ask her now. "Me?"

"No." She laughs. "I mean, yes, of course. But I was talking about your American system of justice."

We've been watching two women argue about whether the first woman's pit bull damaged the second woman's car when it climbed on top of the car to sunbathe. The pit-bull woman is wearing a tube top and has nails that are longer than most people's fingers. The other woman has on sequins. "What's fascinating about it?"

"What isn't?" Talia's eyes widen. "This woman, Judge Judy. She is so wise."

I shrug. "I guess."

"And they let her decide the whole case—they leave it up to her?"

"She's the judge."

"Yes! But she is a woman, and yet they trust her opinion. Had I stayed in Euphrasia, I would someday be queen. I would have been charged with appointing all the magistrates in Euphrasia. But women could not *become* magistrates, for their judgment is warped. They would be inconsistent."

I think of Amber and how she acted sometimes, totally in love with me one day and then like I wasn't fit to carry her used lunch tray the next. It doesn't sound like a totally terrible system of justice to me. Not that I'm going to say that to Talia.

"But if you were queen, couldn't you appoint whoever you wanted? Isn't that part of being queen?"

Talia frowns. "I do not know."

Judge Judy is ordering the first woman to pay for the pit bull's damage. Talia claps with delight. "That is exactly what I would have done."

She looks so cute I feel like kissing her.

That's when my mother walks in.

Mom apparently used the opportunity of me in Europe and Meryl at camp to get some work done. At least she looks "rested," code for the fact that her face is frozen into a stiff smile.

"Jack, darling!" she says through lips that don't move sideways. "You're home!" She blows me a little air kiss.

Meryl, who has come downstairs to witness the scene, mimics it. "Yes, you're home, dear boy!"

My sister's wearing this shirt that says: *I'm multi-talented. I can talk and annoy you at the same time.* An understatement. Except that my sister doesn't actually talk that much. She either sulks or does stuff to try and bait me. Right now, she's carrying around that stupid sketch pad she's completely obsessed with and will never show anyone—probably because she's drawing our mutilated corpses. I glare at her, and she sticks out her tongue. "Aren't you going to introduce Mommy to your friend, Jack?"

"Do you ever brush your hair?" I snap back at her.

"Only for people who are worth the effort."

I decide it's time to give Mom a big hug. "Mom! You look great! I'd forgotten how young you are." I gesture to Talia. "This is Talia, the girl I met in Belgium."

One thing about my mom—she's always calm, like the time last year when Travis and I got caught egging cars on Eighty-second Avenue. Mom stayed calm, calm enough that I wondered if she even cared.

You have to really know her to know when she's freaking. I do. Her smile is wider than when she's actually happy, and her voice is higher.

Now she smiles blindingly. Holding out a hand with nail-polished talons, she squeaks, "How lovely to meet you.

Jack's told us—well, actually, he's told us nothing about you. Are you here visiting family?"

Talia glances at me, then says, "No, ma'am."

Mom continues to smile. "Ah, friends, then?"

Another glance at me from Talia. "In a manner of speaking."

I cut in. "I told you, Mom. She's staying with us."

Silence.

Then Meryl says, "I think there's a *Naruto* marathon on Cartoon Network."

My sister hasn't watched an episode of *Naruto* in at least two years, but I guess it's like how birds and squirrels disappear before a hurricane. The flight instinct just kicks in.

Mom doesn't even seem to notice she's gone. "Seriously, Jack, where is Talia staying?"

I look her straight in the eye. "Seriously, Mom, here."

"Jack has been so kind to me," Talia says in her most princessy voice, "helping me come to America and all."

Mom's eyebrows shoot up. "Talia, dear, would you mind joining Meryl in the family room for a moment?"

"You don't have to do that," I tell Talia.

Talia looks from me to Mom. "I believe I do, Jack. Your mother has asked me to, and it would only be courteous." She curtsies to Mom, then leaves.

Mom watches her go, then turns to me. "What do you mean by this, Jack? First, leaving the tour, which we spent so much money to send you on?"

"It's always about money, isn't it?"

". . . and then bringing home some stranger you met in Europe?"

"You're always after me to expand my horizons."

"By visiting a museum or something—not by bringing home Dutch drifters." Mom still hasn't raised her voice, but her unraised voice is getting a little strained.

"She's from Belgium." I stick with that because that's what her passport says. "And she's got perfect manners—I thought you'd like that."

"That type always has perfect manners."

"That *type*?"

"Grifters, tricksters. They take you in with their perfect manners, and then they swindle you. She could rob us, even murder us in our sleep."

I laugh. "Talia wouldn't do that."

"How do you know that, Jack?"

I stop and think about it. Of course, I know because I know Talia's actually a princess, heir to a throne, who's had a witch's curse placed on her and slept three-hundred-odd years until *I* woke her while looking for the beach. But I don't think that explanation's exactly going to fly with Mom. She'd call the FBI before you could say "grounded until graduation," or she wouldn't believe me.

So instead, I say, "She's a really nice person."

"I bet she isn't even a teenager. She's probably some middle-aged woman preying on young boys . . ."

Actually, she's three hundred.

". . . in those sleazy clothes . . ."

173

"They're Meryl's clothes!"

"She's taken Meryl's clothes?"

I begin to pace. "Does she look middle-aged?"

"Do *I* look middle-aged? It's irrelevant. She can't stay here."

I stop pacing. Why did I agree to take Talia back to America with me? Oh, yeah, because if I didn't, I'd still be rotting in a dungeon. But that doesn't explain why I didn't ditch her at the border. I definitely could have. So why didn't I?

Oh, yeah, 'cause I'm a nice guy . . . which translates to "sucker."

So why do I care if Mom kicks her out now?

I have no idea, but I do. If Mom doesn't let her stay, she'll be all alone in America—a foreign country to her—with no family, no friends, not even the skills to use MapQuest to find someplace to go. And she's so trusting. And beautiful.

God, she'd be dead in a week.

"You can't throw her in the street," I say. "She's just a kid. You wouldn't want someone to kick me out, would you?"

Mom looks down. "She can call her family."

"It's, like, three AM in Eu . . . Belgium. She can't call anyone."

"Tomorrow, then. She can stay tonight, on the air mattress."

"She can't call tomorrow, either."

"Why not?"

Good question. In the family room, Meryl's got the TV on superloud. I rack my brain for any possible, acceptable-to-Mom reason Talia can't call, a reason other than the fact that Talia's family doesn't own a phone. Could I tell her Talia would be a political prisoner if she went back home? Except I'm pretty sure Belgium is a democracy. Mom used to volunteer at a shelter for abused kids, so maybe I could tell her that Talia's dad will beat her if she goes back . . . except I'm guessing Mom's charitable instinct doesn't include taking random abused kids into our house. Finally, I say, "Look, her parents are traveling in America, to the Grand Canyon."

"I'm sure they have cell phones. She can call them."

"I don't think phones work down there." I'm thinking fast and stupid now. "It's all wilderness."

Mom's not buying it. "I'll talk to her." She starts into the family room.

How can you kick a princess out of your house? My mom will figure out a way.

I follow her into the family room. When we get to the door, we stop. Talia's sitting on the sofa beside Meryl, who has her sketch pad with her, and she's actually showing it to Talia. My sister says, "Wow, that's incredible. It really does look a lot better that way."

Chapter 12: Talia

I am banished to the next room to look after Jack's sullen sister so that Jack and his mother might whisper about me.

Hospitality has changed a great deal in the last three hundred years. In Euphrasia, when visitors came to the castle, no trouble or expense was spared—the finest food served upon gold-edged plates, sheets of linen on feather beds. Why, even when Jack came to us in my country's darkest hour, my father ordered a peacock killed for his dinner (that is, before he threw him into the dungeon). The poorest peasant would provide a bed for a weary traveler, even if it was his own bed he was giving up.

Not now. Likely, Jack's mother thinks I will slit their throats if permitted to sleep here. I saw it in her face: fear.

People are very fearful these days. At the airport, we were poked and prodded within an inch of our lives, our shoes removed, our trunks placed inside a special machine which might see inside them, an unreasonable intrusion.

And this is the time in which I must now live, due to wicked Malvolia's curse.

I understand, but I do not like it.

Jack's sister, Meryl, sits upon the sofa, looking at the thing called television, which is blasting like a brass band. The characters in the play she is watching—they are all odd drawings rather than real people—seem quite angry. At least, they are hitting and kicking one another. Meryl, I note, pays them little mind. Rather, she stares at her sketch pad. She does not look up when I enter. I should be friendly to her. Our earlier conversation did not go well, but I have observed my father enough times to know that allies are important. I must make Meryl an ally.

I sneak up behind her and peer over her shoulder.

The drawing is the same one from earlier, the one which the horrid neighbor girl mocked. Now I can study it further.

The detail is striking. The ocean surrounding the mermaid, although only in black pencil, is so real it seems to roil, the sea creatures around her—eels, sharks, octopi—seem actually to swim, and the mermaid herself is so magnificently alive that I can imagine the sea fish and crustaceans doing her bidding.

At the palace, my drawing master, Signor Maratti,

taught me to draw suitable subjects for young ladies—a bowl of fruit or a landscape. But, alas, artistic ability was not one of the fairies' gifts.

Meryl has talent. Although I meant to feign admiration for her work, I do not have to. With deft strokes, she adds a curl to the mermaid's smile. I breathe a sigh.

Meryl jumps. "What are you looking at?" She grabs the sketch pad away, making a nasty scratch upon the drawing with her pencil. "Now see what you made me do?"

I shake my head. "I apologize." I sit down on the opposite side of the sofa from her. She compresses her body into a ball, as if she is protecting her sketch pad from me. She neither opens it nor begins to draw again. Nor does she watch the television. I attempt to watch it, but I do not know what is going on. I clear my throat.

Meryl scowls. "Are you here to talk to me again?"

I would like to talk to her. First of all, I am bored, and second, I would like to know Jack's sister better. But I sense this would be the wrong thing to say, so instead I match her scowl with one of my own.

"Do not flatter yourself." I learned this phrase from Jack. "Your mother sent me in here to bide the time with you so that she and Jack could discuss me."

"Oh, yeah?" Meryl almost smiles. "She's like that. She won't say what she thinks to people's faces. She's too nice. But when your back's turned, watch out."

"I know quite a few people like that."

Meryl slips open her sketch pad, taking elaborate care

to face it away from me. She continues with her drawing.

There is naught for me to do but watch the television show, which appears to be about three friends, two boys and a girl, who wish to be something called ninjas. The girl has pink hair, which is lovely. No one in Euphrasia had pink hair. I know not what a ninja is, and I dare not ask Meryl, so I sit in silence and watch. Bits of it are funny, at least, and I laugh.

Meryl looks up, then back down.

A moment later, I laugh again.

"You like anime?" Meryl asks.

I take this as permission to look at her, which I do. A blank look.

"Anime?" she repeats. "Japanese cartoons?"

I shake my head. "I have never seen one."

"You're watching one now."

"Oh." I look at the screen. The pink-haired girl is hitting someone very hard. "It seems quite lovely. I like how the girl, Sakura, will become a fighter, too, just like the boys. She is rather like Judge Judy, isn't she?"

"Judge Judy?"

I shake my head. "Never mind."

"Sakura's my favorite," Meryl says.

She goes back to her drawing, slightly less sullen. The television show ends, but another of the same begins. Meryl pays it little mind, engrossed in her art. I can hear Jack and his mother talking in the next room, but the blaring television prevents my knowing what they are saying. I stifle a yawn. My eyes begin to close. If I do not speak, I will begin to fall asleep.

Finally, I say, "I am sorry for looking at your sketch earlier."

Meryl sketches a few lines, then says, "Whatever."

"It is just," I say, "that back in my country, I studied with an Italian master, Signor Carlo Maratti."

"Woo-woo for you."

"Oh, I am not bragging. I have no talent whatsoever, I assure you. Signor Maratti despised me. He told my father that teaching me was a waste of his time, and he went back to Italy to paint."

Meryl laughs. "Pretty embarrassing, getting kicked out of *art*."

"Quite. But you have talent, the sort of talent I wished to have."

Now she is holding the sketch pad so that I might catch a glimpse of it, but I do not attempt to do so. Instead, I point at the television. "I like her hair. Is it common in your country?"

But Meryl moves her sketchbook closer. "I don't think it's very good. I can draw people and stuff, but then I have trouble with stupid things like the sky."

I pull my eyes from the television. "May I see?" When she hands it to me, I take a look at it. As she says, the sky looks false against the realistic person and animals. "Ah, I see what you are talking about, although this is really quite wonderful. Have you studied the concept of negative space?"

"I don't take art, actually. My dad says it's a waste of an elective. What's negative space?"

"Signor Maratti was quite enthusiastic for it—it is the idea that instead of observing the positive space of an object, one should draw the shape of the space *around* the object—the mermaid, for example, or this seagull."

"But I tried doing that, drawing the sky first. It still comes out bad."

I look closer. "That is because you drew the outline first. What you must do is draw up to the object, then draw the object afterward. Can I see your pad?"

She hands it to me, and I turn to the first blank page. Then I attempt to sketch the sky around the shape of a bird. "It is quite bad, I know, but the concept is true."

Meryl attempts it herself. I try to nod encouragement without appearing patronizing. When I was her age—three hundred three years ago—I felt patronized by *everyone*. But no, she seems genuinely pleased by my interest in her art. Finally, she finishes the bird, a much better bird than my own, surrounded by a much better sky, and shows it to me. "Wow, that's incredible," she says, smiling. "It really does look a lot better that way."

That is when Jack and his mother walk in.

"Talia," Jack says, "I'm afraid my mom has some bad news."

"Wait a second," Jack's mother says. "Meryl, was that you speaking just now?"

Meryl shrugs. "Yeah."

"And that is your sketchbook?" She reaches for it. Meryl snatches it back. Jack's mother says, "Am I to understand, Meryl, that you have allowed this . . . this . . . girl . . ."

"Talia," Jack says helpfully.

". . . that you have allowed Talia to see your sketchbook?"

Meryl has secreted the sketchbook behind her person again. "She studied with an Italian master. Isn't that cool?"

Jack's mother nods. "Yes." She looks at Jack. "You say her parents will be back to get her in a week?"

Jack nods.

"And you have actually met her parents?"

Jack laughs. "Boy, have I!"

"All right. She can stay the week. But she has to sleep in the study downstairs, on the air mattress."

I wish I knew what an air mattress was.

Chapter 13: Jack

"An air mattress is a strange thing, indeed," Talia says.

"It's rubber," I say. And the study is way too small for it. Talia's going to be wedged between the desk and the door out to the garage, but I couldn't talk Mom into letting Talia stay in the guest room. Too near our rooms. For my own security. So we're putting a princess on an air mattress. By the garage.

"It is ingenious that people of your time have found so many uses for such an unpleasant substance." She feels the top of it. "Is it not possible to put something else inside it, like feathers?"

"Look, I'm sorry. My mom, she's a little weird about things. We're not going to do much sleeping, anyway. We've got that party tonight." I look at her. "Boy, is Amber going to freak when she sees you."

"Amber?" Talia says.

"Yeah, you know, the girl you talked to on the phone. My ex-girlfriend."

"She did not seem very nice."

I shrug. "She's usually nicer." I'm not even sure that's true. I realize that maybe Talia didn't know that Amber's going to be there tonight. "But anyway, you're so beautiful, she'll flip out when she sees you."

"Flip out? I am sorry, but what does that mean?"

"It means she's going to be really jealous when she sees us together."

Talia puts her hands on her hips. "That is why we are going, then? To see this girl, Amber, to make her jealous?"

I don't say anything. I mean, yeah, it's the reason, but when she puts it that way, it sounds like I'm using Talia. Which I sort of am, I guess. But this party is the chance I've been waiting for all summer. Bringing Talia home was just about driving my parents nuts at first—but it will be incredible when Amber sees her and realizes I'm not just waiting around for her. Finally, I say, "Hey, I brought you back here. I talked my mom into letting you stay. I thought the least you could do was—"

"Fine." She looks away. "But should you not be spending your first evening back with your parents?"

I shrug. "My mom's got a meeting tonight, and Dad's out of town. As usual."

Talia nods like she understands, but I doubt she does. Back in her time, mothers didn't go to meetings, and fathers

184

worked on the farm, with their sons by their sides. But she's being nice about it. Actually, she's being nice about everything, the Chinese food that she choked on—I guess they don't have soy sauce where she's from—my weird mother and my weirder sister, and now the air mattress. They don't have *anything* where she's from, and she thinks it's all awesome.

I change the subject. "So, you were actually talking to my sister?"

"Mm-hmm. She seems lovely." I laugh, and she says, "What is funny?"

"It's just . . . my sister and I mostly just insult each other."

"Have you tried talking to her about something which interests her?" Talia pokes the air mattress with her finger.

I shrug. "I didn't really think anything did."

Talia tries to sit down, but the mattress bucks her off. I help her onto it. "In my time," she says, "there was not much to do *but* talk. We had no televisions. We had no telephones—neither the kind in your pocket nor the kind on a table. We had no movies or cars. So we talked. I learned that it is possible to make conversation with anyone, if you figure out what they wish to discuss."

I remember how Talia got me to talk about the gardening thing. I've never told anyone else about that, but with this girl, I sort of feel like I can be myself without worrying about looking uncool. After all, she doesn't even know what "cool" *is*.

But the problem with having someone come to your house and be with you all the time is you start seeing what your life is like through *their* eyes. Like, why *didn't* someone show to pick me up from the airport, or at least call to tell me they weren't coming? Why doesn't Mom have any real food in the house? It's not like *our* food rotted when we were asleep for three hundred years, but that's sort of what it looks like. And why can't I get my sister to talk to me?

"Yeah?" I say. "And what did you figure out about Meryl?"

"That she is lonely, has few friends. She tries to befriend the neighbor girl, who only makes jest of her."

"Jennifer picks on Meryl?"

Talia rolls her eyes. "You do not see what is right before you. But Meryl is a talented artist and finds solace in that. That is what we spoke about. Art."

I don't know what to say to that. I never noticed she had talent. She never showed me her sketches or anything.

"Whooo! This is fun!" Talia's standing on the air mattress now. It's underfilled, and she's trying to walk across it, which is a bit like walking on a surfboard.

"Stop. You'll fall."

"What shall happen if I do? Hit my head and sleep three hundred years?"

"Maybe. Why not?"

"Oh, you are just an old bore! Lady Brooke was always trying to stop me having fun. Well, you cannot!"

"Oh, yeah?" I grab the air pump and turn it on full

blast in her face. "How about that?"

She squeals and covers her face. "Better!" But in the next moment, she falls. I catch her, and for a moment, I hold her there, and I think what it would be like to kiss her. To kiss her again.

But that's silly. I don't even like her, and she's going away in a week. Then I'll never see her again. What I really want is to get Amber back, so kissing Talia isn't part of my plan.

She grabs the air pump out of my hand. "Attack of the ninjas!" She turns it on my face and, at the same time, kicks my legs out from under me. I fall on my butt. "Oh, I am learning from your television."

I don't kiss her. But I do think I'll miss her when she's gone.

Chapter 14: Talia

A party! I am wearing Meryl's "Abercrombie & Fitch" shirt and a pair of blue jeans, both of which are relatively modest. The bathing costume, I place inside my purse, never to see the light of day.

Jack wears a "tank top" and his own bathing costume, which is somewhat more modest than those prescribed for women. Still, it reveals a great deal more flesh than I am accustomed to seeing revealed by the gentlemen at court.

I try to focus my eyes properly on the back of Jack's head or, perhaps, the floor as we traverse the stairs and the hallway on the way to Jack's car. And yet my eyes continue to travel downward, sideways, or in general *away* from their proper destination—for the destination they seek is the back of Jack's legs and other nether regions which have been properly covered in recent days by his trousers.

I remember that delicious moment in the study—that horrible little room next to the place where they keep the cars, where I am to be consigned these next seven nights—when I fell from the air mattress, and I thought Jack was going to kiss me. Was he going to? Will he ever?

I sneak another glance at Jack's legs.

Signor Maratti had a book filled with colored plates of subjects appropriate for young ladies, flowers and fruit and other vegetation. These, he showed me often, the better to reveal my own inadequacies as a painter. But one day, when Signor had excused himself to clean the paintbrushes, I ventured to glance at the book. It fell to the floor and, in my haste to retrieve it, I saw a plate which made me gasp.

I knew immediately why Signor Maratti had not shown me that particular page. One would have thought that the realization of this fact would have been all that was necessary to cause me to avert my eyes in a ladylike manner.

One would have thought wrong.

The picture was of a young man, quite naked but for a bit of leaves where a codpiece would go. I assured myself that, had it not been for that bit of leaves, I *would* have turned the page. What struck me about the picture was how different this young man's body was from my own: muscular where mine was soft, angular where mine was round. I could not quell the momentary thrill at the thought—I knew it was an improper one—of beholding, even touching such a body one day in person—when I was properly married to a suitable consort, of course.

Then Signor Maratti entered, and I was forced to pretend I had been looking at the flowers. I am afraid I did not concentrate for the rest of the lesson, and it was a blessing that Signor himself was old and fat, the better to calm my racing heart and mind.

He never left me alone again.

But now, hundreds of years later, I am beholding a male body, a body which was not even a wish of a prediction of a dream on that long-ago day, and yet I feel the same excitement at the thought of it, the same wondering how it would be to touch it.

We reach the party at good speed, thanks to the service of Jack's car. There are numerous other cars parked on the grassy area in front of the house. To whom do they belong? Will their owners like me? At parties at my father's castle, I was always in the company of Lady Brooke and other female companions, who were under strict orders to keep me entertained, as if I were a fussy infant. There will be no such orders here.

What if they hate me?

I was quite perturbed to find that Jack was using me to make this Amber person jealous. On the other hand, it is gratifying to know that he believes me so beautiful.

Suddenly, Jack is beside me, rapping on the car window. "Coming?"

I manage to rip my gaze from his muscled arms long enough to say, "I am afraid."

He glances at his wristwatch. "They'll all love you."

This seems unlikely, but Jack opens the car door and grips my wrist firmly in his hand. It is so warm, and I remember that he is my intended, my destiny. There is only the obstacle of Amber to be gotten past.

"Do you really think so?" I edge closer to him than I have dared before.

"Sure." He is near enough that I can feel his breath upon me, and with his free hand, he pushes a lock of hair from my face. "You're so beautiful, Talia. How could anyone not love you?"

I hope this is true, of him. I am, indeed, used to being adored. But I was adored because I was a princess. Will I still be adorable when I am merely Talia?

I begin to follow him toward the door. "But what if I say something . . . foolish?" I ask before we go inside.

"Believe me, people will be too drunk to notice."

No one answers when Jack knocks upon the door, so finally we push it open. This is shocking to me. Is there no guard? No servant to announce us? But when we enter, I am no longer surprised.

It is chaos. There is music louder than any that I have heard before. I realize that Jack was correct that I need not worry about saying anything foolish. No one would even hear it. Dozens of people talk and laugh and dance in a most improper manner, and every single young lady at the party is dressed in a bathing costume similar to the one Jack provided. In many cases, they are even less modest.

"Come on," Jack says. "I'll introduce you around."

I am pleased that he does not release his grip upon my hand. It would be terrifying to be lost here. The patio, as Jack calls it, is barely quieter than the house and even more crowded. Here, the crowd centers upon a large artificial lake—the pool—where people are swimming.

My every muscle urges me to stop—nay, to flee—but my mind urges me forward. These are Jack's friends. They must like me. *He* must like me and not think me a misfit from another time.

A portly boy greets us. "Hey, Jacko, you made it."

"Stewy!" Jack slaps the boy's hand. "This is Talia. She's from Belgium."

"Wow, you weren't kidding when you said she was beautiful." He touches my shoulder with a hand that is wet and ice-cold, and he does not remove it. "Does this mean Amber's available?"

"You'll have to ask her boyfriend." Jack guides me toward him, which has the effect of separating my shoulder from Stewy's clammy hand. "Let's get a drink."

"Help yourself. My parents are paying for it." Stewy leans toward me. "I'm looking forward to getting to know you better, Talia."

He leers at me. I try to think of a proper response. As a princess, I might have slapped him or called the guards. Now, I simply turn away. "So kind of you."

Soon, Jack and I have put several chairs and people between ourselves and Stewy, and I am glad of it. Jack thrusts a cold, cylindrical object into my hand.

"Thank you!" I say, staring at it.

"It's a beer." He looks around the patio.

"I am familiar with beer," I say, although I have never drank one and have certainly never seen this sort of container for one. I watch as Jack opens his own beer, then places the cylinder to his lips, his eyes still glancing about.

I do the same. It is so cold that, for a moment, my teeth begin to ache. When I have recovered, I say, "Is Stewy a good friend of yours?"

I have to say it twice before he looks at me, but finally he does.

"He's okay. We go to school together, and . . ." He stops. His eyes suddenly fix elsewhere. I follow his gaze to its end. I see what he has been looking for.

It is a girl. She emerges from the pool, and she is—I would like to believe—no more beautiful than myself, but she wears a bathing suit more revealing than the rest—so revealing, indeed, that I wonder if some of the fabric of it may have shrunk in the water, or if someone played a trick on her. Her auburn hair is long and curly, and although her skin is a shade of tan that ladies of court assiduously avoided through the unrelenting use of headdresses and powder, I suspect this is no longer the case, for every male eye on the patio is suddenly upon her.

But her eyes seek only one person.

"Jack! You're here!"

Jack swears under his breath. "It's Amber."

Chapter 15: Jack

I thought I could handle seeing Amber again, but that was before I saw her. I'd forgotten how she makes me feel—like that time when I was a kid and I got my finger between a plug and a socket. For a second, my whole body tingles, helplessly.

"Jack!" she purrs, managing somehow to insert her body between mine and Talia's before I can move, much less speak. "You're here."

"Hey, Amber," I manage, backing away a step. Not easy. "Nice . . . um . . . bathing suit." *Act cool. Don't drool.*

"You like it?" She steps even closer.

I laugh. "Looks like you found it in the Barbie section at Toys 'R' Us." *Duh.*

"Is that a complaint?" Amber slides her hand down my arm, pausing an instant to caress the muscles, and for a second, it's pretty easy to forget that she dumped me—at a party just like this one, in front of all my friends—because someone with a cooler car came along.

"It's nice," I say.

Beside me, Talia clears her throat, reminding me of her existence. I'm glad Talia's here. She's so beautiful that Amber will know I'm not just sitting around waiting for her . . . even though I kind of am.

"Hey, Amber, this is Talia."

Amber pretend-frowns, then reaches her hand out like she's going to shake Talia's hand. When Talia puts out her own hand, Amber places an empty can in it. "Would you mind getting me a refill?"

I find my voice. "Amber, she's not going to just wait on—"

"I mean, if you were going to get yourself one, too."

Talia looks bewildered but drains her beer. "I suppose I am a bit thirsty."

"Thanks." Amber gives her a big, fake smile.

Talia heads for the cooler, and I face Amber. "That wasn't nice."

Amber laughs. "So I'm supposed to be nice?"

I glance after Talia. Talia's nice. At least, she's interested in other people. I look back at Amber. "Some people are."

"Do you want someone nice or someone fun?" Amber's nails are out, scratching my back where I didn't even know I had an itch. They're long and red, and part of me wants to turn on her and scream, "Go away, witch!" The other part wants to roll over like a puppy, enjoying it.

"I can't have both?" I ask.

Amber moves closer. "I'll try to be nice." She scratches harder, and I can feel her leg against mine. She leans toward my ear. "I missed you, Jack."

"Did you?" I stop looking for Talia. It's not like we're on a date, after all. She's just staying with us. And she knew Amber would be here.

"Uh-huh. You knew I would."

"I didn't know that. You broke up with me. You made out with some other guy *before* you broke up with me."

"Are you still mad about that?" Amber says.

"Still? It just happened."

"Silly! It was a whole month ago." She leans in close, so I can feel her breath against my neck, and scratches harder, until I wonder if I might begin to bleed. If I bleed to death, will she even care? "Look, I was wrong, okay? But you were going away for *half the summer*, and I was going to be so lonely. I didn't want to get stuck hanging around here, dateless and desperate, while you gallivanted around Europe, making out with French chicks."

"So you made out with that other guy because you were going to be lonely?" I say.

"You were leaving. I couldn't stand to think how much I'd miss you." She leans up against me, so warm. "Hey, I called your cell the other day. That shows I was thinking about you, right?"

"I guess." She's totally lying, and I'm totally letting

196

her. The other guy probably left town, and she wants me because I'm here now.

I remember when I stuck my finger in that socket, my dad yelled at me for being stupid. And that's how I feel around Amber. Stupid. The girl makes me stupid.

"How about if I apologized?" She stops scratching and puts both hands on my shoulders.

"That would be a good—"

I don't get to finish because her mouth interrupts me. Like, it's on top of my mouth, rendering me unable to speak.

I'd forgotten how she kissed, too.

When she's finally finished, she says, "Do you accept my apology?"

I know what I should say. *No. Absolutely not. I've moved on. I'm here with Talia, and being here with someone means something to me, even if it doesn't mean anything to you.*

Instead, I say, "Uh . . ."

She kisses me again, her long fingernails in my hair now, and I am fire and water, and Talia was three hundred years ago, or a thousand. Amber is now.

"I missed you, Jack," she says.

Did she really? I want to believe that. It feels good to hear her say it, anyway.

"God, I missed you, too," I say.

We stand there, making out, until someone tells us to get a room. Amber says, "We could go someplace. Are your parents home tonight?"

Which is when I remember. Talia. What am I doing?

She went to get the beer, and she never came back.

"I should find Talia," I tell Amber.

"Don't worry about her," Amber says. "I'm sure she'll find her way home."

Home. I laugh. "You don't understand about Talia. She's . . . she could have gotten lost or something."

"What is she, stupid?"

"No. She's not stupid. She's . . . nice . . . innocent." I remember Talia surfing on the air mattress, talking to my sister, asking me about gardening. Amber never asked me about stuff like that because, I now realize, she didn't care. I could never talk to Amber the way I talk to Talia. She'd laugh at me.

She laughs now. "Innocent? She was here ten minutes ago, and then . . . she went off with Robert Hernandez."

"With Robert?"

Amber rolls her eyes. "She won't be innocent for long."

Ten minutes ago. I calculate. That means she showed up with the beers, saw Amber putting her tongue down my throat, and stormed away, only to fall into the clutches of the biggest player in school. He'll probably try and take her to a bedroom or . . . something.

I pull away from Amber. "I brought her here. She's my responsibility." I stand on my toes, trying to see through the crowd.

Amber looks annoyed and stomps her foot. "So you're going to look for her instead of being with me?"

"I have to."

"But she went off with someone else. Face it, Jack. There's just something about you that makes girls want to make out with other guys."

I turn back toward Amber. "What did you just say?"

"I didn't mean it that way. I was kidding."

"Funny." I laugh. "You just think I'm some loser, don't you?"

She shrugs, but then she says, "Of course not, baby. You're just being silly. She probably went home with Robert."

"Yeah, that's what I'm afraid of," I say. I turn my back on her and start looking through the crowd.

"You're not going to get another chance with me, Jack!" Amber yells.

"I don't want one!" It's hard for me to say that. I know it's not about me with her. It's about the conquest, about winning, about proving to everyone that she can get me back anytime. And yet part of me really wants to touch her some more, wants her to be as into me as I am into her. "I'm tired of being stupid around you."

Then I hear a scream.

Chapter 16: Talia

Jack is not my destiny.

I came to this party to make Jack happy. It did—a bit too happy, if you ask me, because I drove him straight into Amber's waiting embrace.

I returned from fetching the drinks (me, fetching drinks like a common kitchen maid!) to find them locked in a torrid kiss. Jack just kisses anyone and everyone, I now see. It was not special at all when he kissed me. His lips are everywhere.

I turned to run away.

That was when I realized I had nowhere to run. I was in a foreign land, a strange time, alone and friendless, all because I believed Jack—horrible Jack—to be my destiny.

But Jack was kissing some trollop named Amber. Malvolia was right! He is not my true love. I should not even be awake. I should be back in the castle, awaiting a kiss from a respectable prince!

"Is one of those for me?" a voice says while I consider this.

I turn to find myself eye-to-eye with a handsome, dark-haired young man. "I beg your pardon?"

He points to the cans I am holding. "One for you, and one for me?"

I laugh, for it seems preferable to bursting into tears. "Why not?" I hand him Amber's can.

He takes it and drains it down. "Can I get you a refill?"

Finally! A young man who knows how to treat princesses, by fetching and carrying for them. But I say, "I have yet to finish this one."

"Then finish it."

This I do, under his watchful eye. It is cold and tart and fizzy. I still have not worked out how people of this century contrive to keep everything so delightfully cold, even on the hottest of days, but it is lovely, almost worth living three hundred years.

Then I think of Jack. Almost, but not quite.

"Lovely!" I say.

He laughs. "That's a good girl." He takes the can from my hand, then steps away to get another. When he comes back, he says, "I saw you come in with O'Neill."

There is a question in his voice. I answer it. "I am not with Mr. O'Neill."

He glances over at where Jack and Evil Amber are still locked together. "Yeah, I can see. Stupid guy. If I'd come with you, I'd never have let you get away."

I like the tone of his voice almost as much as the tone of the conversation. A young woman clad in a scandalous costume passes by, holding a tray of jewel-colored objects which look to be some sort of confection.

"Want one?" the boy says.

"What are they?"

"Jell-O shots."

I have no idea what a Jell-O shot is, but many people are ingesting them. So, as not to reveal my ignorance, I say, "They look lovely."

"Yes, lovely!" He takes two. I see other people slurping theirs out of the cup like a drink, so I do the same. It is cold, like everything else, and sweet as strawberries.

"Delectable!" I say.

"Delectable!" He laughs. "Here—have mine, too."

I do not argue. I have had little to eat, and my head is spinning. I hope this Jell-O shot will calm it down.

"What's your name, beautiful?" he asks.

"Talia . . . Talia Brooke."

"Well, Talia Talia Brooke, I'm Robert, and I think you're definitely delectable yourself. Did you bring a bathing suit?"

I did, of course, with no intention of wearing it. I note that several other young ladies also appear unable to swim and are simply standing in the water, talking, almost as if the pool is the dance floor. But I am not about to wear such an immodest garment.

"I do not have one with me," I lie.

He frowns. "Sorry to hear that. Don't suppose you want to go skinny-dipping?"

I do not know what this means. Perhaps he can see this by the expression on my face, for he looks annoyed, then away. But I cannot let him leave me, for then I would be all alone while Jack kisses another girl. My head is spinning like a whirligig, I suspect from the beers I drank. I feel about to cast up my accounts like a common drunkard. Still, I must keep Robert with me.

"It is a lovely night," I say. "Perhaps we could go for a stroll."

He looks back at me, smiling. "Someplace dark?"

I blink my weary eyes. "Dark would be nice, indeed." As I say it, I stumble upon my own feet. Robert reaches his hand out to steady me.

"You are so kind and helpful." I glance over at Jack. "I have no idea what I would do without you."

"That's me—Mr. Knight in Shining Armor." He laughs.

"It is true."

We pass the young lady with the Jell-O shots. There is one remaining on her tray, and Robert picks it up and hands it to me. "For you, milady."

"Oh, no," I protest. "You have had not even one."

"I insist." He holds it out to me. It is as blue as a

peacock's feathers. I take it. "Thank you. I am excessively grateful for your help."

"Maybe we can figure out a way for you to show your gratitude later."

"I am certain we can."

He looks so happy about that that I begin straightaway to come up with a plan. Of course, back in Euphrasia, what he is doing is little more than common civility, but this seems to be a century completely devoid of manners and consideration. Therefore, common civility should be rewarded as heroism. If I return home (for it seems I may do just that, if Jack is not to be my husband—horrid Jack!), I could arrange a knighthood for this young man or, at the very least, a medal of some sort.

Jack will be beheaded.

But it is hard to think about it, with my own head so light and floaty. The only time I have felt like this before was once, when Father received a case of that special bubbling wine from France. I consumed almost an entire bottle and, in the end, felt wonderful and terrible and nothing at all like myself.

"Ah, you don't have to do that," Robert is saying.

"Do what?"

"Arrange a knighthood for me. I'm happy to help out a beautiful girl like you, especially when mean old Jack ditched you."

Did I say that aloud? Has the beer done me in?

We stroll through the crowds of people, Robert's hand

204

still steadying my elbow. I swallow the Jell-O shot, allowing it to play upon my tongue as it falls down my throat.

"Where are you from?" Robert tightens his grip. "Your accent's really hot."

"I'm from Euph . . . Europe. Belgium." My head is spinning, and I am barely able to place one foot before the other. Were Robert not supporting me, I would surely fall. I begin to, anyway, or perhaps it is more like floating, flying, jumping from an airplane and landing in a jewel-colored cloud.

And then I feel his mouth upon mine, Robert's mouth, this stranger whom I have barely met. His mouth is upon mine!

I begin to voice my displeasure, but with his tongue in my mouth, it comes out as a moan. We are standing at the far side of the pool, away from the boys and girls playing ball. Robert kisses me again. My brain is in a fog, like the moment—I now remember it—the moment after I touched the spindle when I was falling and helpless to prevent it.

"You're so beautiful, Talia." Another kiss. It is too difficult to fight him in my tipsy state. He kisses me, and then I feel his hand traversing *inside my trousers* toward my nether regions.

"No! Stop it!" My cries are almost soundless. He means to dishonor me!

"No!" I shriek, although in my fog, I fear my shriek is weak. "No!"

Indeed, he ignores my cries, his hot, rough hands searching where they ought not search. I hear sounds around me, people conversing. Does no one notice or care that he is disgracing me before their eyes?

"No!" I pull free of him, raising my hand to slap him, and then I am falling down, down into the cold shock of water.

Water! "Help!" I cry. The icy water sobers me somewhat but not enough. I cannot touch bottom. "Help! I cannot swim!"

I reach for the wall, but in my beer-drenched muddle, my fingers slip away from it, over and over, scraping. Then I cannot see. All I can see is Robert above me, a surprised expression on his face. Does he not understand that I am drowning?

"I am drowning, you fool!" I yell, but the last words are lost as my mouth fills with water. I emerge again, fighting my way up. "I am . . ." I submerge. Is this the end of me, then, the end of Princess Talia of Euphrasia? Shall I meet a watery grave three hundred years too late but not a moment too soon? Will I lie forever on the bottom of this man-made lake with no one to mourn me, no one to know what has become of me?

I submerge for the third, and what I believe shall be the final, time. I lack the strength to fight my way back up. This is the end. This is the end.

And then, all at once, I feel a strong grip upon my arm, someone pulling me up. Once again, I can breathe. I can breathe!

Then I am unceremoniously dumped upon the patio. I take many great, gasping breaths. I lean forward, choking on great quantities of strange-tasting water. There is a hand on my back, hitting me. I choke and inhale, choke and inhale many times before I feel well enough to look upward into the eyes of my savior.

"Come on, Talia, let's go home."

I open my eyes.

Jack.

I collapse against him, feeling his warmth against my cold skin.

Chapter 17: Jack

"Come on, Talia. You're drunk." I'm trying really hard not to hit Robert. I'm in enough trouble without coming home with a black eye I got at some party.

"I' nodrunk," Talia slurs. "Ihadtreebeers. Wehad wine ev'y nighat home."

"See that?" Robert says as Talia falls on the floor. "She's not drunk."

"Well, she's going home, anyway. I'm taking her home."

"Home!" At the word, Talia begins to sob. "Idonawanna-gohome!" She clutches at the patio chairs.

"See?" Robert says. "She doesn't want to go home."

"You really know how to pick them, don't you?" Amber comes up behind me. "What a ho."

"Shut up." I look at her. "You honestly think this is all about you?"

She shrugs. "Who else?"

I get down on Talia's level and start to pry her fingers off the chair. "I don't mean home-home. I mean home with me, my parents' house."

"She's staying at your house?" Amber screams.

"What do you care?" I say.

"Buthey haaate me. Theymakemesleeponairmattress."

Finally, I manage to get Talia up and headed toward the door. A bunch of people are standing around, drinking Jell-O shots, and Talia says, "Ooh! I want another one!"

"Another Jell-O shot?"

"Yes. Hungry."

"Did you have one before?"

"Three," she says, reaching for the girl who's carrying them.

Well, that explains that. I do a quick calculation—three beers plus three Jell-O shots. I try to remember the movie we saw about alcohol poisoning in health class. "I'll get you something to eat." I pull her away from the group and toward the door.

"If you walk out of here, it is over between us!" Amber screams after me.

I turn on her. "It was over a long time ago!"

I put my arm around Talia and lead her out the door.

I'm feeling pretty sober myself, considering I spent most of my drinking time with Amber's tongue down my throat. Still, I drive through McDonald's.

"What are we doing here?" Talia says. She's not slurring so much anymore, but she's really, really loud.

"It's called a drive-thru. You get food here."

"You get food in the car?" She screams it so loud that the drive-thru guy asks me to repeat my order.

After I do, she starts screaming again, "You can drive your car up to a window and get food? We have nothing in Euphrasia! Nothing! It sucked! Sucked, I tell you!" I reach the pickup window, and when the guy hands me my burgers and fries and two large, black coffees, Talia begins to jump in her seat. "This is so coooool! Did you like how I used an American word? *Coooooool!* And *sucked*, too."

I laugh. She's so cute. "Yeah, you're a real American. Have some coffee."

But she's already eating fries. "These are so cool, too! What are they called?"

"French fries."

"They definitely do not suck."

By the time we get home, she's eaten her way through her fries and my own, sticking me with just the burgers, and she's fast asleep.

I'm in luck because my parents are asleep, too. I try to help her onto the air mattress.

Good to know: It's not easy to get a trashed person onto an air mattress, especially when it's not blown up enough. But finally, I get her onto it and tucked in. She closes her eyes again, and she looks so beautiful and innocent, like a little angel, and not at all like a girl who just had three, count 'em, three Jell-O shots and quite a bit of beer. I stand there for a minute, just looking at her. Then I start for the door.

"Jack?" Her voice follows me to the door.

"Shhh," I say. "Don't wake my parents."

"Sorry," she whispers, a really loud whisper.

"What is it?" I say, coming closer to her so she won't have to yell.

"I am sorry," she whispers again.

"You said that already."

"No. I mean about tonight. About drinking too much and going off with that boy, Robert, and allowing him to . . . almost allowing him . . ."

"That wasn't your fault. He's a sleaze."

"And what sort of party was that, anyway? There was no food, no dancing! When Father gave parties, there was a feast! I do not like your sort of parties."

I laugh. "Me neither."

"But I like your French fries. Are they really French?"

"I don't know." I lean to kiss her on the forehead. "I'm sorry about tonight, too." I start to leave the room.

"Jack?" She stops me again. "Do you love Amber?"

"No." I know that for sure. "No. I am totally over the Amber thing."

"Good. She is not a nice young lady."

I open the door, then start to close it again. That's when I hear her voice, real small, like she's trying to be good and not wake my parents. "Do you love me?"

But I pretend not to hear her, because I really don't know.

Chapter 18: Talia

I am asleep on a mattress of Jell-O shots. It jiggles and wiggles, but when I try to bite it, it tastes most unpleasant. Still, I see it, orange, red, yellow, and blue, and it begins to break into individual Jell-O shots, which dance before me, laughing and singing.

Princess, in your dreams we creep,
To dance by light of moon.
Though we may disturb your sleep,
You'll sleep forever soon!

Over and over, louder and louder, dancing dangerously around me. I wish to open my eyes, to run from the room, to stop them. But my eyes remain stubbornly shut. The Jell-O mattress holds me fast. Their whirling motion mesmerizes me, turning to a blur of light and color.

And through it all, I see Malvolia.

I know it is Malvolia because she appears exactly as I saw her three hundred years ago, a humpbacked old woman in robes of black, holding a spindle in a gnarled hand.

But gradually her spine straightens and she is young. The spindle fades, and the room around her changes. It is not a castle but a peasant's cottage made of stone with a thatched roof. Through the windows, I see woods and one lone holly bush. I know that holly bush! I know where she is, deep in the Euphrasian hills, where Lady Brooke and I used to picnic when I was small. Could Malvolia have been so close by? Could she have been watching me all those times?

"Ah, Princess, we meet again! You are well, if intoxicated?"

I do not, cannot, answer. Is she real or merely a dream?

"Cat got your tongue, Your Highness? No matter. I am aware that rudeness runs in your family."

For this, I have no answer, either. The woman, Malvolia, looms closer until her face is the only thing I can see.

"You were wondering if I watched you when you came to picnic with your governess near my cottage on the tallest hill." She laughs at my surprise. She is real, not a dream. I am certain of it, for I can feel her warm, sour breath on my face. "Of course I did, Princess. I watched you from the windows under the eaves. Those who place curses are always curious to see if the accursed one is turning out well.

But that was not the only time I watched. I also watched when you were in the castle. I watched you as you studied naked drawings behind your art master's back. I knew from that that you would not be immune to temptation—to the spindle's lure—and on that fateful day, when you came to me in your quest for more and better dresses, I knew you would be alone."

I gasp. It was my fault for tricking Lady Brooke away. But still, I can say nothing through my sleep, intoxication, and despair. It is as if I have died and am merely a ghost, watching those still alive.

"Do not worry, Princess." The witch's voice is soothing. "You will not have to return to your cruel father. I shall be there soon."

And then she is gone. The whirling, singing Jell-O demons, the shaking Jell-O bed, return. I cannot move. I can barely breathe. In the light from the window, I try to examine my arms and legs. Have the Jell-O demons tied me up? Will they take me away?

Then, suddenly, there is a knock on the door.

It is Malvolia!

No. It is not Malvolia. Malvolia would not knock.

"Talia, are you okay?"

Jack!

The Jell-O demons vanish, wishing to be seen by no one but me.

"Talia?"

I will my lips to form words.

"Yes?"

"Can I come in?"

I straighten the T-shirt and pants I was given in which to sleep. "Yes, please."

The door opens. It is still dark in the hallway, dark everywhere. What time is it in Euphrasia? When Malvolia appeared, it seemed like morning. I could see the sunlight.

"Did I wake you?" he asks.

"No. I mean, yes, but I am glad you did."

"Yeah?" He lights a lamp. I try to turn away from him, that he may not see my face, but it is too late. He does. "Hey, what's wrong?"

"I saw her again!"

"Who? Amber?"

"Worse. Malvolia. The witch Malvolia. She was in this very room."

He kneels beside me and takes my hand. "Nah, that's impossible. My parents have alarms and broken-glass sensors, the works. Not a single witch is getting in this room, no sir."

I have no idea what a broken-glass sensor might be, and the word *alarm* means the palace guards telling of the presence of an intruder. There are no guards around Jack's house, though. "It matters not. Malvolia can get past anything. She has done so already. It was her. She is coming for me!"

"It was your imagination."

"She was in her cottage. She said she would take me

216

there. She has been watching me forever. She knew every-thing about me, and I could see her, even though she wasn't here. She was communicating with me through magic."

"She was in your head."

"Exactly. She's in my head!"

"No. I mean, she's in your mind. It's all in your mind. You had beer and Jell-O shots, so you're dreaming about witches or fairies or whatever they were."

"Jell-O demons!"

"Jell-O demons?"

I nod. "They seemed so real."

"That's because you've never been drunk before. Believe me, last year, Travis and I drank some tequila from his par-ents' liquor cabinet, and I was seeing purple monkeys. That's why I try not to drink much anymore." He pats my shoulder.

"I suppose."

Then Jack takes me in his arms, and although I am still distraught, I cannot help but notice how well I fit in them, my head perfectly right for the crook of his neck. I snuggle closer, enjoying his nearness in a way which would have been scandalous in my time. His arms are safe, warm, and strong, and he whispers, "I won't let anyone take you away."

"But your mother said I could only stay one week."

"I'll deal with my mother. We'll find somewhere else for you to stay. You don't have to go back to your parents if you don't want to."

But if he does not love me . . . I remember Malvolia's words. *"Do not worry, Princess. You will not have to return to your cruel father."* I feel a sudden chill from the air-conditioner blowing on me. I do not know what to do.

"We'll figure out something," Jack continues. "You could sell your jewelry and get an apartment. Or you could be a model, like on South Beach. You know, Stewy Stewart's mom works at a modeling agency. Maybe I can get you in there."

I grip him more tightly. "I do not wish to think about it."

"Okay. It's okay."

He holds me for a long time before saying, "Hey, this air mattress could use some actual air, huh? It must have a leak."

I laugh. "Is that it? I thought perhaps your parents had put me into a torture chamber."

He laughs. "Like yours did? I wouldn't put it past them, but no. It's not supposed to be like that. I'll get the pump."

He retrieves the air pump, then installs it against the proper place in the mattress. It springs to life. He uses a pillow to muffle it. He turns to me.

"Look, about last night, I'm sorry."

"For what?"

"For using you to try and make Amber jealous."

Although I know this is what he was doing, I still feel a bit angry about it. "So, did it work?"

"Oh, yeah. And it was totally stupid. I don't even know what I saw in Amber."

I nod. "Nor I."

"I should probably go. My mom would freak if she caught me in your room. But we'll figure out a way for you to stay."

After he leaves, I settle in on the air mattress. It is certainly nothing like what I am accustomed to, but it is not bad, and I am comforted to know that Jack cares about me. In any case, I manage to sleep a bit. The demons do not return.

Chapter 19: Jack

I don't actually know why I went down to check on Talia. I just had this sort of weird feeling that something was wrong—not that Talia was being visited by the witch Malvolia and her Jell-O minions, but just . . . something.

And I felt responsible for her being here.

I've never actually felt responsible for anyone before.

A lot of things have changed since I met Talia. I'm even working on that sketch of a garden, the one I started on the plane, to show her before she goes. But I don't want her to leave in a week. I want her to stay.

Maybe—probably—that's just the beer talking, but if so, it's talking pretty loud.

It keeps right on blabbing away. I can't sleep, so I take out my pad and start working on my garden design again. I even go online to see what kind of plants will grow in

Belgium, since the garden's for Euphrasia. It looks pretty good. Not that I'd ever show it to anyone, except maybe Talia.

It's three o'clock before I go to sleep.

I wake in a state of total alarm shock to the sound of the cleaning lady vacuuming my room. The clock says eleven.

"Excuse me?" I pull the sheets up to cover my boxers and then realize I slept in my clothes. The events of last night swim before me—Talia, Amber, Jell-O shots, beer, French fries, thinking I was in love with Amber—I'm not in love. I'm also not hungover, but I feel like I am. I can almost hear Talia's Jell-O demons laughing in my head.

But, of course, they weren't real. They were figments of Talia's imagination.

Talia!

She might not have slept as late as I did. After all, she's way more well rested than I am, seeing as how she slept for three hundred years.

If she's awake, she could be downstairs with my family. She might be telling them about her sixteenth birthday ball and the curse and the witch and how she saw that very same witch in our house last night.

And even though Mom pretty much ignores my friends, *that* she would notice.

Or she could be telling them about her Jell-O shot experience, which would get me grounded for sure.

221

Or how I left her to be pawed by that perv, Robert. Ditto.

By this time, I'm out of bed, running downstairs, buttoning my shirt as I go.

When I reach the landing, I stop.

"My governess would not let me read that book—can you believe it? Claimed it was unfit for young ladies' eyes. But I sneaked it out of the library and hid it underneath the mattress. I was quite ill-behaved, I am afraid."

"Ill-behaved?" My mother's voice, the voice she uses on her Junior League friends. "Who would prevent a child from reading *Don Quixote*? It is a classic."

"It had something to do with Dulcinea being . . . er . . . a woman of ill repute. Neither did she permit me to read *Canterbury Tales*. But I studied *The Prince*."

"Machiavelli—an odd title for a young girl to read."

"It was about diplomacy. And, of course, it helped me work on my Italian."

"You read it in Italian?" Mom is impressed.

"Talia had an Italian art master, too, Mom," Meryl says. "What was his name?"

"Carlo Maratti. It was nothing," Talia says.

They're talking about books. My mother loves to talk about books, but Talia's so old that she wouldn't have read most of the books Mom knows. The King James Bible was a new book in Talia's time!

Mom sighs. "I was a lit major in college, but I can't get Meryl to read anything but comic books—"

"Manga, Mom."

"—and Jack reads nothing to speak of."

"Well, Jack . . . he's more of a vigorous outdoorsman, isn't he?"

"Oh, I don't know."

"Yes. Well, he told me how he likes . . . plants."

I clear my throat, the better to drown out Talia telling my mother my deepest, darkest secrets.

"Good morning, sleepyhead," Talia says.

"Jack, you're awake." My mother smiles tightly. "Did you know that Talia speaks four languages and has read *Arabian Nights* in French?"

Talia looks down, all modest. "It is naught. I was in training to be a diplomat."

She *is* a diplomat, I realize, the way she's schmoozing my mother.

"Hey." I stand next to Talia. "I was thinking maybe after breakfast we could go to South Beach and check out modeling agencies."

Meryl sort of snorts when I say that, and Mom says, "We had breakfast several hours ago, Jack."

"Your mother made me something called pancakes. They were a bit like crepes, a dish from Brittany."

"My mother hasn't made pancakes since I was five years old. How'd you rate pancakes?"

Talia shrugs. "Sometimes, when one communicates with others, one produces results."

Like I said, a diplomat.

"Like I'm going to get Talia to help me with my French," Meryl pipes in.

"Exactement," Talia says. "Or like I got you to bring me here and introduce me to your lovely family. You should try talking sometime."

I shrug. "Maybe so."

But it's weird. Talia's not a witch, and yet somehow it's like she's put everyone under a spell, *her* spell. Meryl's talking in more than monosyllables. Mom's making pancakes. And me, I've totally forgotten about Amber.

Chapter 20: Talia

"So a model is someone who wears clothing and is photographed doing so?" I ask Jack as our car traverses a bridge. The water on both sides is deep blue, and for a moment it reminds me of Grandmother's sapphires, then the view from the castle in Euphrasia. What is everyone doing there? And are they sorry I am gone? The light off the water gets into my eyes, and they sting.

"Yeah," Jack says.

"And they receive money for this?"

"Lots of money, crazy money."

"It's degrading, actually," Meryl says from the backseat. She has accompanied us on the car trip, apparently to serve as pseudo-governess, protecting my morals.

"It is not," Jack says.

"I read this book about a girl who became a model, and she had to pose naked!"

"Truly?" I look at Jack.

"No one's posing naked," Jack says.

"No. No one is."

Though I would rather not pose at all. But how else to stay here? If I wish to stay.

On the other side of the bridge, the streets are narrow and filled with people, and the buildings are each painted a different brilliant hue.

"So many colors! Signor Maratti would adore this!"

"Hey," Meryl says, "did you know that Maratti is the name of a seventeenth-century Italian artist? After you told me about your teacher, I Googled his name."

I do not know what Google means, but I say, "Yes. Signor Maratti was—"

I stop as Jack elbows me in the ribs. Quickly, I say, "That was Signor's brother, er, grandbrother . . . great-grandfather or some such."

Finally, Jack finds a place for his car. "Guess we'll leave it here."

"I'll stay with it." Meryl eyes a handsome young man in a very small bathing suit. "I'm going to sketch."

I giggle. "Will you be working on negative space? Or the positive space of that young man?"

"Both." She settles onto the front of Jack's car with her sketch pad.

We leave for the modeling agency. All the women in

South Beach are enormously tall, impossibly slender. Perhaps there has been a famine or a scarlet fever epidemic. I search for the telltale rash on their chests and abdomens (all of which are exposed) but see nothing. Despite their sickly thinness, the young ladies seem quite pleased with their shapes, strutting like peafowl down the bright streets. Finally, we reach a door which says WINIFRED MODELING AGENCY.

"I had a cousin Winifred," I say. "She was a viscountess."

"Yeah. Don't mention her, okay?" He opens the door.

Inside, there is a tree in a pot and a second door, one with glass windows. We step through that door. Jack presses a button, and it closes.

"This is a very strange room," I say.

A moment later, the door opens. The potted tree is gone! The floor outside is a different shade!

"We have been transported to another place!" I clap my hands.

Jack laughs. "Relax. It's called an elevator. It takes you upstairs. Look." He gestures toward a window. I look out. Outside, the sky is blinding blue, and we are closer to it than before. I glance down, feeling suddenly dizzy.

Jack takes my arm and leads me to a door.

"We're here to see Kim Stewart," Jack says. "We have an appointment." He tells her our names.

The skeletal young woman at the desk barely looks up. "Have a seat."

A moment later, a young man enters the room. He

moves as if he is dancing in a ballroom, and his hair is bright green. I wonder if there were always colorful-haired people in other parts of the world. He gestures us into a room with sparkling white floors and white walls lined with glass windows.

"So, which of you wants to be a model?"

Jack gestures toward me. "Her. Who are you?"

He gives us a look as if to say that is none of our business but finally says, "Rafael. I'm Ms. Stewart's right-hand man." He looks me up and down. I feel a chill run through me, as though I were unclothed, but I do not clasp my arms around me to stay warm. Indeed, I fear to move under his gaze.

Finally, he is finished. "No, thanks."

"Excuse me?" I do not know about what, or to whom, he is talking.

"No. We can't offer you representation at this time. Thank you."

He starts to walk away, and I once again feel I can move. "Oh. All right. Thank you." I do not quite understand what "offer representation" means, either, but I do understand that our meeting is over.

"Wait a second," Jack says. "We were supposed to meet Kim Stewart."

The green-haired boy shrugs. "I screen for Kim so she doesn't have to see anyone unacceptable."

"And why isn't she acceptable?"

"Jack . . ." I touch his sleeve. "We should leave."

The green-haired boy turns so he is once again facing

us but not quite looking me in the eye. As a princess, I am unaccustomed to being ignored in this manner, but I begin to suspect that it occurs quite frequently.

"To be brutally candid," he says to the air, "she's too short. And too fat."

"Fat?" Jack and I both say at once.

"These . . ." He walks closer and gestures uncomfortably close to my bosom. ". . . are out of the question. Tyra had to tape hers down when she was modeling. There were designers who wouldn't hire her because of her hips—which were smaller than yours."

"So let me get this straight," Jack says. "Girls can't have breasts? Or hips? But breasts and hips are cool."

The boy wrinkles his nose. "If you say so . . . but you can't make a living off the *SI* swimsuit issue, and horny teenage boys aren't buying couture. Maybe she should try *Playboy.*"

Jack shakes his head. "Don't think so."

"Then there's her hair. This . . ." He picks up a curl like my head is a wig on a stand. "The *Little House on the Prairie* look is completely passé. And there's something about her skin, too."

"What about my skin?" I ask.

"It's just . . . weird. Do you moisturize at all? Your skin looks like you haven't done anything for it in ten years."

Try three hundred.

"Jack!" The door opens, and Meryl rushes in. "Excuse me. Is my brother here?"

I cringe to see her in this pristine setting. Tall and gangly, arms and legs flying everywhere, metal teeth, hair askew, blemishes . . . blemishing. How cruel would this man be to her if, indeed, he finds *me* ugly? She places her hands on nonexistent hips and says, "Come on. You forgot to feed the meter and there's a cop around the corner."

Jack fumbles in his pockets, coming up empty. "We have to go." He starts for the door and, relieved, I follow him.

"Wait!" The green-haired boy begins to run after us. "And who is this?" He's gesturing at Meryl.

Jack laughs. "My kid sister."

"She's breathtaking. So fresh! So . . . thin! This is the type we can use."

"Use for what?" Meryl scowls.

"As a model? Her?" Jack says.

"Yes. Well, once she gets the braces off and starts on Accutane—although we can airbrush most of that out. But she's to die for. Look at that chest—like a little boy!"

Meryl looks down, hair falling into her face. "Yeah, right."

"And the 'tude is perfect."

Meryl laughs. "No, thanks." And yet, I can tell she is smiling a bit beneath her scowl. Why would she not be? This . . . person has just said that I, Princess Talia, gifted by the fairies with flawless beauty, am not pretty while she is a vision of loveliness.

But she looks at Jack. "Didn't you hear me? They're about to *tow* your *car*."

And we leave.

We decide to take the stairs, for the elevator frightens me. Meryl is walking backward, then forward down the stairs ahead of us. "Could you believe him? *That chest . . . like a little boy!*" She breaks up laughing. "Crazy."

"I do not think so," I say as we reach the street and yet another enormously tall, impossibly slender young woman—a model, no doubt—smirks at me. "You are indeed quite lovely."

Meryl makes a face, but then it turns into a grin. "Well, I know one thing—Jen and Gaby would freak if they knew. How'd it go with you?"

I shrug. "I am too fat."

"Excuse me?"

"Aw, they're just crazy," Jack says. "Standards of beauty change all the time. Most of the paintings I saw in Europe, the women were, like, obese."

I know which paintings he's thinking of, and I am indignant. "I do *not* look like a Botticelli!"

"That's not what I meant."

"What did you mean?"

He starts to say something, then changes his mind. "I meant that you're beautiful, and that guy is crazy. We'll find another agency."

I shake my head. "I do not think so."

"Okay. Then we'll go to the beach."

"After we feed the meter," Meryl says.

We cross the street to the beach. It is hot and white and strewn with brown bodies wearing very little clothing. How amazing that being tanned is considered attractive in these times. In my day, only the field hands were tan!

Still, when we reach an empty spot and Jack peels off his shirt to worship the sun, I cannot help but look at him. One thing is certain: *He* is beautiful.

I have been persuaded to wear shorts and a tank top, the better to be ogled by that young man. Jack spreads out a towel, and I arrange myself prettily upon it and pretend to gaze at the ocean. Meryl sits beside me, sketching the sky. I glance at Jack. He, too, is working on something. I wish to ask him what it is, but I dare not intrude. I stare back at the ocean. It is nothing like the seaside in Euphrasia, which I remember from seeing Father off on journeys.

Father!

The ocean is tranquil and blue, and I am lulled into a trance watching its white-capped waves lap at the shore. I could almost go to sleep. Sleep.

Suddenly, the scene before me swirls together with me inside it. The waves rise up and touch the clouds, and from them steps Malvolia.

"Ah, Princess." Her dark form casts a shadow over the sunny beach. "Still unlucky in love?"

I glance at Jack and am pleased to see that he is looking at me. At my legs, to be specific. He admires me, does he not?

Malvolia reads my thoughts. "Aye. A boy admiring

a pretty girl. A rare thing to be certain. But love—true love—is something else."

But I only need more time. I know I can make him love me.

"You were to be awakened by true love's first kiss. That has not happened, and I believe it is time for you to come with me."

No. She cannot take me now. Just a little longer.

"Come with me." The waves leap. The clouds above them darken, and I see Malvolia's hand, reaching toward me, hear her voice, soothing. "Come with me. It will be all right. You know he does not love you."

It is true. I know Jack does not love me, will never love me.

"Then what is there for you? What is there for you if he does not love you?"

Nothing.

"Yes, nothing. Nothing but a family who hates you, a kingdom ruined. Princess, what have you to live for?"

Nothing.

"Come with me." Malvolia's hand reaches closer.

"I will come with you." I rise from the towel and start toward her hand.

"Talia?"

Another step.

"Talia!"

I look down. It is Jack, Jack calling for me. The waves, the clouds, and Malvolia all disappear, as if sucked up by a whirlwind. Instead, there is Jack, half standing before me, a puzzled expression playing upon his face.

"Where are you going?"

I look down. I have walked several steps toward the ocean. Malvolia is gone.

"I thought I might—ah—put my feet in the water."

Jack laughs. "Take off your shoes first."

He kneels before me as if he is about to propose marriage. But instead, he unties first one, then the other shoelace. I am reminded of a popular story of my time, about a girl named Cendrillon, who went to a ball wearing slippers of glass. But, of course, Jack would never know this story. It was told three hundred years ago! Still, when Jack's hand brushes against my ankle, I shiver in the noonday sun.

He stands. "Come on, then." He reaches out his hand and enfolds it in mine, then guides me toward the sapphire water.

Could Jack love me? And can I make him love me before Malvolia spirits me away?

Chapter 21: Jack

"Now what?" Talia says in the car on the way home from South Beach. "If I am not beautiful enough to be a model . . ."

"You're plenty beautiful," I say.

"You wouldn't want to be a model, anyway," Meryl says. "It's dopey and vain."

But I notice she's actually pushed her hair out of her face since that freaky Rafael told her she could be one. And she's been looking in the rearview all the way home, too.

"But what else can I do?" Talia whines.

"Um, you can speak four languages," Meryl says. "You know all about art, and you're some kind of expert in diplomacy."

"But for a sixteen-year-old without a high school diploma," I say, "it's hard getting a job doing those things."

Talia stares out at the water a long time, saying nothing. When she does, she says, "The water here is so blue, like the sapphires in one of Grandmother's necklaces. I used to sneak into Mother's chamber when I was small and try it on. I dreamed of growing up one day to wear it myself. Now I never shall." She looks at me. "Perhaps I should return to Euphrasia."

"To where?" Meryl says.

"Home," Talia says. "To . . . Belgium."

"Why'd you leave in the first place?"

Talia exchanges a glance with me. "It is a long story."

I glance back to say, *Don't tell it.*

"I broke a rule," Talia says, consolidating the long story into a single sentence. "There were horrible consequences, and my father was terribly disappointed in me. He said he wished I had never been born."

"Harsh," Meryl says. "What kind of rule was it—like a curfew or failing in school? Scratch that—you'd never fail in school."

"Not exactly," both Talia and I say together.

"Did you, like, sneak out at night with someone?"

"No," Talia says. "I never sneaked. I was watched constantly, for they were worried I would be pricked with a spindle." I give her a look, and she says, "I mean, that my purity would be compromised."

"Did you wreck your parents' car?" Meryl says.

Talia laughs. "Definitely not that."

"Smoke pot? Get drunk?"

"No," I tell her. "Stop asking."

But Meryl keeps on going, ignoring me. "You didn't kill anyone, did you?"

"Of course not, Meryl!" I say.

"Because Jack's done all those things—except killing someone—and my parents keep forgiving him, anyway."

"Is that true?" Talia says.

"Once, Jack and Travis got picked up by the police for egging cars on Eighty-second Avenue. And one of the cars he egged was the president of Mom's garden club."

"Meryl," I say. "We don't need to talk about—"

"So the doorbell rings at midnight," Meryl continues. "Mom opens it in her robe, and there's two cops standing there. They had a tip from a cashier at Publix that some teenage boys were in there buying ten dozen eggs. The cashier didn't think they were making a soufflé with them, so she called the cops."

"Meryl, will you please shut—"

"You threw *food* at passing cars?" Talia says.

"Just eggs," I say, glaring at Meryl. "Everyone does stuff like that."

"But a hundred and twenty eggs could feed ten families or ward off starvation in the wintertime when food is scarce. Do you have any idea how many hens it would take to lay ten dozen eggs?"

"Yeah, Jack," Meryl says, grinning. "Do you know how many hens?"

Talia keeps going. "It seems dreadfully wasteful and

thoughtless to throw them—particularly at another person's property."

"That's my brother, Jack, Mr. Wasteful and Thoughtless."

"I didn't take them away from starving people," I tell Talia. "I bought them." I never thought about the eggs being food for someone before. How does Talia think of this stuff? Not one other person I know would think about wasting the eggs—not even my parents. When you think of it that way, it does sound sort of . . . "Okay, it was stupid."

"Very," Talia agrees.

"Jack's always doing dumb stuff," Meryl says. "And my parents always forgive him."

"Forgive?" I laugh. "They don't even notice. They never notice anything I do."

"They notice plenty," Meryl says. "You don't have a bedroom next to theirs, so you didn't hear them every night for a week, discussing whether to send you to a child psychologist or military school."

"Military school?" The idea makes me shudder.

"And every time Mom ran into Mrs. Owens—that's the lady whose car Jack egged—she asked Mom if she was getting dear Jack 'the help he needs and deserves.' Mom was totally humiliated."

"I can imagine," Talia says. "Poor lady."

"It was a long time ago," I say. "Can't we talk about the dumb stuff you've done?" Why does she have to embarrass me in front of Talia? I don't embarrass her in front of her friends. At least I wouldn't, if she had friends.

"I never got picked up by the cops."

"You're young. There's still time. Besides, you're learning from my mistakes."

"Are you proud of being a bad example?"

"Be quiet."

But still it's weird. I always thought my parents didn't much care what I did, just wanted me out of their way. Could I have been so wrong about that?

"Parents always forgive you," Meryl says. "Like sometimes, you see parents on the news, and their kid just got busted for murdering a 7-Eleven clerk, and they're like, 'But my Bubba's a good boy. He'd never hurt a fly.' So I'm sure your parents would forgive you for whatever you did."

Talia looks out the window. We've crossed the bridge, and now there's nothing interesting to look at, just gray office buildings on both sides. I remember the beautiful castle and scenery in Euphrasia. Finally, she says, "Do you think so, Jack?"

"I'm not sure." Talia's father seemed like a real stickler, even for a king, and he did say all that crummy stuff to her. But maybe Meryl's right (there has to be a first time for everything). Maybe he'd forgive her, even for ruining their entire country. They're probably worried sick about her—especially considering they don't have any phone or email or even a radio. So it's really like she disappeared into a black hole. But I don't want her to leave.

Talia might have been a little annoying at first. Okay, she was completely impossible. But I realize that's just because she's not like anyone I've ever known before. No one I know would think of the eggs as . . . well, eggs.

If she were gone, I'd miss her.

And I guess I'm feeling a little selfish when I say, "I don't know. But we have six more days, so maybe you should think a little more about it."

Talia nods. "I suppose you are right."

Chapter 22: Talia

I am a coward. I am a cowardly coward, full of cowardice. Part of me knows that Meryl is right, that I should contact my parents, go back home, that they are concerned about me.

But I am less certain than Meryl that my father will forgive me. Jack's mother seems like a lovely person, and I am certain Jack's father is likewise so. But they are not royalty. Neither did they call upon an entire nation to guard Jack from harm, only to have him bring it upon himself by some thoughtless mistake. However many eggs Jack threw, he did not bring ruination upon his family, much less his country.

I tell this to Jack as we eat french fries and pull weeds. We have gone, at my request, to the park where Jack once planted the garden. It is a sad sight, full of thorns and none too very many flowers. But, with our help, it looks quite a bit better. I have even touched dirt now! Jack is right. It does smell clean, like the air. After an hour, we walked to the McDonald's nearby and got french fries. More french fries!

"Who knows if Euphrasia is even a country anymore?" I pull a large weed. "And if it is not a country, then my father cannot be king. He could never forgive me for that."

"Maybe he could do something else," Jack says. "Like, take a computer course." But he looks unconvinced. He sticks a handful of french fries into his mouth. On the other side of the park, children play a game. They are dressed in matching shirts and short pants of gold and ruby and emerald and orange. The object of their game appears to be to kick a spotted ball into a net while preventing the other team from so doing.

At the palace, I often stood by the window and watched the peasant children. Their lives seemed consumed by work. Boys helped their fathers in the fields. Girls milked cows and gathered eggs. But they did play, when the work was done. I watched them sometimes from the windows, and I wished I could join them.

There is a large tree nearby, an old one with moss hanging from it. I nudge Jack.

"Teach me to climb that tree! I have never climbed one."

Jack looks at the tree, dubious. "That's a hard one."

"Would it be difficult for *you*?"

"No, I . . ."

"Then show me. I am stronger than I look."

He nods and walks to the tree. "You have to get a good grip first. There aren't any low branches, so you use your fingers. Then, dig in with your feet."

I try it. It is far more difficult than I had imagined. "What if I fall?"

"I'm behind you. I'll catch you."

This seems to help, for I am suddenly able to dig my feet in and climb a bit.

"Good," Jack says. "Now, grab that branch above you and pull yourself up."

I do. I do! And next thing I know, I am sitting upon the branch.

"Now, grab the next one and get up on it," Jack says.

But I am already doing that. It is easy, now that I have started, and soon I am so high that the park seems to swim beneath me, and Jack is climbing up behind me. When we reach the highest branch I dare, I sit upon it and look down.

The earth spins below me, and yet it is fine, like everything has been today. So what if I cannot be a model, if I am no longer considered beautiful, if Malvolia is trying to catch me. I am climbing a tree! And I am doing so with Jack.

He comes up behind me. "You did it."

I nod. We sit there a moment, watching the children at play.

"Why do you suppose this has happened?" I ask Jack.

"What has?"

"You. Me. You finding me after all those years. Of all the people who could have stumbled upon Euphrasia, why you?"

"I said I was sorry about not being a prince."

"No. It is just . . . odd when you think about it. Had you and Travis not been in Belgium, and had you not been bored and looked for the beach and taken the wrong bus . . . I might still be asleep. Or some Belgian boy might have found me. In any case, I would not be here."

"It is weird when you put it that way," he says.

"Yes. Do you know the story of King Arthur and the Sword in the Stone?"

"I saw the movie with Keira Knightley. But they didn't concentrate on the stone part—mostly it was about Keira in a breastplate. She was Guinevere."

Guinevere in a breastplate? How interesting. "Arthur was the son of a king who died," I say. "He was raised by Sir Ector, a knight. No one knew he was heir to the throne. Then, one day, a strange stone appeared in a churchyard. In the stone was a glittering sword, and written on it, in letters of gold, 'Whoso pulleth out this sword of this stone and anvil is rightwise king born of all England.'"

I swing my feet a bit and continue.

"Many knights tried to take the sword, but none could budge it. So a day was chosen when all could try, and jousts were held as well. Sir Ector and his son, Kay, and Arthur also came. But when it was time for the joust, Kay found that he had broken his sword. He asked Arthur to ride back for another. When Arthur returned to the castle, he could not get it. That was when he remembered the sword he had seen in the churchyard. The guards were away, and the sword was there, alone. Thinking only to get a sword for his brother, young Arthur took the hilt and drew the sword from the stone."

I love this part!

"Why could he take it out when no one else could?" Jack asks.

"He was meant to be king. Destiny. Do you believe in destiny, Jack?"

"I'm not sure."

"Do you not think, Jack, that perhaps it was destiny, you going to the castle? Do you think you were destined to be the one to wake me?"

I wait. If he believes in destiny, perhaps he will believe that *he* is my destiny. I sit, feeling the wind upon my face. Below, the boys are finished playing. They run their several ways, some stopping at the newly weeded garden.

"Hey, would you look at this?" one of them says.

"Yeah. Someone got rid of all the weeds."

"Cool."

What will Jack say? What will he say?

Finally, he says, "I don't know."

"You do not know?" The words explode from me like cannon fire, and some of the children look up at us. "But what do you think? Surely you must think something, sometime, you silly boy?"

It is useless. I was wrong to believe that Jack could be my destiny, my beloved. He cares not for me at all. He thinks of nothing but play.

"Never mind," I say. "It is of no import."

"But you didn't let me finish. I was going to say that I don't know about destiny. I don't know if there even was a King Arthur, or if that's just some dumb story."

I sigh, not merely because I adored *Morte d'Arthur*, but also because Jack is missing my point entirely.

"But what I do know is that everything's different since I've been with you. I'm different. Like being here. I might have thought about coming here, but I wouldn't have. I'd have been out partying. You made me remember. I don't know if I was destined to wake you up, or if it was just dumb luck. But I'm glad it happened this way."

"Are you?" I ask.

He nods. "Before, I'd say I didn't want to do what my dad wanted, but I knew I'd end up doing it, anyway. I'd go to college and major in what he wants me to major in and do what he wants me to do, and one day I'd wake up and I'd be sixty and with all my decisions made for me."

His voice is soft, and he smells of dirt and the air above us, and it is a clean smell.

"And now?" I say.

"Now, maybe I won't."

I nod. This is where he should say that he is in love with me, that I have changed his life and that he loves me for it. But he doesn't. Is it because he is shy? Or because he is too young to say such a thing? Too scared after Amber?

Or is it merely because he does not love me?

The worst of it is, I am falling in love with him. Before, I was merely trying to make him love me. My own feelings were meaningless. But now, I, Princess Talia, am in love with a boy, a boy who does not love me back.

Jack takes his telephone from his pocket and looks at it. "I guess we should be going. Meryl just texted that my dad's actually coming home for dinner."

"Really?" I try to swallow my disappointment. "I look forward to meeting him, and you can discuss some matters with him as well."

"Some matters," meaning, of course, his hopes and ambitions. I am one to talk, having run away from my own father. Still, I suspect at least *some* things are easier for those not to the castle born. While Jack's father may be angry if Jack fails to follow in his path, it is the tradition of a mere generation or so, not the divine right of kings. And Jack will only be disappointing his own family, not an entire kingdom.

Jack says, "Yeah, maybe. Can you get down?"

I look, and I am dizzy again, but I say, "I think so."

"I'll catch you if you fall. Or you can fall on me." He starts to climb down.

When we reach bottom, I say, "Jack, what is a garden

club?" When he gives me a questioning look, I say, "Meryl said that you egged a car owned by the president of your mother's garden club."

Jack shrugs. "I'm thinking it's a club for ladies who like to . . . garden."

"So then your mother is interested in plants as well?"

"I guess."

"And you have never told her of your shared interest?"

"I never . . ." He shifts his knees. "I mean, she wouldn't care. My dad wants me to go into his business. He's in charge."

I laugh. "You do not know the first thing about women, do you?"

"What's that supposed to mean?"

"Even in my time, we knew that men were not in charge. Oh, they might bluster as if they were. But when it came down to it, we women bore much of the influence. Often, my father would make some grand pronouncement in the evening. And the next morning, he had changed his mind. After a while, I realized that it was my mother who had changed it, quietly, in the night."

Jack appears to think about it. "So you're saying . . ."

"I am saying that perhaps your mother would be your ally. It would be diplomacy."

When we return, Meryl is outside in the front yard, sitting underneath a tree. She clutches her pad to her, clearly interrupted in the act of drawing by Jennifer, the wicked

248

girl from the next house. As Jack and I approach, I hear the word "weird."

"Hello, Meryl," I say, loud enough to interrupt Jennifer's cruel talk.

The girl immediately breaks from Meryl, but not due to any guilty conscience about disturbing her. No, she has other motives..

"Hi, Jack," Jennifer says, throwing her chest out and prompting me to clutch Jack's arm in a most territorial and un-princesslike manner. Nonetheless, the tramp runs her hand across his arm. To his credit, Jack seems uncomfortable at the attention.

"Meryl," I say, "how is that new drawing coming along? I am dying to see it."

She smiles. "Really?"

"Really. I have thought of little else." This is not true, for I have been thinking of how to make Jack fall in love with me. But Meryl does not have to know that, nor does Jennifer, who is rather a junior version of Amber.

"I've been working on it all day." Meryl takes it out to show me.

Jennifer laughs. "That junk. I've seen her drawings. They suck."

I start to defend Meryl, but she interjects. "A lot you know. Talia thinks they're good, and she studied art with Carlo Maratti!"

"Who's that?" Jennifer's derision shows on her face.

"And you know what else, Jennifer?" Meryl continues.

"My brother isn't going to like you, no matter how much you stick your boobs in his face. Right, Jack?"

Jack sort of nods. Jennifer's mouth takes on the appearance of one of the suits of armor in the castle hall, when the hinges have rusted out and the face mask hangs open.

"Come on, Talia." Meryl gestures for me to follow her.

I do so, without a backward glance at Jack, but I am amazed. I have changed things. I have helped Meryl to stand up to Jennifer. I am sure of it. I have changed Jack, too. I know it. But is it enough? Perhaps if I can help Jack to speak with his father, it will make him love me.

Chapter 23: Jack

Talia's grabbing my arm all the way down the stairs. I don't know if it's because she's nervous about having dinner with my parents (both of them, here for dinner on the same day!) or just that guys held out their arms to help girls back in her time. I sort of like having her hold on to me. But I bet if my dad sees her holding my arm, he'll see it another way. "Clingy," he'll say. That's what he used to say about Amber.

But maybe it would be okay if it was the guy's idea. So right before we go into the kitchen, I take Talia's hand off my elbow and put it in my hand. I give it a squeeze. She squeezes back. "It will be okay," I say.

"I might say the same to you."

Then we walk into the kitchen. My dad's there in his suit and tie, like every other day of my life, so it's weird that I have this urge to throw my arms around him, like I did when I was three and he went out of town, to say, "Daddy."

But I don't.

"Dad, this is Talia, the girl I met in Europe. She's staying with us."

"Nice to meet you, Talia. Have a seat." As soon as she does, he turns back to me. "So, Jack, it's lucky, your coming home early. Ed Campbell was telling me he's looking for a summer intern for his office."

I'm torn between annoyance and annoyance—annoyance that my dad's not even going to bother disapproving of Talia. Instead he's going to ignore her completely. And annoyance at the idea of a summer internship. Like, couldn't he say hello at least before he starts trying to turn me into him?

I know what that means—my dad talked one of his golf buddies into offering me a job making copies and fetching Starbucks to "get a feel for the business" and look good on my college apps. Boring. Talia says I should tell my parents what I want. But she doesn't know what that's like when you're a regular person, not a princess.

"Um, I don't think so, Dad. I sort of have other plans for the summer."

"Partying and going to the beach?"

"No. Not exactly." *Although what's so bad about that? I mean, I am seventeen years old with my whole life to work.*

"Good, then. So I'll tell Ed you can come in Monday."

It's Thursday. I should probably be happy he's at least giving me a weekend before he destroys my summer. But Talia's staying a week.

Dad's talking about what a great opportunity this is, blah, blah, blah. . . .

"Mr. O'Neill," Talia says, "I believe what Jack was trying to say is that he has other plans for an *occupation* during the summer."

"Excuse me?" Dad gets that line that he always gets between his eyes whenever he talks to me. "Young lady, I don't believe I asked—"

"She's right, Dad," I say. "I was thinking about putting up some flyers at the grocery store, about doing gardening. It would be, like, starting my own business."

"Gardening?" Dad laughs. "Jack, you're not eight years old anymore, and we're not poor, either. This internship will look great on your college applications."

Here we go with college applications.

"I like plants, okay?"

"Well, that's just ridiculous. What are you going to do—work at Home Depot?"

Mom holds up a bowl of string beans. "Beans?" When I shake my head, she says, "Enough about work. Tell us about your trip, Jack."

Then she starts talking about it herself. She's memorized my entire itinerary, starting with Day One, Museum One and starts going through it. I answer, trying to avoid the words *boring* and *lame* and also trying to keep from looking at Dad. We're talking and laughing like everything's okay, but I know it's not.

When I finish, Dad says, "So, I'll call Ed and tell him you can start Monday?"

"I told Talia you'd never listen to me."

"This was Talia's idea, then?" Dad says.

"Yeah. I mean, no . . . I mean, the gardening business was my idea. Trying to tell you about it, like you'd actually care what I want, that was Talia's idea."

"We just want what's best for you," Mom says, "and for your college—"

"I don't even want to go to college."

Which stops her for about two seconds. Then she turns to Talia. "Talia, you must have been to so many museums growing up in Europe. Which is your favorite?"

"Can I be excused?" Meryl says.

"Yes, dear." Mom turns back to Talia. "Now, as I was saying . . ."

I say, "You can't just change the subject and expect things to go away."

She stops in midsentence, looking at the bowl of rice like she's trying to decide whether to try and change the subject yet again. But finally she looks at me.

"The reason I change the subject, Jack, is because it helps me to ignore the fact that my son, the child I bore and raised from infancy, has no interest in anything we want, no respect for—"

"That is not true," Talia interrupts.

Both Mom and Dad stare daggers at Talia, but she continues. "I have known Jack only a week, but already I can tell how much your opinion means to him. When we were traveling in Europe, you were in his thoughts and conversation the whole time."

Is that true?

"Young lady," Dad says, "I hardly think this is any of your business."

"No, it is not. But perhaps as an outsider, I can see more clearly. Jack does respect your opinion. He craves your approval. But he feels that the only way he can get it is to deny his true nature and do exactly as you say."

Mom looks at me. "Is that true?"

I nod.

Talia continues. "It was my idea that Jack should tell you where his real interests lie, in gardening, in being with the earth. I said I was certain caring parents like yourselves would understand."

"Young lady," Dad says. "I don't know who you are or where you're from, but you have no idea the sort of pressures a boy like Jack will face, the competition . . ."

"Dad," I say.

Talia holds out her hand. "You are right. I have no idea, and it is none of my business, and I was taught to obey my parents. But sometimes it is just impossible to obey blindly. Sometimes a child must strike out on her own. A child cannot be a child forever, whether that means not touching a spindle or . . . or . . ."

I know, of course, that she's not just thinking about me but of herself and her own parents. I think what she's saying is pretty profound.

Dad looks away. "I'll tell Ed you'll be in Monday."

"I won't be there." I stand. "Come on, Talia."

"Jack!" My mother tries to follow me.

"Sorry I ruined our family dinner," I say.

Talia follows me out. "That did not go well."

"It's not your fault. It never goes well."

She purses her lips in that cute way she does. "It certainly makes me think about my own situation."

She means about leaving, about going home. She's still thinking about it. I don't want her to go. Yet I have no idea how to get her to stay. I was hoping maybe my parents would give in, let her stay a little longer, at least until the end of summer. After the mess at dinner, that's not looking very good.

Thing is, I'm falling in love with her. But my parents wouldn't want to hear that, either.

The next morning, Talia beats me downstairs again. When I finally make it to breakfast, Talia whispers, "It did work!" Then, louder, she adds, "Your mother has been telling me of a lovely garden nearby, where she volunteers. Will you take me to it?"

"I'm sorry," I say, "I seem to have walked into the wrong room. My mother is talking to you about gardening?"

"About Fairchild, Jack," Mom says. "You must remember.

I used to take you there all the time with me when you were younger, and you loved it. But I never thought you'd have any interest in it now that you've grown up."

"Jack is very interested," Talia says. "Right, Jack?"

"Yeah. That'd be cool."

I remember going there with Mom, and then we just stopped. I figured she didn't want to be seen in public with me anymore, once I was a pimply-faced thirteen-year-old. Could it have been that she just didn't think I'd want to go? Was I that much of a jerk?

Mom nods, like she's answering yes to the last question. "I'm happy you want to go. It's been a while since I've seen you taking a real interest in anything, other than partying."

"He has some other interests of which you are unaware," Talia says.

"Okay, enough talking about how I don't have any interests," I say, wanting to end the subject. "Why don't we have breakfast, then go?"

Talia laughs. "Once again, you have slept through breakfast."

Chapter 24: Talia

For lunch, we eat something called a hot dog, which Jack's mother very kindly volunteers to prepare. She must have slaved all night, for it seems like quite an elaborate blend of sausages and spices on specially made oblong bread, and there are several sauces available. I try some of each, red, green, and yellow. The yellow one is my favorite, and I marvel that Jack's mother went to so much trouble, and also that Jack said his mother could not cook. "Might I please have one with only the mustard sauce?"

"Wow," Jack says. "Most girls I know only eat lettuce and diet dressing. They're afraid they'll get fat."

"I never get fat," I say, "although I know the man at the modeling agency said I was. In truth, I appear to be getting thinner." I hold out the waistband of one of the pairs of jeans Jack bought in Europe. It fit well then, but now it is much too large. I wonder privately if this is part of the fairies' gift. Modern ideals of beauty have changed, so it may be that I have changed with them. In my day, it was considered preferable for a woman to have meat on her bones, the better to show that she could afford food and prove healthy for childbearing. In my day, the young ladies at the pool party, or Meryl's tormenters, Jennifer and Gaby, would have been thought quite poor and sickly. Only the peasants were so skinny.

I mention none of this to Jack. Talk of hips for child-bearing would only scare him. That may be why men prefer young ladies to be slimmer now. They do not wish to marry and have children at a young age anymore. Ladies the age of Jack's mother are plumper. I also note that standards of male beauty and "hotness" have changed little.

I look at Jack. He would have been thought quite hand-some in my time.

I sigh. *Quite* handsome.

"Hey," Jack says. "Earth to Talia. Come in, Talia."

I do not know what this means, so I look at Jack.

"'Sup?" he says, which is his way of asking what I am thinking. I can hardly tell him I was thinking how hand-some he is or how nice it might be to bear his children, so I say the first thing that comes to mind.

"Will your mother and Meryl be accompanying us to the garden?"

"Doubtful." Jack reaches for the red sauce. "My mother never accompanies me anywhere." Jack's mother says nothing

259

but raises her eyes and looks at Jack a long time.

"Well, I know I'm not going," Meryl says. "Who'd want to go on some boring old nature walk?"

I am rather glad at Meryl's refusal. I like Meryl, but she would merely present an impediment to getting Jack to fall in love with me. Already, last night, she annoyed him greatly by singing a song about "Jack and Talia, sitting in a tree." It probably did not help that we actually *had* been sitting in a tree that very afternoon.

"I wish you were going," I tell Mistress O'Neill. "I imagine you have great expertise and could teach Jack and me a thing or two about gardening." I smile at her.

"What a lovely, polite girl you are."

"She means not like that Amber chick," Meryl says with a mouthful of hot dog.

"Yes," Mistress O'Neill says. "That is exactly what I meant."

I try to blush and look downward as I was taught, but secretly I am checking Jack's expression at the mention of Amber's name and sitting upon thorns to see his response. To my relief, Jack does not seem too perturbed by Meryl's comment. Indeed, he does not even tell her to shut up.

"Thank you. I was told to respect my elders, even the peasants." Realizing my mistake, I cover my mouth. "I mean, not that you are peasants, only that you are older than I . . . or rather . . . I mean . . ."

"Quit while you're ahead," Jack whispers behind his hot dog.

"Ahead?" Meryl says. "She just called Mom an old peasant."

"It is quite all right," Jack's mother says. "I won't go with you, but I hope you have a nice time, since you will only be here a few more days."

Oh, I have fouled things up now. His mother hates me. She walks away.

Jack is smiling at me. "Don't worry about it." He touches my shoulder.

I feel myself blush and look away, nearly overturning my water in the process. But I glance sideways at him, through my fingers so that he might not guess my motives.

In my time, I would have been expected to marry the man my father chose. But now, that man—any man he might have chosen—is dead. I can choose whomever I want. Would I choose Jack, were he not my destiny?

He is handsome. I have grown accustomed to the out-landish clothes now worn by gentlemen in this time, and the hair. In my time, men's hair was much longer, with curls flowing well past the shoulders or even wigs in the style of Louis, Dauphin of France (whose son, Louis, used to come visit our palace until he became engaged to a princess from Sardinia). It was quite elegant when compared with the shaggy styles favored by boys Jack's age or the strange, short cuts of their elders.

And Jack is kind. True, I forced him to take me with him. But after we had made good our escape, nothing stopped him from abandoning me in Belgium or France.

At the time, I assumed that no one would leave a princess, but I now realize many would. Nothing save his own kindness required Jack to bring me through those countries, to purchase clothing for me, obtain a passport, fly me across the ocean, or bring me home to meet his parents. He did it for me—much as that man gave his coat for his wife.

And yet, he is a mere boy, unready for love, perhaps, and certainly unready to marry.

No. He is handsome and kind. He is wonderful and funny and enjoyable to be with. I remember being with him, up in that tree. And there is a tingling in my shoulder where he touched me.

If only I could make him love me.

But I am beginning to realize that being a princess does not mean I will be given everything I want. No, it is up to me.

At the garden, Jack pays our admission, then asks for directions to something called a "tram tour." We traverse a path of dirt and rock, and Jack directs my attention to various plants and flowers. This is a beautiful place, with the sort of exotic blooms I imagined seeing on travels to India or China. Blossoms of purple, yellow, fuchsia, and red fill my eyes like the raiments of bridesmaids at a fairy wedding.

"So beautiful," I say half a dozen times, in part to express joy in what Jack loves—gardening—but also because it is indeed beautiful, like nothing I have seen before.

On the tram tour—a tram being a sort of open bus—I sit

closer than strictly necessary. "I am a bit afraid," I say, although it is a lie. "Do you mind if I sit closer to the center?"

Jack shakes his head. "I'll hold you, if you want."

Thrilled, I present my hand, but he does not take it. Instead, he places his arm around my shoulder. He is so close I can almost feel his heartbeat.

He turns his face toward me and looks at me. "Okay?"

"Yes!" The word is a gasp because, in that moment, with his face mere inches from mine, I think—I hope—he might kiss me. And I want him to, not merely because of the curse or my father or wanting to prove that he is my true love, but because I want, once again, to feel his lips upon mine. He moves closer.

But then, the tram slams to a stop. Jack and I are jostled apart, and at the same time, an old woman says, "None of that shameless behavior here."

Jack and I light from the tram, putting a seemly distance between us, so as not to offend the old woman's eyes, but Jack was going to kiss me. I know he was. Perhaps later.

And then we reach a pool with the most wondrous of flowers. My eyes widen.

"Something, isn't it?" Jack says.

"Yes. Something." I can still feel the sensation of Jack leaning toward me, our lips about to meet in a kiss. Jack grasps my hand.

Before me, floating in shallow water, is the most enormous flower I have ever seen. No shy young rosebud, this. The plant is taller than a child of eight and, although closed, it is wider than my shoulders and pursed like an enormous pink mouth covered in spiny whiskers each as long as my fingers.

"Magnificent!" I say.

"Victoria water lily," Jack reads. "It says here it can get to be six feet across."

"Oh, my."

"Nothing like that in Euphrasia, huh?"

"No. Nothing at all." I glance away, and when I look back, it is almost as if the thing has moved.

A man standing nearby interrupts. "You have to come in the morning, though. That's when it's open."

"Really?" I keep my eyes glued upon the lily. Its petals seem to shake.

"Yes. They open in the evening and close at ten each morning."

Jack laughs. "Then I'll never see it, right, Talia?" He nudges me.

But I do not look at him. I gaze only upon the bud because, despite the man's words, despite the late hour, it does, indeed, appear to be opening, nay, not merely opening. It appears to be . . . speaking.

"Dear Princess, the time has come," the open bloom says. Its voice is deep, as if coming from the bottom of the pond.

"Who . . . what are you?" Although I know.

"Oh, Princess." The plant's voice changes. "You know exactly who I am."

Malvolia!

"What do you want of me? Why do you keep . . . ?"

"I want my spell fulfilled."

"It was fulfilled. He loves me. I know it."

"You know no such thing." The flower's voice is mocking. "I think not. I was cheated. You said yourself that he does not love you."

"I said nothing of the sort."

"You thought it. It is the same thing."

"Talia?" I hear Jack's voice, far off in the distance. I try to answer but can't.

Now the bloom appears to have grown, rising up through the murky water.

"Talia! Say something!"

"Come, Princess." Green leaves fill my vision.

"What do you want from me?"

"I want my due." The flower has turned into a vine. Each spiny whisker has become a curved tentacle, reaching for me. The green leaves are no longer the green leaves of Miami but rather the trees in the Euphrasian hills. I am in Euphrasia.

"Come, Princess, come with me."

And then everything goes black.

Chapter 25: Jack

"Talia? Talia!"

I try to catch her as she begins to fall. Is she sick? Freaking out from the heat? Unable to stand the sight of a giant, sexual-looking water lily?

"Talia?" I nudge her, at first gently, then harder as I realize her body's limp.

Is she dead? Did her heart just realize it was three hundred years old and stop beating? No! She can't be dead. No!

"Talia? Say something!" My whole body is quivering, but I have to stay calm. I have to help her because she is the only one who can help me.

Now other people are crowding around, asking if she's okay, saying they'll call 911, shoving and pushing, grabbing and poking, until I can't breathe.

Breathe!

I feel my heart crashing around in my chest, almost as though it isn't tethered down.

"Anyone know CPR?" a woman says.

I shove the gathered spectators away and kneel beside Talia. What I mean to do is CPR, like I learned in my junior lifesaving course, but somehow, when I kneel beside her, when I hold her in my arms, my mouth near her mouth, the events of the past week—Talia in the castle, in the dungeon, on the airplane, at the party, at dinner, even Talia gazing at that water lily—all swim before me like a river, a waterfall, and as on that day in the castle, I grab her. I press my lips against hers.

I kiss her.

I kiss her long and hard and like both our lives depend on it, which maybe they do.

"Don't go, Talia," I murmur.

Go? Don't I mean die?

I kiss her again, harder. But this time, I say, "Please, Talia, I love you."

She stirs.

I pull away, stare at her. She stares back, eyes widening. "Jack?"

"Are you all right?"

Her white hand flutters to her even whiter forehead, and she says, "I was flying."

"Flying?" I'm aware of people around, a woman with a concerned face, a man who offers a water bottle, which I take, but I focus on Talia. "Where were you flying?"

"Not where." She winces at the water I splash on her face. "Not where but when. I was flying back in time, flying in the airplane back over the ocean, to Europe, then to Euphrasia, to the tower room where I lay those three hundred years. I actually *saw* the three hundred years, Jack. Euphrasia was invisible to the world, but it was there. I was there. I saw the seasons change through the window. And then I saw my birthday eve, and every birthday before that, every Christmas and state occasion. And finally, I was a little girl, playing in the Euphrasian hills with Lady Brooke, and there was a cottage. Jack—a stone peasant cottage with a holly bush beside it, a cottage I always saw but never paid much attention to." She stops to breathe, shaking. "And in the eaves of that cottage was a window, and in that window was a face, the face of the witch Malvolia. She was calling me, saying I had to come back and do it all over again. I was back. She took me to her cottage on the highest hill in Euphrasia, where I used to picnic with Lady Brooke. I was there."

"No. You were here."

"I was there. I could hear you saying, 'Talia, Talia, say something,' but I could not answer, for I was not here. I have to do it all over again."

"Why? This makes no sense."

"Because the spell was to be broken by the kiss of true love—I knew that. That is why it is all wrong. You do not love me, and that is why Malvolia pulls me back to her."

"Because I don't love you?"

Talia nods.

"But I do love you. Didn't you hear me say that, too?"

And as I say it, I realize it is true. I love Talia, not just because she's hot (even though she is), and not just because she's kind and thoughtful and smart, but because she makes me be all those things when I'm around her. "I'm a better person when I'm with you. I don't want to stop being that person. I don't want you to go."

"Really?"

"Will that be enough for her, for Malvolia, to make you stop having these creepy dreams?" I don't really believe Malvolia is appearing to Talia, but I know that Talia believes it, and I want to make it better for her. "Does it matter that I love you?"

I see her think about it, really think like she's doing a crossword puzzle or a sudoku, not just trying to think of an answer to a guy who said he loves her. I tell myself it's because she fainted, because she's freaking out or sick.

"Talia?" I try to meet her eyes, which have glazed over. Is she going to faint again?

But she shakes herself awake. "Yes?"

"Do you love me back?" Because maybe that's the problem. Probably. Probably she thinks I'm a jerk compared to the princes she could've had.

She looks off into the distance over my shoulder.

She smiles. "Yes, Jack, I love you."

I feel myself grin, even though loving Talia was something I never thought I wanted. Now, though, it seems so perfect. Talia talks to me. Talia knows me. She doesn't think I'm a stupid party boy. She even likes my kid sister.

"I love you, too, Talia."

She laughs. "I know."

Chapter 26:  Talia

I love him. I love him and he loves me; at least he says he does. Is it enough for Malvolia?

It must be. It is not like the world is absolutely crawling with eligible bachelors, dying to marry a three-hundred-sixteen-year-old princess. And besides, Jack is the one I want, the one I love.

"I love you, too," I say, and mean it.

It will have to be enough, for in the moments before Jack revived me for the second time with his kiss, I saw what Malvolia meant when she said, "Come with me."

"Come with me, Princess." Her voice was so soothing, lulling me like the ocean's waves outside the castle in Euphrasia. I almost wanted to go. "Come with me."

And simultaneously, I felt my body falling and part of

me—some other part, dare I say my soul?—floating ahead of it, into the center of the water lily, then through the water and down, down, until finally I was back in Euphrasia. Malvolia was with me, towering over me, a spindle in her hand.

"Will you kill me?" I asked, not as if this was a terrible idea—for my body felt light and floating, as if I had taken opium—but merely as a point of fact.

"No, Princess." Her voice was the same, but I could see that her smile was false, as though her lips were trying to express one emotion while her eyes showed quite another. The eyes were true, and they were cruel. "Not yet."

That was when Jack kissed me, and I woke to his declaration of love. He was my savior once again.

And yet, even as Jack declared his love for me, I thought I heard Malvolia's voice in the distance, calling me back.

Chapter 27: Jack

Talia and I spend the next few hours walking around Fairchild, looking at the plants and kissing. It's a cool place, and I get a lot of good ideas for my garden design, which I plan to show Talia. I tell her about it, and she says she's really looking forward to seeing it.

She doesn't imagine she sees Malvolia again. I'm hoping that now that I've told her I love her, maybe she'll get over this guilt trip she's on about it not being true love's kiss that woke her, and she'll stop thinking that Malvolia's going to take her back to Euphrasia.

"It seemed so real," she says. "She even brandished a spindle."

"It's all over now."

"And then I was in her cottage."

"Her cottage?"

"Yes, I told you about it before—a peasant's cottage atop the highest hill in Euphrasia."

"No, Talia." I stroke her hand. "You were right here the whole time, at Fairchild. I saw you. It was a dream."

"I hope so."

After Fairchild, we come home and kiss some more and discuss what to do about the huge problem of her not being able to stay here after a week. We decide to think about it tomorrow. Dad's working late, and Mom's shopping with Meryl. So we get some pizza, then watch television.

It all falls apart when the eleven o'clock news comes on. The newscaster is saying something about a father searching for a missing daughter. She was last seen with an American youth.

Talia gasps. "Father!"

I look. It's the king. He's standing on a street corner. He wears a crown and his king clothes. He holds a painting of a beautiful blond girl.

Talia.

The headline onscreen says MISSING GIRL.

Talia stares, horrified, at the screen. Then she moves closer, as if she has forgotten the difference between television and reality.

"Father," she says. It's a whimper.

"Maybe it's not that bad," I say.

But I know it is. They show the king again, looking tortured worse than when he ate the tough peacock. "How long has the girl been missing?" asks the reporter.

"She is not a girl," says the king. "She is a princess. The heir apparent to the Euphrasian throne."

"Ah, a princess. I see." The reporter smirks. "From *Euphrasia*."

"They do not believe him," Talia says. "They think him insane."

"And she has been missing several days, a week," the king says.

"Had you argued?" the reporter asks. "Could the *princess* have run away?"

They're flashing a 1-800 number over the king's head, to call with tips.

"Argued, yes," says the king. "You could say that. But my Talia, she would never run away. She was sheltered, innocent in the ways of the world. She could not go out on her own. She would . . . she would . . ." He looks like he's going to cry. "She was the light of my life! Of all our lives! No matter what. If she has been kidnapped, or worse, I do not know what I shall do."

"Do you suspect foul play, then?" the reporter asks.

"I do not know," says the king. "Perhaps. There was a boy. . . ."

I groan. "He thinks I kidnapped you."

The news goes to another story, a story about the sudden decline of a forest on the Belgian border, but Talia still stares at the television.

"It's okay, Talia. We'll fix it all."

"Okay? It is most assuredly not okay. While I have been

frolicking in America, my parents, who have lost everything, believe I am lost to them as well. I have frolicked,
Jack! And drank and partied. And my parents are in such
agony that my father—who has never seen a car or a bus,
let alone a television camera—has somehow gotten out of
Euphrasia and found this Belgian news station, all in the
hope of finding me, his most beloved daughter. The light
of his life."

"Yeah." It does sound pretty bad when she puts it that
way.

"We must call."

"What?" I'm thinking of what they said about foul play.
I didn't kidnap Talia, but sometimes things get messed up.
What if they think I did? "I don't—"

"We must call. My father is suffering."

"Wait!" She's leaving. She's going to get on a plane, and
I'll never see her again. "I understand. You're right. You
have to call."

"I am horribly selfish and thoughtless." She tries to grab
the phone from me.

"No, you're not." I hold it away from her. "You're nice.
You're going to call now that you know he wants you back.
But couldn't we just wait until morning?"

"Morning?"

"It's the middle of the night. It's later there. Everyone's
probably asleep. That news show wasn't live. It couldn't
have been. And I'm just a little worried that they'll think I
kidnapped you."

"But you did not. I will tell them you did not."

"But they might not believe you. They might think you have . . ." I try to remember the name of it, this thing I heard about on television, where victims bond with their captors. ". . . Stockholm syndrome."

"Impossible. I have never even been to Sweden."

"Still, your dad threw me in a dungeon once. What's to say he wouldn't . . . misunderstand again? Couldn't we just wait until tomorrow when my dad's home?"

It sounds crazy, but I'm thinking maybe Meryl was right. My parents *have* bailed me out a bunch of times when I've screwed up. No, they haven't been perfect. Sometimes they've been total jerks. But they're the only parents I have, and I don't want to go through this alone.

"I promise," I say, "I'm not trying to get you not to call them. I know it's the right thing to do. It's just . . . I want my dad here, too."

Talia nods. "All right. Tomorrow, then."

Chapter 28: Talia

Tomorrow.

Tomorrow I will speak to Father, perhaps even go back to Euphrasia. Will it be the same Euphrasia I have always known, or will it be irreversibly changed?

It matters not. As soon as I saw Father's dear face on that television, all thought of anything else evaporated, replaced by only one notion: I must find him. I must let him know I am all right.

I settle down on the air mattress. Finally, it has just the right consistency, the correct amount of air, and now I am leaving. I remember that first night when I was visited by the Jell-O demons and Jack came in to comfort me.

Dear Jack . . .

Will I ever see him again?

In my time, if someone journeyed from Euphrasia to

America, one might never return. But now, there are airplanes, cellular telephones, even something called email. Surely, I will be able to see Jack again. After all, we love each other.

For the first time since waking from my long sleep, I am able to rest.

The Jell-O demons do not return. Instead, when I open my eyes, it is morning and Malvolia stands before me.

"You got away," she says.

"I was rescued," I reply, "by my true love's kiss."

"Rescued? You cannot be rescued."

She grabs my hand, and I see a spindle in her other.

"No!" I scream it, but nothing comes out. Still, my throat hurts as if I have screamed. It feels flaming and raw. The old woman's claws dig into my hand.

"No!" I manage to say. "I must go back to Father." It is probably best that Malvolia does not know this, for it is not a sentiment destined to win her over. Still, I struggle. The room is dark, and I can see little. The old woman pulls at me, and although I try to rise and struggle against her, I am unable to find purchase on the tight air mattress. I fall backward. My arm feels as though the veins are being stripped from it, and I hit my head upon something, a chair.

Then everything goes from black to blacker.

Chapter 29: Jack

"Jack!" Meryl's banging on my door. I look at the digital clock, and the number burns my eyes. Seven o'clock. In the morning? Seven AM shouldn't even exist, especially in summer.

"Go away!" I yell.

"It's important! Mom wants you downstairs."

"And I'll be there in an hour or three."

"It's about Talia!"

Talia. I'd forgotten about Talia and the news, but now it all floods back—the euphoria of loving her, the agony that she's leaving, that I'll lose her.

"Jack!"

"Give me a second, okay?"

When I get downstairs, Mom and Dad are both there. Both.

"Where's Talia?" Mom holds up a newspaper. It's open

to an article called "Leads Sought in Case of Missing Belgian Girl."

"It's Talia," Meryl says. "She's a runaway."

"Did you know, Jack?" Mom asks.

"No. I mean, yes, sort of. I mean, not exactly."

"What, exactly, Jack?" Dad asks. "Did you help this girl run away from her family? You didn't . . . kidnap her?"

"It wasn't that way," I say.

"What way was it?" Dad asks. "This sort of thing could ruin your whole life, keep you out of coll—"

"Must we make everything about college, Evan?" Mom says. "The girl clearly wasn't kidnapped. Did she look kidnapped to you? She was having a great time."

I give her a grateful look, and she says, "Why don't you just tell us what happened, Jack?"

I nod. They'll find out, anyway. "But you have to sit down, and you have to believe me."

Dad grumbles that he's not sure he can believe me about anything now, but Mom gestures for him to sit. I pour out the whole story of Talia and me, and how we met, and how we escaped. At the end of it, he says, "That's impossible."

"*I* wouldn't believe me, either, not if I hadn't been there and seen it with my own eyes. But it's true. There was a castle and a king and a queen, and Travis wanted to try on the crowns, and there was this princess. It was Talia."

"It's not that we don't trust you, Jack," Mom says. "It's just that it seems so—"

"Look!" I hold up the newspaper. "This picture they

281

put of her. It's not a photo. They didn't have photos then. It's an oil painting. And look what she's wearing."

I point. In the portrait, Talia's wearing a crown.

"Hey," Meryl says. "Here's the story again."

Channel six is running last night's interview, but the reporter's saying, "The man, mad with grief, claims that he comes from another world, another time."

And there's Talia's dad. He has no crown on, but other than that, he looks pretty much like the Burger King again—especially in his robe. It's that red and gold curtain material they wear only in pictures of royalty.

I turn to Dad. "Do many of the guys you hang with dress like this? I'm telling you, he's a king. When Talia and I saw the report last night—"

"Last night?" Mom says. "You saw the report last night?"

"Uh-oh," Meryl says.

"You knew about this last night, and you did nothing?" Dad demands. "Jack, I knew you were irresponsible, but—"

"I'm not being irresponsible, not this time. Talia wanted to call her dad, and I agreed she should. But I was scared, too. I was worried they'd think what you thought, that I kidnapped her or something. So I wanted to wait until you were here and ask you what to do."

"You wanted what?"

"I guess it sounds lame now, not doing something right away, but you hear all the time about teenagers getting interrogated by the police without their parents there and even *confessing* to stuff they didn't do just because the police think they're guilty, and I don't know, I just thought maybe you'd know the right thing to do. You usually do. So I told Talia we should wait."

"You thought that I could help you? Well, that's . . . something." Dad looks surprised, and for the first time since I got up this morning, maybe the first time in a year, that line he gets between his eyebrows when he talks to me disappears. He looks at the television where, once again, King Louis is crying. The line returns. "But now, I believe we must call and reunite this man with his daughter."

Mom nods. "Why don't you go get Talia?"

I start toward the study. I'm surprised Talia isn't already awake, considering she's been up and eating pancakes hours before me every day. But maybe, like me, she's trying to put off calling her dad for as long as possible. Maybe she doesn't want to leave.

I knock on the door of the study. "Talia?"

No answer. I knock louder. "Talia? Wake up, sleepy-head!"

Nothing. "Talia?"

I try the door. Locked. Why locked? She wouldn't lock it. I'm not even sure she knows how to use the lock. I beat on the door, screaming, "Talia! Talia! Talia!"

Nothing. Nothing. Nothing!

She fainted yesterday. What if it happened again? Or she choked? Passed out?

"Talia!"

Finally, Mom shows up with a hairpin. We pick the lock, and I open the door.

The room is empty.

Chapter 30: Talia

I am in blackness. It is not like sleep but like being inside a coffin, away from everyone, everything, closed in with no light anywhere.

Was this what it was like when I slumbered before? Do I slumber again?

No. I am certain there were no dreams in my three hundred years' sleep. But were there visitors? Did the fairies check on me or did Malvolia herself? Did they see me?

In the still, black nothingness, I return to sleep.

Chapter 31: Jack

"She must have left," Mom says. "She was probably anxious to talk to her father, and she locked the door to keep you from finding out she had left."

"She wouldn't do that, and she'd tell me if she did." But I wonder if that's true. Talia was hot to call her dad, and I stopped her because I was afraid. But maybe she wanted to call so bad she sneaked out and found a pay phone. After all, she's already run away once.

I hear my cell phone ringing in my room. Thinking it's Talia, I bolt out the door.

"Talia?"

"Dude, you're in a big mess."

Travis! Travis, calling from Europe.

"Where are you? Do you know anything about Talia?"

"I know King Kong and his goons tracked me down

with the tour, and they're trying to torture me for information. I keep telling them I don't know anything. They finally let me use my phone, so I'm calling you. You've got to make her call home."

"She's not here."

"She didn't go with you?"

"No. Are you with her parents?"

"I'm with her dad in Brussels. It's been a super barrel of laughs, let me tell you."

"Sorry. She hasn't called there? It's been all over the television stations here."

"Here, too. They all think she's with you, but they don't know who you are. They keep calling you 'the American youth.'"

My sister Meryl comes in. She's carrying something in her hand, two somethings. The first is Talia's jewelry box. Her jewelry box! She'd never leave without that, so she must be coming back.

I can't see what the other object is, on top of the box. I walk closer.

"Jack? Jack, are you there?"

"Yeah, I'm here. She's not with me, Trav, honest."

I'm standing in front of Meryl now. I pick up the object on top of the box. It's long and slender and looks hundreds of years old, and even though I've never seen one before, I know exactly what it is.

It's a spindle.

"I have to go, Trav. I'll call you later." I close the phone.

"What is it?" Meryl demands.

"She hasn't called home," I say. Now Mom's joined Meryl in the kitchen. "I think she's been kidnapped."

"Kidnapped?" Mom says. "That's impossible. I looked at the windows in that room, and they're not broken. They haven't even been unlocked. And we have alarms on the doors."

"A witch wouldn't need to break a window or, if she did, she could fix it."

"A witch?" Meryl says.

I nod. "Her father and his goons aren't going to be able to find her. We have to go to Euphrasia."

Chapter 32: Talia

When next I waken, it is daylight, and I am alone. I feel the mattress beneath me. It is not made of rubber, nor filled with air. As I run my hand over the coarse ticking (for there is no sheet), I feel a small, sharp pain. A pinfeather! The mattress is made of down!

I look out the window. At first, all I see is blue sky and a large chestnut tree shadowing the grass. Then my eyes grow accustomed to the light, and I make out shapes—a holly bush, the thatch of a cottage roof hanging down, and in the distance below, the spire of a castle.

I am home! I am in Euphrasia!

Chapter 33: Jack

"Euphrasia?" my mom says. We're back in the kitchen, telling Dad.

"That's where she's from. Her country." I remember Talia's words: *She took me to her cottage on the highest hill in Euphrasia, where I used to picnic with Lady Brooke.*

"But there's no way she could be back in Europe," Mom says. "She couldn't get a flight out that late, even if she left the second you went to sleep."

My parents still aren't believing the magical princess stuff. "I know. I know it sounds crazy. But I'm not saying she took a commercial airline."

"What are you saying, son?" my dad asks.

I feel completely stupid telling him what I'm thinking. It *is* stupid, thinking Malvolia took her through some *portal* to Euphrasia. It's more than stupid—it's crazy.

290

But so is a princess who sleeps for three hundred years only to be awakened by a doofus like me. Crazy things happen.

Just not to Dad.

Still, I have to try and make him understand.

"She said the witch was taking her to Euphrasia, yesterday when she fainted at Fairchild. I thought she was crazy. I told her so. But now she's gone. She's gone, and it's my fault for not believing her."

"Jack . . ." My mom rubs my shoulder. "We can look around the neighborhood. She can't have gone far without a car. But if we don't find her, I think you'll have to accept that she ran away again."

"She didn't," I say. "She wouldn't run away, and she especially wouldn't run away and leave this." I gesture toward the spindle. "And all her jewelry, too."

"Hey, here's what I was looking for," Meryl says from the computer. She points to a Wikipedia article she's been reading.

"Not now, Meryl," Dad says. He's taken out one of Talia's necklaces and is examining it.

"No, listen for once!" She reads, "'Carlo Maratti drew ridicule at the end of his life for claiming to have been the art master to Princess Talia of Euphrasia, a nonexistent country. And then, one day, he lost his memory entirely.' That was Talia's art master."

"I don't understand," Dad says. He holds up a sapphire to the light.

"So, Carlo Maratti died in 1713. Jack's telling the truth, Dad. She's really from the seventeenth century. She's really a princess, too! If you'd talked to her, you'd know it's true."

Dad looks at the computer screen, then at the necklace. "Dana, maybe we should listen to the boy."

"What?" I say.

"What?" my mom echoes.

"He seems pretty sure of himself, and besides, I wouldn't mind seeing the place."

"What place?" Mom asks.

"Euphrasia. It sounds fascinating."

"So you actually believe me?" I forget for a second how upset I am about Talia. I'm glad my dad doesn't know how Wikipedia works, that anyone can just add stuff, that Meryl could have put those sentences in the article.

"You believe what you're saying, don't you?" Dad asks me.

I nod. "Talia told me that Malvolia would take her to a cottage on the highest hill in Euphrasia."

"But why can't we simply call her parents and tell them to check there?" Mom asks.

I think of the empty air mattress, the pillow with the indentation of Talia's head. The spindle.

"Because I may need to be there, to rescue her."

Chapter 34: Talia

"What do you want from me?" The words are a cry to the room, to no one, to Malvolia, whom I know is there somewhere, looming like a black bat.

But there is no answer.

Is she away? Would she take me here, all the way to Euphrasia, and simply leave me, free to come and go as I please? It is impossible. It is too simple.

And yet I hear no sign of Malvolia. Indeed, the room is perfectly silent, silent as only Euphrasian rooms are. American rooms always had noise, the blare of the television, or even at the dead of midnight, smaller sounds, like the tick of a clock, the buzz of a computer, or the constant whoosh of air-conditioning.

There is no air-conditioning in this cottage, Malvolia's cottage, but it is cool nonetheless, for it is high up in the

Euphrasian hills and is shaded by a chestnut tree. I breathe in the fresh air, Euphrasian air which has not been processed or filtered in any way. It smells like my childhood, and I sigh as I remember Mother and Father. After the sigh is true Euphrasian silence. Can the cottage be empty? Dare I chance walking about?

What have I to lose? And the cottage is small. Surely, if she were lurking, I would hear her. She would hear me.

I rise.

I am still dressed from last night, in a pair of blue sleep trousers and a T-shirt. My feet are bare, and I step lightly on the unpolished wooden floor. I tiptoe to the door, which has a window in it, and then stand by that window, gazing out. No one in sight, not even a shepherd boy with his flock. I will leave. I will go to my family.

I glance behind me. No one there. I open the door.

"Going somewhere, Princess?"

Chapter 35: Jack

Even though I say it's not necessary, Mom insists we drive around the neighborhood, looking for Talia. We even look at the nearest Trailways bus station and ask if they've seen her. "I didn't even know there was a Trailways bus station," I tell Mom. "What are the odds that Talia would find it?" But Mom says we should leave no stone unturned.

So when we've finally turned every stone (and haven't found Talia), we head back home and go online to order a plane ticket.

"Get two," Dad says.

"Two?"

"One for me, one for you."

I heard Dad before when he said he wanted to see Euphrasia, but I didn't think he was serious. The thought of ten plus hours on the plane with Dad doesn't do it for me.

"Don't you have work or something?" I ask him. He always has to work.

He shrugs. "I can move some things around."

"But I can go by myself. I went by myself before."

"The last time you went on a trip by yourself," my dear little sister says, "you sneaked away from the tour group, went to a nonexistent country, and kidnapped the heir to the throne. So, understandably, Dad's worried about what will happen if he sends you back."

"Shut up," I say.

"That's not it," Dad says.

"What is it then?"

Dad thinks a minute. "I want to see this Euphrasia. Besides, if it's really like you say, with witches and curses and kidnappings, it could be dangerous. If this Malvolia has really been plotting against Talia for three hundred years, she's not going to give up easily.

Wow. He actually listened and believed me.

"Okay. Then I guess we should get going."

And that's how I end up spending the next twenty-four hours alone with my dad, flying to Brussels and then driving to Euphrasia.

Chapter 36: Talia

Caught! I feel Malvolia's icy fingers upon my bare arm.

"Going somewhere?" she says.

"Merely home. I thank you kindly for bringing me this far."

"I am afraid not." With her claw, she draws me around, then into the room.

"What interesting . . . attire," she says, her black eyes scanning my pajamas. "You cannot go home like this. It is hardly what one would expect of a princess."

"Are you going to torture me? Chain me to the wall?" Then I realize I may merely be giving her ideas which she had not yet considered. So I am quiet.

"Nay, Princess. You have done me no harm."

"Then you will allow me to leave?"

She shakes her head. "It is upon your father I seek revenge. You are merely a pawn."

I, who have studied the game of chess, know that it is no good thing to be a pawn. Pawns are eliminated quickly while kings and queens stay to fight the battle.

"So you plan to . . . kill me? But surely this is not necessary. My father adores me, and he will pay whatever you wish for my safe return."

"Whatever I wish?" Malvolia looks into space, considering. "What I wish is to see your father miserable and heartbroken, as he has made me."

She leads me to a table set up for sewing. Cuts of fabric lie all around, and I realize they are meant to be parts of a dress, a dress the exact shade of my eyes. The gown is unfinished, panels unsewn, buttons lying beside it on the table.

"We will create a beautiful dress for you, Princess. That is what is important to you, nay? To have the most beautiful dress? Now you shall sew it yourself. And then I will deliver it to your father, wrapped around your dead body."

"My dead body!"

"Revenge is not a pretty thing, Princess."

She means not only to kill me, but first to use me to sew my own shroud. I look into the old woman's black eyes, and I see something I have never seen before: hatred. This is what Father and Mother sheltered me from, protected me from.

I realize, too late, that Father and Mother were right.

They were right, and I shall never be able to tell them. I shall never see nor speak to them again.

Out the window are the verdant Euphrasian hills. I shall never go home.

No. This is impossible! It is impossible that I should live three hundred years only to die in this manner. Perhaps it was my destiny for my life to end like this, but must I accept this fate?

"Was it not enough to make me sleep three hundred years?" I ask. "Can you not consider yourself avenged and let me go?"

"Come now, Princess." Malvolia's voice is like the rocks under carriage wheels. "It is time to sew your lovely dress."

Why should I sew? I want to ask her. *Why should I, a princess destined to become queen, sew a gown for myself only so I can be killed?*

But then I look at the dress. It is pieces, only pieces, which would take days, maybe a week, for even a skilled seamstress to sew. I have never sewn anything in my life, and if my skill at painting is any indication, my hands are lacking in dexterity. It will take a long time—long enough for someone to rescue me?

Jack. I dare not hope that Jack . . . and yet, I told him the exact location of Malvolia's cottage. Of course, he thought me daft at the time, but now perhaps he will remember. Perhaps he will come here in time to rescue me before Malvolia . . .

"Time to sew," the witch repeats.

"I do not know how to sew," I say, sweet as pie to this old lady who would murder me. "You will need to teach me."

"I fully intend to."

"But please . . ." I remember the story of Scheherazade in *Arabian Nights* (which Lady Brooke tried to prevent my reading), who put off her death night after night by dawdling at her storytelling until her captor changed his mind. "Might I have breakfast first? I will sew better on a full stomach."

The old woman's eyes appraise me, attempting to catch a lie. But finally she says, "You do look thin, Your Highness. I will fix you breakfast. You may set the table."

I glance out the window again. There is no one in the distance, no chance of rescue.

No chance but Jack.

Chapter 37: Jack

After we book the plane tickets, I call Travis and ask him to tell Talia's dad to look on the highest hill in Euphrasia, where Talia and Lady Brooke used to go for picnics. He says he'll tell them.

"But . . ." I say.

"What?"

"Be careful, okay, when you go there. Talia was really scared of this Malvolia chick. She could be dangerous."

"What's she going to have—an assault weapon?"

"Worse," I say. "She's got magical powers."

In all the activity, I try not to think about the fact that Talia's gone, that I might never see her again, that she might even be dead, and that if I'd just listened to her in the first place, I might have been able to prevent it.

But I have lots of time to think about that on the airplane.

I wonder how many times in my life I would have been able to prevent something, change something, do something different, if only I'd listened to someone. I don't know, but when this is over, I'm going to try and listen a lot more.

I spend about three hours sitting in the plane seat (one good thing about going with Dad—he sprung for first class), listening to my iPod and contemplating life. That's a lot of contemplating for me, but I can't sleep. I'm too worried about Talia. I wish I could use my phone and call Travis. I wonder if it really would interfere with the plane's signal. Still, it would suck if the plane crashed, and if Travis is back in Euphrasia, his phone won't work, anyway.

Dad's been sitting doing work, paying zero attention to me, which is what I'm used to, anyway. So I take out my garden design and start working on that. But even then I can't concentrate, because when I try to decide what kind of flowers would grow around the trees in front of the castle, that gets me thinking about Euphrasia and that hill. Where is it? And is Talia really there?

Dad taps my shoulder. "What's that you're working on?"

"Huh?" Instinctively, I cover the design with the sleeve of my hoodie.

"That." He points. "What is it?"

"Oh." I try to look casual. "Homework. Math." This is the best way to get rid of parents, I've found. They don't want to get stuck helping with math.

"In the summer?"

Stupid.

"I'm trying to get ahead." He should like that.

He nods. "It doesn't look like math. It looked like a design of some sort."

"Geometry. They make us do maps and plans."

I took geometry in ninth grade, but I doubt Dad will remember that.

"I thought you took geometry in ninth grade."

Nabbed. "Yeah, but next year I'm taking trig, and that's got a lot of geometry in it, so you have to remember—"

"You took trig last year," Dad says. "Never mind." He goes back to his work.

I try to go back to mine, but now I feel bad about Talia *and* sort of bad about blowing Dad off. I just figured he'd think it was stupid. In fact, I *know* he will. He already said gardening was stupid. But, on the other hand, I do complain a lot about Dad blowing *me* off. And he did seem happy when I'd said I was waiting for his advice. And I *am* surprised that he knows so much about what classes I've taken.

I start to turn the paper toward him, to show him, then change my mind. I can't take the chance of him saying it's stupid. He's finally starting to believe me about stuff, to treat me like I'm not just some dumb slacker. But if I start talking about gardening again, I could ruin it all.

I keep working on it until they turn off the lights. I could turn on my overhead light, but I decide I should at least try to sleep so I'll be rested for tomorrow.

I wonder what Talia's doing right now.

Chapter 38: Talia

The old lady fixes me breakfast. I wonder, at first, if I should eat it, but then I realize that if she wished to kill me now, she need not poison me. Indeed, she might easily have killed me already.

After breakfast, I dawdle about, clearing the dishes, looking out the window at the chestnut tree. Would that I could climb it, be free once more. Malvolia reproaches me. "I should have known not to expect much work from you."

Considering that she intends to kill me, this seems only reasonable. But I finish the dishes, and then Malvolia begins the chore of teaching me to sew.

Breakfast was a silent meal, but afterward, as we are sitting together at the table, it occurs to me that I should use the diplomacy skills that were the work of years. After all, perhaps if I talk to her, she will begin to like me, rather than see me merely as a spoiled extension of my hated father. Then she may be less likely to kill me. At least, it is worth a try.

"You sew extremely well," I say as she shows me how to fit the pieces together.

"I am not sewing, Princess. You are."

"No, but I meant the dresses you made for me that day. Perhaps you do not remember it, for it was three hundred years ago, but they were the loveliest I had ever seen. Were they made with magic?"

She shakes her head. "Nay. Magic can sew a dress, but it cannot design one. To make a beautiful gown, one needs skill, not merely arts." There is an unmistakable hint of pride in her voice.

"Well, you certainly have skill." I have managed to thread the needle and am now attempting to make a knot in the thread. "I have none."

"I was a seamstress by trade, before your father destroyed me."

"My father?"

"Oh, drat!" The old woman looks past me to the window. "How have they found me?"

I turn, looking for what she is talking about. At first, I see nothing. Then, far off in the distance, I spy a man on horseback, then another. I recognize the shape of the larger one. It is Pleasant, one of the castle guards, the drunkard who watched Jack that night in the dungeon. They ride toward the cottage. I am saved! I am saved!

"They are coming for me!" I cry.

"Silence!"

And then, when I try to cry out again, I find that I cannot. My mouth will make no sound.

"And sit still." As soon as she says it, I cannot move. "Much better. I do not know how they have found me. My location has been secret since before your birth. But they shall not thwart me."

I know how they found out. Jack! Jack believed me, and he remembered—the highest hill in Euphrasia. Jack has contacted my father somehow. They are coming for me.

But they will not find me, for the old woman is now, with surprising strength for one over five hundred years old, dragging my stiff body across the room. She kicks aside a rag rug, and I see a trapdoor under it. She opens the door, and proceeds to pull me down the cellar stairs. The staircase is long and steep, and I fear there may be rats at the end of it. I suppose I should be happy that Malvolia at least drags me by the arms, lest my head bump against each step. But this is small comfort when rescue is so close.

Finally, we reach the bottom of the stairs. It is pitch-black, and Malvolia drags me to the corner, throwing a blanket atop my unmoving form.

"Rest, Princess," she says.

Her footsteps move away, but I cannot see her. I can see the smallest bit through a hole in the blanket, and only when she reaches the top do I spy her face. She has changed into someone else, not Malvolia, not the old thing who displayed the dresses at the castle that day, either, but an entirely different old lady, a sweet and kindly looking one, one I have never seen before.

She shuts the trapdoor, and I am left in darkness.

I hear Malvolia walking around upstairs, maybe pulling the rug over the trapdoor or, perhaps, even enchanting the door itself. Then there is silence and blackness and nothing. I struggle to move, struggle to speak, but there is no way. Finally, I stop. Will I stay this way forever? Will she remove the spell after they leave? And what does it matter, if she intends to kill me, anyway?

Upstairs, I hear the two men enter.

"We have to search the house." I recognize the voice of Pleasant.

"Oh, me!" A high-pitched old lady's voice. "Must ye? I am afraid I have not cleaned too well."

"King's orders," another voice—my father's guard, Cuthbert, who is not renowned for his wit—says. "We shan't be a minute, ma'am."

"Ah, me. Can I get ye a cup of tea, gentlemen?"

"No, ma'am. We will just look around."

I hear the two clumsy oafs walking about, overturning things, and all I can do is hope—just hope—that they will see the trapdoor.

"What is this about, then?" Malvolia asks.

"The king's daughter," Cuthbert says.

"The pretty one with the curse on her? How is she?"

"She's disappeared, ma'am. The king believes it was the doing of the witch Malvolia."

Malvolia laughs. "Do *I* look like the witch Malvolia, then? Were I a witch, I would be able to free meself from this rheumatism."

Cuthbert laughs, too. "King's orders. Is there a cellar here?"

"Nay. 'Tis only a small cottage, and I can barely keep that."

"We must have a look around, nonetheless. The king requires it."

I hear them walking toward the door. I am saved! I am saved—although possibly a mute paralytic for the rest of my life.

"Ye look parched," Malvolia says. "Would ye not care for a wee bit of port?"

"We should not," says Cuthbert, who is clearly the conscience keeper of the two.

"Should not, my arse," Pleasant says. "'Twas a long ride and a hot day—and a fool's errand if ye ask me. There is nothing here."

"Indeed," Malvolia says. "Nothing but an old lady offering a nice bit of port. Please join me, for I hate to drink alone."

Something—a fly or even worse—crawls onto my cheek under the blanket. I wish to scream, to flail, but I can do nothing. It is as if I am already dead, and maggots are munching upon my face.

"Aye, we should have some," Pleasant goes on. "There is naught to drink at the castle."

Can the dead hear the living? I wonder. And, if so, would that be a comfort or a curse?

"True," Cuthbert says.

And then I hear the clinking of a bottle and tankard and the scraping of chairs.

"Did you know," Malvolia says, "that Malvolia was once employed at the castle?"

"Truly?" Pleasant says.

"I seem to remember hearing something of it," Cuthbert says. "She was a seamstress. That was before this whole spindle business."

Malvolia employed at the castle? How strange. And stranger still that my father never mentioned it to me.

The fly has left my nose and lit upon my hand. No, they are two separate flies.

"Do ye wish more?" Malvolia asks.

"You are too generous, ma'am."

"Nay. I am grateful that you are out, protecting us all."

I hear the clink of glass once again. I know how it will be. The wine will be poured and the bottle drained, and the guards will leave, saying they saw nothing. They will not return. And I—I shall spend the rest of my days (what few are left) sewing my dress and waiting for death.

Where is Jack?

Chapter 39: Jack

When we reach the airport in London, I call Travis, who stayed the night outside Euphrasia in order to meet us when we get there.

"Did they find her?" I ask. "Was she where I said she'd be?"

"No, man. They sent two guys up there, but they said all they found was some harmless old lady."

So Talia was wrong. I hadn't thought of that.

"Maybe it was another hill, another cottage."

"They're checking every cottage on a hill, but let me tell you, it's not a crack crime scene investigation team."

I remember how easy it was to escape the dungeon and take Talia with me. "Guess not. They should check every cottage in the kingdom."

When I get off the phone, Dad says, "No luck?"

"Nope." I look at him, daring him to say it was a waste of time coming here.

But he just says, "They're going to be boarding in a few minutes. Better get our stuff together."

I do, and as I'm sitting on the flight from London to Brussels, I think of something: If Malvolia is a witch, she can probably disguise herself.

Chapter 40: 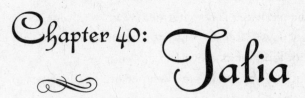 Talia

It is twenty minutes after Cuthbert and Pleasant stumble from the cottage before Malvolia releases me from the cellar and from her spells. I have twenty minutes, therefore, in which to wonder what shall become of me. Will I be killed viciously, violently, or merely left here until I die of starvation?

For one thing I am grateful that Malvolia intends to deliver me to my father. At least he will know what happened to me, that I did not merely run away with a young man.

Although, in fact, I did do that.

But I cannot resign myself to this fate. I must return to Father to make amends. If I am not to be saved, I must persuade Malvolia to release me of her own free will.

So when I am freed from the spells, I do not complain,

as I am inclined to do. Rather, I simply stretch and say, "Thank you, ma'am, for releasing me. After not moving for so long, it feels wonderful to wiggle one's toes." I grace her with my sweetest smile.

But the old witch is not charmed by my gratitude. Nay, she merely says, "Relish your movement while you can. You are not long for it. Now, on with your sewing."

So much for her seeing me as a person, but I do get to sewing with a diligence I never felt for anything resembling work in my former life. I love the feeling of the cold silk between my fingers and, indeed, enjoy seeing it become a dress. Were it not for my situation, I would find it quite satisfying to learn to sew, for I have never done anything so useful before.

This I tell Malvolia, who grunts, "I am not doing it for your entertainment, but enjoy it if you must."

For the next hours, I sew in silence, the only sound being the steady rhythm of needle in fabric. Finally, the old woman, seeming pleased with the length of my stitches, which I have purposely made minuscule, to take up more time, allows me a small supper of bean soup. I hope that she will not require me to sew any more for the day. I wish to extend the job over as many days as possible.

Over supper, I glance at the departing sun and play with a streamer of silk in my lap. I have stolen it from the leftover scraps for I love its feel. "This is excellent soup," I say. I eat slowly, one bean at a time.

"Surely not what you are used to at the castle," she barks.

"Surely not. Mistress Pyrtle, the cook, was no artist with soups. Too salty. But you must remember that?"

No response. I try again.

"I heard you tell the men who came that you used to work at the castle. Is that true?"

Malvolia's black eyes narrow. "You know 'tis."

"I know nothing of the sort. I was told nothing."

"Indeed?" She thinks upon it a bit, staring at the horizon. "No, I am not surprised at that. Why would your father tell you anything other than that I was evil, bent upon your destruction?"

And is that not the truth?

But I say, "Mainly, we discussed what I must avoid—spindles—something I did not do very well. We discussed it . . . frequently."

Malvolia laughs. "The spindle-pricking was inevitable. With my spell, I assured it was so. I took great amusement in seeing your father's pathetic efforts to prevent it."

To protect me. I wonder why, if it was so inevitable, the old woman bothered to come to the castle herself on the eve of my sixteenth birthday, to present me with the spindle. Was she nervous?

As if hearing my thoughts, Malvolia says, "I brought the spindle myself because I wanted to see that it had been done, so I did it myself."

Nice. But I say, "I am glad you told me that it was inevitable, for I have been blaming myself, or rather, Father has been blaming me."

315

Malvolia laughs. "That does not surprise me. Aye, he was always one to place blame."

"What did he blame you for that you did not deserve?" I cry out. "You cursed me. You made me sleep three hundred years! And now, when I have been wakened, you are making excuses, saying that the curse was not properly broken, so that you might bring me back."

I should not have had such an outburst. Now that the scalding words are out, it is impossible to push them back.

"I am speaking of before that, Princess, when I was but a seamstress in the castle, and he was an all-powerful king."

"What happened?" Can there be a reason for Malvolia's animosity other than merely not being invited to the party?

"'Tis of no import." She gestures toward the table. "Clear the dishes, and if you can do so with no more impertinent questions, I will allow you to read to me instead of sewing away the evening. My eyesight is too poor to see the stitches in the waning light, and I do not trust your clumsy hands."

I suspect her eyesight is perfect. Still, I follow her instructions, then read to her from the only book in the house, the Bible, until the light wanes so that I cannot see, even with a candle.

Chapter 41: Jack

The flight to Brussels is only an hour. Travis meets us at the airport.

"Dude!" I say when I see him at the rental car place. "Thanks for coming."

"No worries, man. I wanted to get out of that castle before the king threw me in the dungeon as an accessory."

My dad finishes renting the car and says to Travis, "So you believe all this, then, the kingdom and the curse, and that there's a princess being held by a witch?"

Travis shakes his head. "I know it sounds like we're smoking weed, Mr. O'Neill, but Scout's honor, I saw it with my own eyes. And I had to help out because I feel sort of responsible, seeing as how we woke them up and everything."

My dad nods. "It's important to fulfill one's responsibilities." He looks at me.

"Can we go?" I say. "Talia could be getting stabbed to death with a spindle right now."

I'm not really serious when I say it, but after the words come out, I sort of am. I want to see Talia again. I want her to be okay. And I want it to be now.

Chapter 42: Talia

Malvolia does not bind me or place me under a spell during the night. Rather, she enchants the locks on the windows and doors so that I cannot escape without her knowledge. Jack's family had a similar invention in the twenty-first century, an alarm system, it was called.

When morning comes, I return to sewing. The bodice is nearly finished but for the buttonholes. The skirt should be short work. I hope I might live another night.

I stop to admire my handiwork.

"Keep at it," Malvolia snaps. She has been in a particularly sour mood today.

"I am sorry. It is just so . . . lovely." I must try again to strike up a conversation with her. It is my only hope of survival. "You have been kind to me. Were you to release me, I would speak to Father on your behalf. I would persuade him to make amends . . . for not inviting you to my christening party."

"Your christening party? Is that what you believe this to be about?"

"That is what I was told, and you have not told me otherwise. Is it not the case?" I make one small stitch, then pause, awaiting her response.

"No. It is not." She glances at the stitches, and I believe she will hurry me on, but instead she says, "Were I you, I would not be so determined to live. Your father is angry for what you did. You have destroyed his kingdom. Indeed, it may not be a kingdom at all, and he may not be a king. And as for your marital prospects, any prince you might have married is dead. What have you to live for?"

It seems that if I had nothing to live for, allowing me to live would be far worse punishment than killing me. But I say, "I am in love."

"Impossible." But the old lady leans toward me. "With whom could you be in love?"

"His name is Jack." I abandon my sewing entirely. "He is the boy who kissed me awake."

"A commoner who woke you under false pretenses. He was not your true love—merely some youth who stumbled upon you and thought you pretty."

"This may have been true. But as time passed, we fell in love. He was kind, and he watched over me." Malvolia does not attempt to silence me, so I continue on, telling her of Jack, of running away, of the airplane and the party and Jack's parents and, finally, of the moment when he said he loved me. "You were there for that," I tell her. "At least, I thought I saw you in the face of the water lily."

"Aye. I was there. And you say you are in love with this boy?"

"Yes. I was not at first, when he woke me. But as I grew to know him better, to see how kind he was, not merely because I was a princess, but because he liked me, I grew to love him."

Malvolia's face is thoughtful. "Indeed. And what did you say this boy's name is?"

"Jack." The syllable comes out as a sob, not merely due to my sorrow at not seeing Jack, but for another reason. "He cared for me, and I fear he will be destroyed if I die. He is innocent in this."

"And he loves you, too?"

I nod. There is something in Malvolia's black eyes, a humanity I have not seen before.

But then she says, "We have wasted enough time. Back to your sewing."

I start slowly again, admiring the beauty of each and every stitch. After some time, I say, "Please, Malvolia. Will you not tell me why you hate my father so? You intend to kill me. The least you could do is explain why."

"The least I could do is nothing." She gestures at me to return to my sewing. "And you had better to ask why *he* hates *me* so much, for it was with him that the animosity began."

I nod. "Then tell me that. My parents were far too inclined to keep me in the dark, and I am afraid there is much I know not."

"Indeed. What you know not would fill books."

For a long while, the only sound in the room is the smooth silk against the roughness of my cotton sleep pants. But finally, she says, "Did you know that your family had another babe before you?"

"That is a lie!" I say, and I am certain it is. Had I not been told that I was my parents' only child? That they had dreamed of having a babe? That I was the answer to their prayers—the sole answer?

"Indeed, then, they did not tell you much. Two years before your birth, your parents had another child, a boy named George."

A boy! And named for my grandfather George. How happy my father would have been to have a male heir. Still, it cannot be true.

"I was employed as a seamstress in the castle, as were many of the kingdom's fairies."

I know that Malvolia is a witch, not a fairy, but I elect not to press this point. Rather, I lay down my sewing and listen to her story.

"As after your own birth, your parents planned a lavish christening party, and I—as the most accomplished seamstress in the land—was assigned to make the clothing for the occasion, a christening gown for your brother, and a dress for your mother.

"The christening gown was the work of many weeks. It was made of cotton imported from Egypt, and the skirt was over three feet long. The bodice was smocked and embroidered, and the skirt was sewn with hundreds of seed pearls.

"The day before the christening, I entered the nursery, that I might try it on the babe to make certain it fit his wee form." The old woman's eyes grow misty with memory. "Lady Brooke was with him, but he slept. He looked so peaceful, lying upon his stomach, thumb in mouth. Lady Brooke asked me if I might keep an eye on him while she checked on his bath. She was then quite young and stupid, and I suspected her errand might have had more to do with flirting with one of the gentlemen of court than the baby's bath. Still, I agreed. In the nursery, I could sew undisturbed by Lady Brooke."

I smile at the idea of imperious Lady Brooke ever being a silly girl. Malvolia does not see me, though, so engrossed is she in her own tale.

"Besides, I enjoyed seeing the sleeping babe," she says. "He was beautiful. So she left me there. The babe slept on, so I engaged myself in sewing more and more seed pearls to the train of the gown. I stayed an hour, and when I sewed the last, Lady Brooke had not returned, and the babe had not yet awakened. Annoyed at this waste of my time (for I had still your mother's gown to finish), I approached the crib to check upon the babe."

Tears fill her eyes, and I know what is coming, know

why my brother was never spoken of by my parents.

"I expected to see the baby sleeping peacefully. Instead, I saw an infant, blue and still. Dead."

The fabric slips from my lap to the floor.

"I tried mightily to revive him, shaking him, even slapping his little cheeks. Then, failing this, I tried magic. It was then that Lady Brooke entered the nursery. Seeing the baby dead, and me standing over him reciting incantations, and perhaps fearing repercussions for leaving her post, she began to scream. She screamed so loudly that everyone came, and when they did come, she concocted a story of how I had put a spell on her to remove her from the room, the better to suffocate the baby.

"All who came believed her, for I was a solitary being, not well liked by the others. And soon, the king heard tell of it, and in his grief, he had me removed from the castle. He wished to kill me, but I was too clever, with knowledge from my hundreds of years of existence. I outwitted him. I slipped into my realm, and later I disguised myself so that he could not find me. Still, he declared that, evermore, I should be known as a witch and not a fairy, and I was ostracized by one and all."

"But it was not your fault!" I say.

"Nay. I loved the babe. It would have been my pride and joy to see a prince wearing a dress of my creation. But no one would listen to me, and I felt lucky to escape with my life. From that moment on, I was ostracized as a child killer. It was not fair. It was not fair."

I remember my fear at Father's anger. I touch her black-clad shoulder. "No. It was not fair."

"But I will make it fair," she says. "I was accused of killing one of King Louis's children, when I had not done so. If I kill the other, 'twill be the perfect revenge."

I look away, eyes filling with tears. She will kill me. It is all over. But I cannot let that happen. I swallow my tears and turn to her. "Good fairy, I am sorry for your misfortune. My father was, indeed, wrong to accuse you in such a way. It was cruel."

The old woman nods. "Aye, it was. And it is for that reason that I must seek justice."

"But killing me for my father's cruelty is *not* justice. Can you not see that?" I allow the tears to run down my cheeks and implore her. "I am not my father. To kill me would be just as great an injustice as was done to you. Please do not do this."

I wait for her response. She starts to speak, then stops and looks down. Finally, after a long while, she says, "You had best return to your sewing."

I do, wishing that I might have a quantity of seed pearls to sew on, to prolong the job. But, of course, I do not ask. It is no use. It is no use.

Chapter 43: Jack

We get into Euphrasia at high noon, with Dad wearing dress shoes and carrying a briefcase and a laptop. The hedge is a lot smaller, so it's easier to push through. But I see Dad's eyes get big when he sees the place. It looks even more like Colonial Williamsburg than before. Now there are a bunch of people in old-fashioned clothes doing old-fashioned things like watering horses. The plants are still dead and the paint is still faded, but the people are alive.

"I didn't believe you," Dad says. "I thought I was indulging you."

"I know."

"It's amazing. All this . . . for three hundred years."

We walk farther until we come to the castle. My dad's trying to check his BlackBerry when I hear a voice cry, "There he is!"

And another. "Seize him!"

And soon, two meaty hands are clenched around my neck while another guy grabs my arms.

"Hey!" my dad yells. "Hey! What's going on here?"

"This is the villain who has taken my daughter," the king says. "Tell me where she is."

Here we go again. "I don't have her. Please! I came to help you look for her."

"We already went to the cottage on the highest hill. She was not there."

"You went already? You know, it's kind of hard to talk with this gorilla holding my neck. Any chance he could not do that?"

The king gestures to the guard to let go of me, which he does—slowly.

I say, "Did you go to Malvolia's cottage yourself?"

"Of course not. I cannot climb hills. I have henchmen to do that for me."

I look at the henchman. "Hey, aren't you the same guy who was guarding the dungeon the day I escaped?"

The guy nods sheepishly.

"You did a great job then. Is it possible you missed something when you went to the cottage?"

"Nay. Cuthbert here was with me, and he'll tell you there was naught in that cottage. Right, Cuthbert?"

They exchange a look. "Right."

"And you searched the whole cottage, Pleasant?" the king asks.

Pleasant?

"Yes, sire," Pleasant says.

"From top to bottom?"

"Aye," the smaller one, Cuthbert, says.

"Even the cellar?" the king asks.

"Nay, there was no cellar," Pleasant says. "But we looked in all the closets."

"They looked," the king says. "And now there are more men out, visiting every house in Euphrasia. I will leave no stone unturned in the quest for my daughter."

"Then let me go, too. I want to look for Talia. You could send these guys with me."

The two guards don't seem too happy about the idea of going out again, but they can't exactly say that, so they just grunt.

The king looks at me and Travis, obviously seeing two able-bodied guys who can help look for his daughter, and says, "Very well. If there is anything you can do, I will not stop you. I only want to see Talia again. I said . . ." He looks away. "I said horrible things to her. I do not want to go on living if I cannot set them right. And you . . ." He glances at Dad. "You will stay with me, as assurance that they will return."

And so Travis, Cuthbert, Pleasant, and I go to look for Talia.

Chapter 44: Talia

The bodice is finished, and Malvolia's design for the skirt is quite plain. It will be short work. My life may end tomorrow, or tonight. I gaze out the window at the night sky, at the stars which are brighter in Euphrasia than anywhere with electric lights. I try to sew slowly. A tear falls from my eye. I use the strip of silk which I have secreted in my waistband to wipe it away. It is hard to believe I once so wanted a dress like this. Now I shall have it, but at what cost?

"Keep working," Malvolia says.

I sigh, then return the fabric to the waistline of my pants against future tears. I begin to sew the skirt, using even more minuscule stitches.

"I have decided something," Malvolia says after a time.

"What is that?" I say, although I dare not hope she has

decided to let me go.

"I have decided not to kill you. 'Tis not your fault that your father was unjust to me, any more than Baby George's death was my fault. 'Twould be wrong for me to kill you."

"So I may go?" I almost drop my needle from joy. "Thank you!"

"No. It will not do to let you go. But I will give you a chance at life."

"A chance?"

"You almost fulfilled the terms of my curse. You slept three hundred years, and you were awakened by a kiss. But I am less certain than you that 'twas love's first kiss. After all, the young man did not wish to marry you."

"People do not marry at sixteen in the twenty-first century."

"Ah, that is true indeed," Malvolia says. "In this century, everyone thinks they are going to be something called a rock star. But it does make it harder to say, 'They lived happily ever after.' So I have decided on a test."

"A test?"

"Aye. I will finish this dress, for you are the slowest seamstress I have ever encountered."

"I went slowly on purpose, so you would not kill me!"

". . . and after I have finished it, you shall wear it, and I shall prick your finger with a spindle."

"Again?" I am not pleased with this turn of events.

"Again. You will fall asleep, and I will place an enchantment upon you that will surpass Flavia's sickly spell. You will wake only if kissed by a young man who is truly your love, truly your destiny, one who would walk miles and face torturous tests to find you. If he does, you shall be free."

"But . . . but the castle guards were already here. You told them I was not within. How will he even find me?"

"I said it was a difficult test. True love would look a second time. True love would not be thwarted. True love would not accept no for an answer. He would search the world and certainly look again and again in every cottage in Euphrasia until he finds you."

"And if he does not?"

"Then you shall sleep forever."

A second tear falls upon the green skirt. I love Jack. I do. But to rely upon his diligence seems rather a tall order.

"Stop crying on that dress," Malvolia barks. "'Twill stain."

Then she takes it from me and begins to sew.

I sit dumbly a moment, crying, looking at the tree just outside the window. It is a windy day. I go to pull the streamer of fabric from my waistband to dry my tears. I stop.

"Excuse me," I say.

"What now?" the old woman mutters.

"I wonder if I might perhaps go outside."

The old woman laughs. "And escape? 'Tis not likely." She continues her sewing.

"But I thought . . ." I feel the lump of fabric at my waist. "I mean, I know you are a powerful fairy. Surely, there is some spell you could perform to prevent my escaping. It is merely that I wanted to breathe the fresh Euphrasian air before you put me to sleep again. It may be my last chance."

Malvolia chuckles. "Not too confident in your beloved, then?"

I shrug. "I am. But you have set a difficult task for him."

She thinks upon it a moment. "Very well. I suppose there is no harm in it. But if you venture beyond that stand of pines, 'twill be the last thing you do."

I nod, looking at the chestnut tree, which is closer. "I only wish to feel the wind in my lungs."

Then, before she can protest further, I stand and walk toward the door, hoping she will not see the bulge from the streamer of fabric in my waistband.

Chapter 45: Jack

I've been to more cottages than I ever wanted to see in my life. Weird thing about being in a place with no mass communication—where I come from, if a celebrity gets photographed getting into a car with no underwear, everyone in the world knows about it in fifteen minutes. But here, people don't know really basic stuff like:

1. The princess is missing;
2. They've been asleep for three hundred years;
3. It's now the twenty-first century.

So we have to keep explaining it to them over and over. We must have walked twenty miles. The sun is setting, and there's no sign of Talia.

The road sort of dead-ends into a hill.

"We should go back," Pleasant says. "We can look more tomorrow."

"We can look more today," I say.

"Nay," Cuthbert says. "There are no houses near here. 'Twill take us an hour to reach one."

"What about that one?" Travis points to a lone cottage at the top of the hill.

"We were already there. That was the first one we looked in," Pleasant says.

"That's the cottage on the highest hill?" I say. I feel a chill wind whip across my chest.

"Aye. We had to climb all that way on a fool's errand."

I stare up at the cottage. Everything around it looks overgrown, even more overgrown than the rest of Euphrasia. My feet hurt, and I want to stop walking as much as the next guy. Maybe Talia was wrong about the cottage. After all, it was just a dream she had. Maybe she's not even in Euphrasia. Maybe I'll never see her again.

"Okay." I start to walk away, trying not to think too hard about what walking away means, that I'm giving up. No, I'm not giving up. We'll look more tomorrow. I glance back at the cottage one last time. The trees are blowing back and forth, almost like a hurricane.

Something catches my eye, something in the tall chestnut tree not far from the cottage door.

I nudge Travis. "Do you see that?"

"What?"

"Look," I say, "in that big tree."

I remember Talia's description of the old lady with the roomful of green dresses. *There was a lady, an old woman.*

It was she who brought the green dresses.

The color of her eyes.

Finally, Travis looks.

"Do you see it?" I say.

He nods. "But that doesn't mean . . . It's just a ratty old piece of . . ."

"It means something. We have to go up there."

Chapter 46: Talia

Malvolia sews with alarming speed. But after all, she is a fairy—or a witch, depending upon whom you ask. Within two hours, the skirt is finished and attached to the bodice.

"Put it on," she says.

Must I? But I do not say it, for I know I must. I know Malvolia believes she is doing me a favor by not killing me, a favor in the name of true love, so to doubt that Jack will come for me would be to say that our love is not strong enough to warrant the chance she is giving me.

It is strong enough. My doubt is founded merely upon Jack's immaturity. I know Jack loves me, but he is young and not always serious, prone to mistakes. In his own words, a screwup. So while I know down to my fingertips that he loves me, I am not so confident in his ability to thwart Malvolia . . . or my father.

And still, because I cannot say this, I try on the dress.

It is beautiful. If I must sleep another three hundred years, at least I shall be a vision of loveliness.

"Thank you," I say, "for giving me this chance."

"You do not wish it, I can tell."

"That is not true. I am very grateful to you. If—when— my beloved wakes me, I will speak to my father about you, to persuade him to forgive you."

"That is kind. I know you fear your young man will not find you. But if he loves you, he will."

I nod.

"And who would not love you, Princess? Even I, mad for revenge could not bring myself to kill you. You are well past the insolent brat I met three hundred years ago. You think of others besides yourself: your parents, Jack, even me."

I nod again.

"And now, my dear, I must ask you to lie down." She leads me to my little feather bed in the corner. I glance out the window at the chestnut tree.

"What will you do to me?" I say. "Will it hurt?"

"Nay." She looks off as if to something in the distance. "It will be just like last time you slept, only this time I suspect it will not be for three hundred years. Now, we must make haste."

337

At that, she pulls a spindle from behind her back. "Make a wish." Her voice is hypnotic. "Then touch the spindle."

I wish that Jack's love will be strong enough. . . .

"Touch it, my dear. . . ."

Chapter 47: Jack

We've been climbing the hill for an hour, and the cottage looks no closer than before. In fact, it looks farther away. The wind is pushing against us at every step, and Pleasant isn't being very pleasant about it. Neither is Travis.

"I want ale!" Pleasant whines. "We have already been to this cottage!"

"I bet they're serving dinner at the castle right now," says Travis. "And it's not like we can just go to a drive-thru or something if we miss it."

I glare at him, and he says, "I'm just saying . . ."

"Don't just say," I tell him. But it's getting dark, and soon we won't be able to see to walk.

"Hey," Travis says. "Would you look at that?"

"What?" I say.

"I spit my gum out by an oak tree before. There it is."
He points at the tree.

"What do you mean? You spit your gum out just now?"

He shakes his head. "Like, twenty minutes ago. I spit it out, and now it's there. It's like we've been going in a circle."

I look. He's right. There's a piece of green gum.

"It's probably someone else's gum."

"Are you kidding? They don't even *have* gum in this place. That's *my* gum. We've been here before."

"But that's impossible. We can't be going in a circle. We've been walking uphill." But a lot of things do look familiar, like that funny rock over there that's shaped like a wedge of cheese.

Travis shrugs. "Weird, right?"

I look up at the cottage. It's stone, like Talia said, and at the top of the hill. And still as far away as ever. I shiver in another gust of wind.

"We have to keep walking," I say.

After another five minutes, it's almost completely dark. I hear Travis's stomach growl.

"I am going back," Cuthbert says. "There's no way we shall reach it tonight. Look." He gestures down the hill.

I look. We're near the bottom, as if we've been sliding backward. Has someone placed a spell on this hill? Not impossible, not here. But if someone has, that someone must be Malvolia. That would mean I'm on the right track, that Talia's here.

I look up at the top of the hill, at the cottage so far away. A light burns in one of the windows. Is Talia there? I remember what I saw in the chestnut tree. She is.

I make a decision. I turn to Pleasant, Cuthbert, and Travis. "Look, guys, why don't you go back to the castle and have dinner?"

That's all Pleasant and Cuthbert have to hear. They say their good-byes and go. Travis tries to protest. "Bud, if you want me to stay . . ."

"I don't. I have a feeling this is something I need to do myself. All by myself."

"Well, if you're sure . . ." I can tell he's dying to leave.

"I'm sure," I say.

"Okay." He turns and walks away before I can change my mind.

I keep going up the hill. The sun is down now, and the moon is barely a sliver. The only light is the light in the window of the cottage. I can see someone moving inside. Is it Talia?

I pass the wedge-shaped rock again.

"Are you messing with me?" I yell up toward the cottage.

No answer but the wind in the trees. It's not that late. My body is still on Miami time, so it's really not. But I'm hungry and tired from walking so far. I look at my watch. I've been walking uphill for four hours, wearing sneakers, getting nowhere.

An hour more. Then another in the pitch darkness. I can't see where I'm walking, but once, I feel something sticky on the bottom of my shoe. Travis's gum. I look up at the cottage, still so far away. This is the hardest I've ever worked, the most exhausted I've ever been. But still, I keep walking against the wind.

If Talia's not here, then where is she? Did she run away in Miami because she didn't want to go home? Could she be on the street somewhere? Could she be dead?

An hour later, I pass the same wedge-shaped rock. But something is different. By the dim light of the skinny moon, I can make out a shape lying beside it. I walk closer and reach out to touch it.

It's a blanket and a pillow. There's something attached to the blanket: a piece of paper. I take out my cell phone to use as a light.

Sleep, it says.

Although I want to resist, I can't. I fall down almost like I'm fainting and go quickly to sleep.

But I don't sleep well. I have this strange dream where I'm playing *Jeopardy*, and the host is this weird old woman in black. I know from Talia's description that it's Malvolia. We're on Final Jeopardy, and the category is "Princess Talia."

The old woman reads the question.

"What was the name of Talia's art teacher?"

I look at her. "What if I don't remember?"

She fixes me with a dark stare. "True love would remember."

The other contestants, Pleasant and Cuthbert, are already writing. The *Jeopardy* music begins to play. When it's almost over, I suddenly remember Meryl showing me the Wikipedia article yesterday.

I write, *Carlo Maratti.*

I wake with a start before I can find out if I got it right, if I won the game.

The sun has risen, and maybe it's getting in my eyes, because now it looks like I'm a quarter of the way up the hill.

How did I get there? Did Malvolia really appear to me in my dream, the way she did to Talia? Did she ask me that question, and did I move closer because I got it right?

Beside me is a loaf of bread, a wedge of cheese, an apple, and a jug of water. Although it grosses me out to eat something that just appeared on the ground, I have no choice. I'm too hungry. I eat some of the bread and cheese, drink the water, and save the rest for later. I don't take the blanket or pillow with me. They're too heavy, and I hope not to need them. I begin to walk. As soon as I start, the wind, which had been silent, begins to howl again.

It's just like yesterday, except now I'm closer to the cottage. It looks like a normal cottage, like every other cottage in Euphrasia. What if it's just a mirage? I'm clearly hallucinating.

But the fullness in my stomach tells me I didn't imagine the bread and cheese. I keep walking. I don't see the gum or the wedge-shaped rock. Instead, there's a line of bushes that looks like a dinosaur and a clump of blue flowers. I see them over and over, like I'm on a treadmill.

Again, at the end of the day, it gets dark. Again, I find the blanket and pillow. Again, I sleep.

This time, I'm playing *Who Wants to Be a Millionaire*. I'm on the million-dollar question, and it's multiple-choice.

"What is Princess Talia's fondest wish?" Malvolia reads. "A—to fall in love? B—to travel? C—to be a great queen? D—to please her father."

They all seem like pretty good answers. She wants all those things. "I can't decide."

"Then you will fail." Malvolia looks a lot happier about that than the host of *Millionaire* usually does. "Of course, you could take the prize you have already earned."

"What's that?" I ask.

"A first-class ticket back to Miami . . . with your father questioning why you wasted his time in this manner!"

I groan. "Hey, wait!" I try to remember when I watched this game. What were the rules? "Do I have any lifelines left?" I ask Malvolia.

She looks annoyed. "You can phone a friend."

Phone a friend. Phone a friend. But who would I call? Travis is here in Euphrasia, and my other friends don't even know Talia.

Then I have an inspiration. "Can I call Talia?"

Malvolia sighs. "She is on your list."

I hear the sound of a ringing phone, then Talia answers.

Thank God she remembered how to answer the phone. But where would she get a phone?

Oh, yeah. Dream.

"Hello?"

"Thirty seconds," Malvolia says.

"Hey, Talia, I'm trying to get up this hill to save you, and I need to know: What's your fondest wish? A—to fall in love? B—to travel? C—to be a great queen? D—to please your father?"

Talia laughs. "Oh, silly, you know the answer to that one."

"No, I don't. That's why I called you."

"But you do. I told you about it, remember?"

"No. No! Just tell me!" She's maddening. But that's Talia.

"When we went to get the passport, Jack. Think."

The buzzer rings, and Malvolia says, "Time's up. What is your answer?"

And suddenly I remember Talia, that day at the passport guy's place. She was so excited about the airplane. She clapped her hands and said, "It is my fondest wish to travel!"

So that's what I tell Malvolia. B. Final answer.

Again, I wake before I can find out if I got the question right, if I won the million dollars. Again, I look around and find that I have moved up the hill. Now I'm at the halfway point. There's food and water. I eat and drink. I wonder if it's even worth it to walk uphill, since by now I'm pretty sure that my getting there is more tied to answering questions in my dreams. But I have a feeling Malvolia wants me to walk. I'm tired and have muscle aches where I didn't even know I had muscles. I need some Bengay bad.

But I walk. Everything swims in my head and I wonder what I'll be asked next. I can barely concentrate for it. Still, I push uphill, against the wind.

When I collapse on the blanket for the third time, I dream that I'm playing Trivial Pursuit with Malvolia. We're sitting in my parents' house, and I'm looking across the game board at her. We both have all the wedges, and I'm in the center of the board. Malvolia reads from her card.

"What is Princess Talia's full name?"

"Full name? She had seven or eight of them!"

Malvolia holds up her hands. "'Tis difficult to win. Oh, and you must recite them in the correct order."

"Wait a second," I say. "I used to play this game with Meryl all the time. This isn't how it works. I get to *choose* the category for the final question."

Malvolia shrugs. "All right, then. Choose."

"I want a sports question."

She chuckles. "There is no sports category in this version of the game."

"So it's like, what, the Silver Screen edition?"

She hands me the box.

I read, *Trivial Pursuit: Insanely Difficult Edition.*

I look at the instructions for the list of categories:

Yellow—Neolithic Civilizations

Green—Theoretical Physics
Pink—Twelve-tone Composers
Blue—Sino-Tibetan Languages
Brown—The Norse Saga in Literature
Orange—Princess Talia

"Uh-huh," I say.

Malvolia drums her fingers on the table. Her nails are long and purple. "Which category do you wish to try, then?"

"These are impossible."

"Not if you are smart."

Well, that kills it. "I'll take the Princess Talia question. Just give me a minute."

"Very well."

She continues drumming her fingers on the table. I glare at her, and she stops but begins to whistle the *Jeopardy* theme song, like Meryl used to do when I was trying to think of the answers. I put my hands over my ears.

Talia Aurora. I remember Aurora for her grandmother. Then, there were three kings' names, in alphabetical order. What were they?

"I'm gonna wi-in," Malvolia chants.

"No, you're not," I snap.

"I think I am."

I put my fingers *in* my ears and begin to hum. *Talia Aurora Augusta* . . . Three kings, then three queens.

"There is a time limit for this," Malvolia says, loudly enough to be heard even with my ears stopped up.

"No, there isn't."

"Yes, there is." She sounds exactly like Meryl.

I throw the rules at her. "Find it, then."

"You lose points for your rudeness."

"I'd be able to think better if you'd be quiet."

She is, for a second while she examines the rules, and in that time, I hear Talia's voice.

"Talia Aurora," I repeat after her. "Augusta Ludwiga Wilhelmina Agnes Marie Rose . . . of Euphrasia."

In an instant I am awake and three quarters of the way up the hill. There is no food beside me this time, and the wind howls louder than ever before. Is Malvolia angry that I got the hard question right? It doesn't matter. I'm almost there, and I need to keep going.

This time, when I walk, I do get closer to the cottage. I see the distance closing, and I can examine everything more carefully. It's just an ordinary cottage made of stone, with a thatched roof and big windows in the attic. Shouldn't it be a dark castle like in *The Wizard of Oz* or maybe guarded by a three-headed dog like in *Harry Potter*? But it's special, for now I know for sure that Talia's inside.

Chapter 48: Jack

I reach the top of the hill, the cottage door. A chill wind howls across me. The door flies open.

But how could it be open? It's too easy.

I walk inside. There's no Talia. No Talia. Instead, there's only Malvolia, Malvolia in the flesh. I've never seen her, but I recognize her from her piercing, black eyes.

"Where's Talia?" I say.

The old woman shakes her head. "She's here, if you can get to her."

"Get to her? I got past your never-ending hill. I answered your questions."

She chuckles. "Mere trivia. To be worthy of a princess, one must face a dragon."

"A dragon? I can't . . ." I picture getting fried by a dragon. But then I think about it. I couldn't answer any of those questions, either, and yet I did. I wouldn't have thought I'd be able to walk uphill for three days, but I did. I was motivated, maybe for the first time in my life. So if I have to slay a dragon, maybe I can do that, too.

"Do I at least get a sword?" I say.

"'Tis not that kind of dragon," she replies.

"Then what . . . ?"

She moves aside to reveal a part of the room I hadn't seen. It's a sort of office setup with a desk and chair. In the chair sits my dad. He has a stack of paper about three feet high in front of him and another, marked URGENT, to the side.

"Can this wait, Jack?" He gestures toward his work. "I'm a little busy."

"I didn't . . . I came to find the princess. You know that."

"To be worthy of a princess, you must face your dragon," Malvolia says. "Your greatest fear." She gestures toward my hands. I look down and see that I'm holding the notebook where I've been drawing my garden design. I glance at Dad, then at Malvolia. "You mean I have to show it to him?"

Malvolia nods. "Your greatest fear."

Outside, the wind whistles through the trees. I take one step toward the desk. Then another. "Dad? I have to tell you something."

Dad tears his eyes away from his work. "What is it?" He looks back at his papers. His phone and his cell phone both start ringing at the same time.

But I hold out the book. "I . . . it's just something I've been fooling around with."

Malvolia clears her throat, and when I turn, I see her disapproval.

"No, that's wrong," I say. "I've been working on this. It's a design. My design for a garden."

My dad opens it. For a long moment, I can only hear the pages and the wind outside. I can't look at Dad, so I look out the window at the chestnut tree, the one I saw before with the streamer of green fabric blowing at the top. I'm sure now that Talia is here. She climbed the tree, like I taught her, and tied the green fabric to the branch, so I would see it, so I would come rescue her.

"So?" Dad says.

"So I want to do this," I say, "to do landscape design. I'm good at it."

Dad rolls his eyes. "You think so?"

I can tell he doesn't, but I say, "Yeah, I do."

And then the dragon does the thing I most feared. He doesn't breathe fire. He laughs. Uproariously, as if he's never heard anything more hilarious in his life. There are tears running down his face, and between gales of laughter, he says, "You, a landscape designer? You!"

"What's wrong with it?" I fight the urge to stomp my foot. I'm reverting to infancy around my dad, but I know I have to hold my ground.

Dad clutches his sides to contain his hilarity. "I pay a guy fifty bucks a month who has more talent than you!" He holds out some brochures for business schools, brochures that seem to have materialized in a third big pile on his desk. "Here's what you need, an education, a degree from a good school—I'll pay someone off to make sure you get in and get through. And then, after that, I can get you a job."

"You'll get me a job? Why?"

"Haven't you noticed, Jack? You're a loser, a slacker. You've never succeeded in anything in your life, no matter how much we do for you. We have some hope for Meryl, but the only way you won't be a complete embarrassment to your mother and me is if you let us control every aspect of your life."

"That's . . ." I feel wet heat behind my eyes, and I try to control it. I have to stay calm. "That's not true."

"Loser. Party boy. You couldn't even get Amber to stay with you."

"Amber?" This is so out of left field I don't comprehend his words for a second. "I don't even want Amber."

"But you see, that's what you do. Whenever anything gets difficult for you, you walk away, you give up. You couldn't keep Amber, so now you want this girl. When you fail to save her and she dies, you'll decide you didn't like her, either. That's just your way. You've never been serious about anything in your life. You're a screwup."

I can barely see his face through the clouds of anger inside me. How dare he say that about Talia? How dare he even compare her to Amber? "That isn't true. I love

Talia. I'm serious about her."

Dad starts to laugh again, so hard I have to raise my voice to be heard over him.

"And I'm serious about this, too, about landscape design. This is what I'm going to do with my life. If I go to college, that's what I'm going for."

Dad stops laughing, and I think he's finally hearing me. "Listen to me, Jack. If you're serious, I'm going to get serious with you. To make it in a field like landscape design, you have to have talent. And the fact is, you don't." He reaches for my drawing, which is under a pile of B-school pamphlets. "This isn't any good. It sucks."

"It . . ." I stop. "What?"

"It sucks."

Sucks? Dad would never say *sucks.*

And that's when I realize this isn't the real Dad. He's just a fake thing, a test Malvolia came up with, like all the game shows. In fact, maybe this Dad is all in my head, my worst fears of Dad. In which case, the way to pass the test is by standing up to him. I take a deep breath.

"I'm sorry you think my design sucks . . . Dad. But that's what I'm planning on doing with my life. And the other thing I'm planning on doing is rescuing Talia. So if you could please get out of my way, I'd really appreciate it."

"You can't speak that way to me. You can't show such disrespect." He's tearing out what little hair he has with one hand while pushing papers to the floor with the other.

"I know you don't really feel that way. You came all the way to Euphrasia. You wouldn't have done that if you thought I was just a stupid slacker. And when I see the real you, I'll be sure and show you my designs. I'm excited about them, and I bet you'll like them, too. But now . . ."

I gesture toward him, and he vanishes into thin air. I was right.

I look at Malvolia, who is still there. "Did I do it? Did I pass the test?"

She gestures toward something in the corner. "Only one more."

And then I see her. There, on a mattress on the floor, is Talia. Or, at least, Talia's body. Is she dead? Or just sleeping? I rush to kneel beside her. I take her hand. There's a pulse.

She stirs slightly. She's breathing.

I shake her. Call her name. Nothing.

But then I know what I have to do. I don't know if my kiss will be enough, if she loves me enough, too, but I need to try. I lean over and think about Talia, about meeting her, being in Europe with her, then in America, how she was with Meryl, my parents, how she actually cared about the stuff I cared about and didn't think it was stupid. How I loved her. I love her.

"I love you, Talia," I whisper.

I put my lips to hers.

She stirs.

She wakes.

"You are here!" Talia says. She looks around the room. "But how long have I slept? A year? Or twenty? Are you an old man? Let me see your face."

I laugh. "It took me three days to climb the hill."

"Days? Merely days? But where . . . ?" She glances around. "Where is Malvolia?"

I look behind me. Sure enough, she's gone. "She left."

"Oh, no," Talia says. "But she was kind to me. She showed me how to make this dress."

"It's beautiful. You're beautiful."

I hold my hand out to Talia. I want to touch her and not stop touching her, to prove to myself that she's real and alive and here. "I think we have to go."

"In a moment." She pulls me toward her and kisses me a bunch more times, on my cheeks, my hair, even my eyes. I throw my arms around her and hold her a really long time until finally the cottage door starts banging with the wind, and the noise reminds me that everyone's waiting for us, Talia's parents and the people in the castle. And Dad, too.

"We should go," I say.

She nods and allows me to help her up. With a final glance around the room, we leave, closing the door behind us.

As we descend the hill, she says, "Do you know what I was thinking, Jack?"

"What?" I stop to kiss her again. I rescued this princess, so I should be able to kiss her all I want, as long as she wants to, too. The wind, which had been roaring in our ears, has stopped.

Afterward, she says, "I think you were my true love all the time. That must be why I woke. Malvolia was wrong."

"You think?"

"Yes, but she had her reasons. I wish I knew where she went. Perhaps if we come back another day . . ." She gestures uphill at the cottage, then gasps.

I look at what she's looking at but see nothing. The cottage is gone.

"Well, that's the end of that," I say. "Hey, maybe we can walk a little faster? I'm hungry, and like I said, it took me three days to walk up here."

"Yes," Talia says. "And I need to see Father. We must talk."

She starts to run, and because we're holding hands, I run, too. We run down the hill so fast it feels like we're flying.

Chapter 49: Talia

When we reach the castle grounds, I clutch Jack's hand.

"What's wrong?" he says.

"I am frightened."

"Of what?"

"Of what? Let us see . . . Father was already angry at me a week ago for destroying his kingdom. Now add to that the offense of running away, getting on an airplane, leaving the country, losing my jewels—"

"Oh, I forgot to tell you, Meryl found the jewels. I brought them with me."

"All right. Not the jewels. But nonetheless . . . *and* the offense of falling in love with a commoner." I gaze up at him. "Not that *that* is an offense to me, my dearest."

He rolls his eyes. "Of course not."

"But Father may possibly disagree with me."

"Understood. He's been in a bad mood."

"So do I not have reason to be frightened?"

But at that moment, the castle door is thrown open and a mob descends—not only people, although every scullery maid, cook, lady-in-waiting, groom, and guard is there, but also animals, the palace dogs and cats and chickens and cows and horses, and even the five fairies, Flavia, Celia, Violet, Leila, and Xanthe, all pour forth from the castle door to see me, to greet me, their beloved princess.

At the head of the group are Father and Mother. I drop Jack's hand—he will forgive me—and run screaming into their arms.

"You are not angry at me, Father?" I ask as soon as I can easily breathe under his embrace.

"No, no, my dearest."

Mother says, "Your father lost his temper, dear. But now, he realizes you could not have helped what happened. You were dealing, after all, with the forces of evil."

I remember Malvolia's story of the baby, and I know I should protest. But on the other hand, Malvolia is gone, and Mother and Father have stopped being angry at me. There will be time to straighten out that matter in the future. And I *will* straighten it out.

"I am so glad to be home!" I say, and we hug some more.

Behind me, I hear a tiny voice—Flavia's voice—saying, "He was her true love after all!"

"Besides," Father says, "I believe we have it all settled now, how Euphrasia will survive in the twenty-first century."

"You have?" I say.

"Yes. Perhaps we should discuss it over breakfast."

We adjourn into the castle. The dining table is laid for a small group, a dozen or so, and Mother is all smiles. "Did you know," she says, "that they have something called a truck now, which moves so quickly that it is possible to bring in food and other necessities from Belgium and even France?"

I beam. I did know that. I move closer to Jack, for it has occurred to me that—true love or not—we may not be long in each other's company. He must go back to America, for school, and I will stay in Euphrasia with Father and Mother. But we are together now, and I shall make the most of it.

"Evan." My father turns to Jack's father. "Tell them about Royal Euphrasia."

"What's Royal Euphrasia?" Jack and I both say together.

"Well, it's an idea King Louis and I had, a joint venture between the Euphrasian government and my company. King Louis was concerned that now that Euphrasia is visible again—now that the hedge is gone—the kingdom might be vulnerable to some sort of outside takeover. King Louis might be overthrown. He did not want that, so we had to think of a way in which Euphrasia could support itself."

"Support itself?" I think of the world I have seen, a world of airplanes and computers, photographs and televisions. How can Euphrasia possibly compete?

But Jack's father continues. "See, when the kids were little, my wife and I liked to go to these tourist attractions—Colonial Williamsburg, Medieval Times . . . remember, Jack?"

Jack nods. "That was fun."

"So when I saw this place, I thought what a great idea it would be to develop Euphrasia as a tourist attraction. It would be just like Williamsburg, only real, with real people from the seventeenth century, and maybe we could open some cute little hotels where people could actually *live* like they did in your time."

"With no toilets?" Jack says.

"I have to admit, I really do like toilets," I say, although I am ready to say I like anything at all if it will make Father happy. "Perhaps we could have *some* toilets."

"But you see, Talia," Father says, "in this way, the people of Euphrasia could continue to live as they are accustomed. And I would be able to continue being a king, and you a princess. The curse caused the world to forget us. But once they find out that we are here, that we are back again, there may be a movement to change things."

I nod. I remember seeing Euphrasia from the airplane. It was small, but it was there.

"Of course, we'd need to do some painting and repairs before we could open," Mr. O'Neill says, "and maybe get some better costumes for people."

"But what they are wearing is authentic," I say.

"Oh, I know," Mother says. "But Mr. O'Neill explained that there is authentic and there is *authentic*. People want things to be more colorful, and not have the townspeople running about looking like mushrooms."

And in a second, I think, *I could sew the clothes. Would they allow me to sew?*

"And we'd need to do some better landscaping, too," Mr. O'Neill says. "I've just found this design my son has been working on."

I hear Jack draw in a breath. "You found that?"

I draw my breath, too. Jack told me, on the way back, how he showed his landscape design to the dragon father Malvolia created. He told me that, in this vision, his father laughed at him, ridiculed him. I pray he will be strong. I dearly hope his father will not hurt him.

"So . . ." Jack kicks the ground with his shoe, not making eye contact with his father. "Do you like it?"

Please let him like it.

His father nods, smiling. "It was the inspiration for all of this. Once we found this, it helped us to visualize, and that's how the whole plan got started. You have talent, Jack. You can work with the landscape designers to help us achieve a really great look for Royal Euphrasia."

"But . . ." Jack stammers. "But I thought you wanted me to go to business school."

"That was before I saw what a talent you had for this.

Your mother and I hadn't realized you had an interest in landscape design. For a while, we worried you weren't interested in anything. But now . . ."

It is as Meryl said. Jack's parents were worried about him, as mine were about me.

"Jack has a talent for gardening," I say, "a great affinity for the land."

Jack's father nods. "You can help us with Royal Euphrasia in the summers."

"Really? I could stay here and work on it?" Jack asks.

"Well, for the rest of the summer . . . and then you could come over for Christmas break and spring break and, of course, college."

I know how Jack detests talk of college, but now he says, "Yeah, that'd be cool. I could go to college in Europe and maybe major in landscape design." He glances at his father, whose face is inscrutable. "I could minor in business, so I'll be able to help you with this."

"But you'd better get your grades up, if you want to be able to do that," his father says. "And maybe take French."

"That'll be easy," Jack says. "With my girlfriend over here, and me over there, I'll have lots of time to study."

"So you approve of Jack . . . Jack and me?" I say to Father.

Father laughs. "Of course I do. Clearly, he was your destiny. And he and his father are saving . . . how would you say it, Travis?" He looks at him. ". . . our Euphrasian behinds."

I gaze into Jack's eyes. I would like to kiss him again, but that would be impossible, with our fathers here. Still, I move toward him and grasp his hand.

I hadn't noticed Travis before, but now he interrupts. "Hey, can I be in charge of food? Maybe we could open the first Euphrasian hot-dog stand."

I clap my hands. "Yes! I love hot dogs! Can you make them, then?"

We all laugh, and I know it will be all right. It is finally all right.

Two Years Later

Talia

"Are you ready?" Jack asks.

I survey his attire. He is not dressed exactly as he was when first we met. I know all too well what marketing people are now, and they and Jack's father had their ideas about the costume. So instead of swim trunks under his jeans, Jack wears artfully "destroyed" blue jeans, and the flag T-shirt is replaced by a clean, plain one. I chose white, the better to show off his tanned good looks. He is still as handsome as he was that day.

"As ever, my love," I say, adjusting my green gown. "But there is a little time, is there not? Might we look out the window?"

"We might." Jack offers his hand, and we walk to the window. It is three stories up, and below, where the moat once was, a lengthy queue has formed within velvet ropes.

There are so many little girls in line. Some wear crowns, and others are even dressed like me, in satiny green gowns which cost many Euros! To one side, a woman circulates, selling spindle-shaped holders covered in pink and blue spun sugar candy. Several fairies flutter around in the trees, watching at a safe distance from the crowd.

"All to see us?" I ask Jack.

"I told you, this stuff's really popular. At Disney, they reenact the Sword and the Stone every day."

I well know it. Last summer, Jack and I went on a tour of all the Disneys (Florida, California, Paris, and Tokyo) as well as Colonial Williamsburg and Plimoth Plantation, in preparation for the opening of Royal Euphrasia. I know all about tourist attractions and lines of people. Indeed, we had to relocate the scene of Jack's and my first kiss from the tower room to a larger venue (formed by knocking out several walls between the guest bedrooms and adding a grandstand of seats), the better to accommodate the crowds.

"Why do you suppose they are all here?" I ask.

"They want magic in their lives, I guess," Jack says.

"Magic like we have?" I look into his eyes.

"It will be even bigger, once the movie comes out," Jack says.

"Yes, but we will not be here then."

It is true. Come fall, Jack will be off to England to study Landscape Architecture in Manchester, while I will be in Paris, studying fashion. It is my aim to design elegant clothing for young ladies—clothing to make them feel like princesses and not show their bellies. Actors will play the parts of Jack and Talia at Royal Euphrasia after we leave. But for now, and every summer and winter break hereafter, Jack and I will meet in Euphrasia. And someday, we may live here together in the castle. When it was remodeled, many of the rooms were blocked off so that Mother, Father, Jack, and I, and even our future children, might have a place to stay.

But first, there shall be adventure. And travel. And when I return to Euphrasia, it will be because I wish to settle down, not because I have to.

"Dear Jack," I say, "it has all worked out so perfectly!"

He sweeps me into his arms for a kiss, a lengthy one that makes me forget everything that has come before it, and indeed, all the people outside. It continues until we are interrupted by the clearing of an elderly throat.

"Ahem. Perhaps you should save that for your audience."

It is Malvolia. Jack and I pull apart from each other . . . guiltily.

"The christening scene went well, then?" I ask her.

"Indeed." She rubs her hands together. "I had those wee ones more scared of me than they would be of any roller coaster." She smiles.

"You are, indeed, quite frightening," I say.

I spoke with Father about Malvolia. It was a good deal of work to persuade him that he might have been wrong in exiling her. But I pointed out that Lady Brooke had been none too careful in watching me that fateful day. When he sent for Lady Brooke to discuss the allegation that she had lied about Prince George, it was found that she had disappeared from Euphrasia entirely. Grudgingly, thereafter, Father agreed reluctantly that a fairy dressmaker might be of some use in the castle, on a probationary basis, since there were no children about for her to harm. The other fairies helped us to search for her within her realm. Once she heard of the possibility of forgiveness, she allowed herself to be found. She proved such a godsend that he has allowed her to continue on, playing herself in the daily shows. In rehearsals, when she disappeared into a puff of smoke, the assembled onlookers were amazed at the special effect. They searched far and wide and could find no trapdoor. I expect she shall long be with us.

Now, she begins to laugh and does her trick again. In an instant, she is gone.

Travis appears at the door. "Are we ready?" he asks.

I can hear the sound of many feet trooping up the castle steps. I take my place on a pretty velvet sofa under a frieze of flowers designed and drawn by Meryl after the original tapestries were destroyed in the remodeling. I commence to feign sleep. I can hear the audience filling in their seats. A Royal Euphrasia employee welcomes them to the show. Then, Jack and Travis enter stage right.

"Wow, she's hot," Travis says.

"I know," Jack says, and I can feel him leaning closer to

me. "But she's asleep, like the rest of them."

They go through a bit of scripted dialogue, Travis trying to persuade Jack to kiss me, Jack resisting. Finally, Jack says, "Look, I want to kiss her, but not in front of you. Why don't you go downstairs and look around? The princess and I need some time alone."

Travis leaves, and Jack leans even closer. He kisses me. I rise from my sleep.

It is magic! The audience applauds, and we are on our way to happily ever after. Again.

Ever wonder what it was like for the Beast?

Read an excerpt from

BEASTLY

also by ALEX FLINN

I had planned on picking Sloane up in the limo, giving her the corsage, and then reaping the benefits of all that advance planning by at least making out with her in the limo. After all, my dad had spent big, and it was supposed to be the most important night of my life. Being a prince had to be good for something.

That's not how it went down.

First off, Sloane practically burst a vein when she saw the corsage. Or she would've, if there was any room for any bursting in that tight dress she had on.

"What are you, blind?" she demanded, her already toned arm muscles sticking out more from clenching her fists. "I said my dress was black. This totally clashes."

"It's white."

"It's *off*-white. Duh."

I didn't see how off-white could clash. But hotness had its privileges.

"Look," I said. "The stupid maid screwed up. It's not my fault."

"The *maid*? You didn't even care enough to go buy it yourself?"

"Who buys things themselves? I'll get you flowers another time." I held out the corsage box. "It's pretty."

"Pretty cheap." She knocked it from my hand. "It's not what I asked for."

I stared at the corsage box on the floor. I wanted to just leave. But at that moment, Sloane's mom showed up with all the latest technology necessary to take both still and action photos of Sloane on my left side, Sloane on my right side, Sloane slightly in front of me. The camera was recording and Ms. Hagen, who was single and who probably wouldn't have minded an intro to my dad, was cooing, "Here's the future prince and princess." So I did what the son of Rob Kingsbury would do. I kicked the cheapo corsage aside and smiled nice for the camera, saying all the right things about how beautiful Sloane looked, how great the dance would be, blah, blah, blah.

And then, for some reason, I picked the corsage off the

floor. Another petal had fallen, and I put it in my pocket with the first one. I took the box with me.

The dance was at the Plaza. When we got there, I handed my tickets to the girl who was checking them. She looked at the corsage.

"Pretty flower," she said.

I looked at her to see if she was kidding. She wasn't. She was probably in my classes, a sort of mousy-looking girl with a red braid and freckles. She didn't look like she belonged at the Plaza. She must have been a scholarship student because they made them do all the grunt work like taking tickets. Obviously, no one had asked her to the dance, or ever bought her flowers, not even a cheap, broken rose. I glanced at Sloane, who was having a joyous reunion with fifty close friends she hadn't seen since yesterday, since all the girls blew off school the day of the dance to get pedicures and spa treatments. Sloane had spent most of the ride griping about the corsage—not exactly what I'd planned—and she'd still refused to wear it.

"Hey, you want it?" I said to the girl.

"That's not nice," she said.

"What?" I tried to remember if I'd ever picked on her. Nah. She wasn't ugly enough to tease, just a total zero, not worth my time.

"Goofing on me, pretending you're going to give it to me, then taking it back."

"I wasn't pretending. You can have it." It was so weird that she even cared about a stupid rose. "It's not the right color for my girlfriend's dress or something, so she won't wear it. It's just going to die, so you might as well take it." I held it out to her.

"Well, since you put it that way . . ." She smiled, taking it from me. I tried not to notice her crooked teeth. Why didn't she just get braces? "Thanks. It's beautiful."

"Hey, enjoy it."

I walked away sort of smiling. Why had I done that? I for sure wasn't in the habit of doing favors for uglies. I wondered if all poor people got that excited over stupid little things like that. I couldn't remember the last time I was excited about anything. Anyway, it was fun, knowing Sloane would eventually stop whining and want the rose, and I'd be able to say I didn't have it.

I looked around for Kendra. I'd almost forgotten about Kendra, but my timing was, as usual, perfect because there she was, slinking into the front entrance. She wore a black and purple dress that looked like a costume for *Harry Potter Goes to the Prom* and she was looking for me.

"Hey, where's your ticket?" one of the ticket-taking drones said to her.

"Oh . . . I don't have . . . I was looking for someone."

I saw a flash of pity on the ticket taker's face, like she knew exactly what was going down, loser to loser. But she said, "Sorry. I can't let you in without a ticket."

"I'm waiting for my date."

Another pitying look. "Okay," the volunteer said. "Just stand back a little."

"Fine."

I went to Sloane. I pointed at where Kendra was loserishly standing. "Showtime." That was when Kendra spotted me.

Sloane knew just what to do. Even though she was pissed at me, she was the type who'd never miss the opportunity to cause another girl permanent emotional damage. She grabbed me and planted a big kiss on my lips. "I love you, Kyle."

Sweet. I kissed her again, not repeating what she'd said.

When we finished, Kendra was staring at us. I walked over to her.

"What are you looking at, Ugly?"

I expected her to cry then. It was fun to kick the nerds, make them cry, then kick them some more. I'd been looking forward to this night for a while. It almost made up for the corsage crap.

But instead she said, "You really did it."

"Did what?" I said.

"Look at her." Sloane giggled. "She's all dressed up in that ugly dress. It makes her look even fatter."

"Yeah, where'd you find that?" I said. "A trash heap?"

"It was my grandmother's," Kendra said.

"Around here people buy *new* dresses for a dance." I laughed.

"So you're actually doing this, then?" she said. "You really did invite me to a dance even though you had another date, just to make me look stupid?"

I laughed again. "You actually thought someone like me would take someone like you to a dance?"

5

"No, I didn't. But I hoped you wouldn't make my decision so easy, Kyle."

"What decision?" Behind me, Sloane was cackling, chanting, "Loser," and soon other people started in until finally the whole room was buzzing with the word so I could barely think straight.

I looked at the girl, Kendra. She wasn't crying. She didn't look embarrassed either. She had this intense look in her eyes, like this chick in this old Stephen King movie I once saw, *Carrie*, where this girl developed telekinetic powers and took her enemies out. And I almost expected Kendra to start doing that—killing people just by looking at them.

But instead she said in a voice only I could hear, "You'll see."

And she walked out.

Don't believe in magic?
It's time to get CLOAKED!

Read an excerpt from Alex Flinn's next novel,

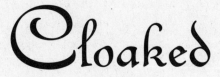

It takes nearly five minutes for the elevator to reach the penthouse floor. I knock and hang around like a stalker until another Mount Everest of a guard asks what I'm doing there.

"I was . . . I work at the hotel. I'm bringing the princess's shoe." I hold it up.

"I take zis!" The guard plucks it by the strap and starts to close the door.

"But I . . . she . . ." I slump over. She's probably still asleep. Can it really end here, my one big chance?

His hand's on the doorknob. "You have been paid?"

I nod. "But—"

"Zen go on your way." And the door slams.

That's that. I head back for the elevator. It was stupid, me thinking I could talk to the princess about anything but her broken strap. I mean, who am I? Some poor slob who works in a hotel. I should be happy I got to meet her at all. Someday, I'll probably tell my grandchildren about it. And they'll assume it's dementia setting in.

But still, I feel like going downstairs and banging something with a hammer until it's obliterated. Victoriana said she wanted me to deliver the shoe personally. I went to a lot of trouble. It's not right that the guard is keeping me out. He's not any special person. He's only a guard, just like I'm only a shoe-repair guy. He's no better than—

"Pardonnez-moi?" Mister Everest is back.

"What do you want now?"

"It is ze princess who wants. She says I must ask you to come into her suite."

"So she *did* want me to deliver the shoes in person?"

"Oui."

"So I was right? I wasn't just lying to get to see the princess?"

"Yes, yes. Is zat not what I just say?"

I'm savoring this. "So I was right, and you were . . . what's the word I'm trying to think of here . . . ?"

The guard's face is purplish. "Leesen, you leetle pipsqueak. If you do not wish to see ze princess, I will be happy

2

to tell her you left ze building."

"Okay." I follow him into the suite.

I've never been in the Royal Suite before, but it's bigger than our apartment. Flowers decorate every flat surface, so it looks a little like a funeral, without the body. There's even an aquarium with a small shark swimming between the anemones. The guard leads me through one room, then another, until finally we reach a sitting room, decorated in blue and white to blend with the cloudless sky outside its glittering French doors. The princess sits in a big wicker chair. She's dressed all in white, golden hair flowing down her shoulders, wearing the shoes I've repaired. I notice, with satisfaction, that the left shoe is a bit shinier than the right.

She doesn't look hung over. She doesn't look like she only got four hours' sleep. She looks like a marble statue of an ocean goddess. If I ran into her at Wal-Mart, I'd still know she was a princess. I stop, then bow low.

"Please." She gestures me up. "Please, zis is not needed."

I stand. She says something in French to the guard. He shakes his head, but leaves, muttering something and glaring at me. The door closes, slightly louder than necessary.

I am alone with the most beautiful girl I've ever seen. Please, God, please, don't let me say anything stupid.

"Allo, Johnny."

I start at my name, that she remembers it.

"Did I get it wrong. You are Johnny, *non*? Ze boy who watches me?"

"I don't . . ."

"It is nothing to be ashamed. Everyone watches. But I have to sneak to watch zem."

"Sneak?" So she *was* there, all those times I thought I saw her. But why?

"Sit." She gestures at a chair.

I do, tripping over my own feet as I go, almost falling into her lap. "Sorry."

"It is all right." She stares ahead, saying nothing, like she's waiting.

"The shoe, it's okay?" I have no idea why I'm here.

"Shoe?"

"The one I repaired? I should have asked you for the other one, so I could polish both, so they'd be perfect. I could still." I'm babbling. I'm babbling. Make me stop.

She glances at me, then her shoes, and finally, it seems to dawn on her what I'm talking about. "Oh, *oui*. Ze shoe is lovely." She lowers her voice. "Ze shoe, it was—ow you say—a ruse."

"A ruse?" I whisper.

"*Oui*. A ruse. I broke ze strap in order to speak wiz you, and I pretend to be drunk so ze guards would not suspect my duplicity."

"You pretended to be drunk? But you reeked of *mojito*."

"I had *one*, and I kept ze mint in my pocket to chew."

"But you were stumbling and acting, um . . ."

"Crazy?" She rises and stumbles across the room in per-

4

fect imitation of a drunk. When she comes back around, she slumps against my chair. "Zis, I do all ze time."

"But why?"

"Many reasons. For ze press, mostly, so zey will see me as harmless, someone to be ridiculed and never suspect ze turmoil in my country, ze turmoil . . ." She touches her chest. ". . . in here."

"Wow." Meg will freak when she hears this. "So . . . ?"

"I needed to speak wiz you about a matter of ze utmost importance. I needed to see you . . ." She glances at the door. "Alone."

She places finger to lips then tiptoes to the door and pulls it open. A guard falls into the room. Victoria barks several sentences to him in French. The guard retreats, and this time Victoriana stands by the door until she's sure he's far away before pulling it shut.

"What did you tell him?" I ask.

"Zat if I catch him eavesdropping again, it would mean not only his job, but also his children would be kicked from ze Alorian soccer training team."

"Harsh."

"A princess needs her privacy." She walks to the French doors. "Let us go out."

"Isn't that dangerous?" I picture sharpshooters, waiting on the beach, or the Zapruder film of the Kennedy assassination we saw in history. "Couldn't someone . . . ?" I mime a gun.

Victoriana shakes her head. "*Non*. Sadly, ze person who

5

is ze greatest danger to me wants me very much alive."

I follow her out. The ocean roars, and seagulls' cries surround us. Victoriana closes the balcony door. When she turns around, there are tears in her aquamarine eyes.

"Please," she whispers. "You must help me."

5/10

Once upon...today?

Modern Fairy Tales *from*

ALEX FLINN

NOW A MAJOR MOTION PICTURE

READ IT
BEFORE YOU
SEE IT!

Ever wonder what it was like for the Beast?

BEASTLY

ALEX FLINN

It's not the story you think you know.

HARPER TEEN
An Imprint of HarperCollinsPublishers
www.harperteen.com